The
Three Day Club

By
Randall Probert

The Three Day Club

by Randall Probert

www.randallprobertbooks.net

email: randentr@megalink.net

Cover Illustrations by
Brian Colby
Bethel, Maine

ISBN: 978-0-9852872-3-8

Published by
Randall Enterprises
P.O. Box 862
Bethel, Maine 04217

Dedication

I would like to dedicate this book to all retired Game Wardens and those who have fallen while on duty. The following poem I found in a copy of the International Game Warden magazine and the author is unknown.

Warden's Reward

A man knocked at the heavenly gates;
His face was scarred and old.
He stood before the man of fate
For admission to the fold.
"What have you done," St Peter asked,
"To gain admission here?"
"I have been a Game Warden, sir,
For many and many a year."
The pearly gates swung open wide;
St Peter touched the bell. . .
"Come and choose your harp," he said
"You have had your share of hell."

Preface

As many of the stories are based on true events and happenings, I have taken the liberty to change some names and add my own touch here and there, so not to embarrass or poke fun at anyone. My only intent is to provide an enjoyable read. Where and when I could, I have used the person's real name. Many of the stories are my own, although the book is not about me.

Though the stories are based on true events, they may not be in chronological order.

Randall Probert

CHAPTER 1

Ian Randall yawned and then drove along the old I.P. dirt road in T7-R6 with his head out the window, trying to stay awake. He yawned again and then pulled over to the roadside near Weeks Brook and poured the last of his coffee into his cup. The coffee was cold, but he was hoping the caffeine would keep him awake long enough to get home at Knowles Corner.

He yawned again and finished the coffee. At 10 P.M. the night before he had received a telephone message from a frantic Boy Scout Master that three of his youngest boys had wandered off after supper and hadn't returned. The scout troop had put in at the bridge on Wadliegh Brook in T8-R7. They were to spend the first night camped below the Narrows on Grand Lake Seboeis and then the next day canoe to Snowshoe Lake and down the river to the campsite and bridge at the Matagamon Road in T6-R7.

John, the Scout Master, couldn't leave the other six boys there and go very far in search of the lost boys, and they couldn't very well canoe safely out of there during the night.

John had noticed a plane with floats at the old forestry camp when they went out onto the lake. His only hope now was if the plane was still there. He had not heard the plane take off and he knew he would have been able to hear it.

He chose the biggest and strongest boy there, Michael, and told the rest, "We are going to canoe back up the lake and hope the plane is still there and see if whoever is there can get a message out for us. You boys are to stay right here and do not go off exploring. Keep the fire burning, but not raging. Michael and I will be back as soon as we can."

As they canoed back through the narrows, Michael asked, "Will they be all right, Mr. Smith?"

Not wanting to worry Michael, John replied, "They'll be just fine. Tired and hungry, but this will be a good lesson for all three boys."

As they were leaving the narrows, John could see three men loading the plane with their gear. He hollered and waved his paddle and said, "Don't leave! I need to talk with you!"

One man held and steadied the canoe while John explained his problem. He wasn't sure who he was talking with, but figured he owned the plane and the cabin. "As soon as we get back to base at Shin Pond, I'll call the game warden for you."

"Thank you. I surely do appreciate it. But I must get back to the other boys now. Thanks again."

Ian didn't get the message until 10 P.M. Knowing he would probably be all night and into the next day, he made two thermoses of coffee and a lunch and threw them into his back pack, along with extra batteries and dry socks. He thought about asking his Uncle Jim Randall, who lived just below the Kathadin Hunting Lodge on Rt.11 at Game Warden Curve, to help. Uncle Jim knew that country probably better than he did. But he decided against it. *No....I guess not. You have had your share of lost people and you're probably what? Seventy-two years old now or so?* Ian knew his uncle would come out if he asked him, but he had indeed had his share of lost people—even though he didn't look or act his seventy-two years.

He turned north at Knowles Corner, the junction of Routes 11 and 212, and then turned west onto the I.P. road in T7-R5, which would take him to the Snowshoe Road in T7-R6, and then to the Lost Pond Road in T7-R7, which was only about a mile and a half from the narrows on Seboeis Lake.

He drove past Keith MacEllroy's camp on Lost Pond and followed the old winter logging road as far as he could.

Before leaving his pickup, he radioed the State Police Barracks in Houlton and advised Scotty of the situation. Then he shouldered his pack, closed and locked the doors and looked at his compass for a heading below the narrows. From where he was and in a straight line, the distance probably wasn't more than three quarters of a mile. It was now 11 P.M. He looked up at the sky and the stars were out bright. *Good night for a walk.* Ian always found it easier to walk in a straight line in the dark than during daylight, but tonight he had several obstacles to walk around. . .a rock slide on the back side of a hill, a beaver flowage and a tangle of raspberry bushes.

He walked into the campsite at the narrows just after midnight. John was still up and sitting by the fire and suddenly surprised to see Ian walk in from the shadows and bushes. He didn't think he would see anyone until well after daylight the next morning.

John stood up and said, "I'm certainly surprised to see you here tonight. Especially walking in from the woods like that. I wasn't expecting anyone until morning."

John poured Ian a hot cup of coffee and explained what happened.

"Where are the boys from?"

"These three are from Rhode Island."

"So I'm assuming not very woods wise."

"Only what they have learned from scouting."

"I don't expect our plane will be able to fly come daylight. The weather report said fog and low clouds are supposed to roll in after 3 A.M. and hang around all day."

All the boys had a compass but had not had any experience using one in the big woods. "I'm going back in the woods and see if I can pick up any sign at all. If I don't come back tonight, at first light send two boys to canoe along this shore down to the south end and then back up along the same shore. Send out two more boys an hour later and then the last two. You stay here. Do you have a handgun with you?"

"Yes, a .357."

"If the boys come back or are picked up in one of the canoes, fire three shots about five seconds apart."

Ian left and was able to find John's track in the starlight and followed those until John had turned back. He hadn't gone very far. Ian started making circles trying to find the boys' trail. Half way through the third circle, he found where the three boys had walked through some loose dirt. They were traveling due east. Ian set his compass but continued following their tracks. When he lost the tracks he would continue east and then make another circle until he found their tracks again.

He kept up this routine all night and sure enough, at 3 A.M., clouds rolled in and the stars were gone. *As long as it doesn't rain.*

An hour later Ian had followed their tracks out to the Snowshoe Road and instead of turning south, the tracks headed north, into deeper woods. Thinking the boys wouldn't leave the road now, Ian picked up his pace. Only occasionally did he stop to look for tracks to make sure they had not turned back into the woods. And to see their tracks, Ian had to turn around with his back in the direction they were traveling and shine his light on the road. This way he was able to pick up the shadows produced from the treads on their boots. This was the only way he could see their tracks at all on the hard gravel road.

Certain now the boys would never leave the road, he only stopped to look for tracks when he came to the junction of another road. At the junction of the La Pomkeag Road, the boys had taken this branch. Ian knew of a camp that was close to the road and hoped the boys would stop there. The camp used to belong to Hank Carson, a biologist in Ashland. But John and Mimi Burmingham now owned it and had turned the camps into a sporting camp. "Oh, I hope they stop there," he said out loud. But he still had at least another three miles to go to reach the camp.

It was 4:30 A.M. now and the cloud cover was lightening. He picked up his pace again. At 5:30 A.M. he could see the camp as he rounded the last corner. The three boys were lying under a tarp asleep.

He stepped up on the wooden porch and walked towards the sleeping boys. He thought they might awaken, but they didn't. He pulled the black tarp off of them and still they slept on. He prodded one with the toe of his boot and finally this one awoke and stared up at Ian. Then he woke his two friends.

They had hiked about seven miles from their campsite at the narrows and they were rightfully tired. Ian shared his lunch and coffee with the boys and then said, "Well boys, we're going to have to walk back to your campsite." He had already tried his portable radio, to call for someone to bring in a pickup, but because of the fog and low clouds, his radio was useless.

When the boys had finished eating their meager breakfast of Ian's lunch, he said, "The only way back to your campsite is to walk."

"All the way back, mister?" one of them asked.

"Afraid so. But we'll walk the roads until the last leg."

The boys had had two hours sleep and were full of energy, but it wouldn't last for long. Ian had been up now for 36 hours.

*   *   *   *

After the first mile of hiking, the boys were tired. Ian was sore and lame all over but he knew better than to stop. He slowed the pace during the next mile and then picked it up again the next and so forth all the way back to the campsite. They had left Burmingham's camp at 7 A.M. and at noon they were back at the campsite. The other six boys in the canoes had returned for lunch.

John fixed Ian a cup of coffee and two hotdogs cooked on sticks. While the hotdogs were cooking, Ian wrote down the information he would have to have for his report.

As he started to leave, John and all the boy scouts kept thanking Ian over and over. He reset his compass to find his truck and left. As tired as he was he didn't stop until he was sitting behind the steering wheel of his pickup. After he had

11

turned around and on his way out, he radioed the state police barracks and advised he had located the three boys and returned them safely to their campsite and he was on his way home.

* * * *

Ian yawned again and pulled back on the road for home. It was 2 P.M. and he could see Rt. 11. Someone was calling Ian on the radio. "Houlton, 2256. Ian, wake up."

"Go ahead, Scotty."

"I just received a report of a plane crash near where you are, in T7-R6. This is coming from the radio operator at the Houlton International Airport. Two men in a Cessna 172. The pilot radioed first that he was having engine problems and was beginning to circle Umcolcus Lake and ditch it in the water. But two minutes later he radioed back that he had completely lost the engine and was going to try to bring it down between the trees on to the Umcolcus dirt road a short ways from the landing at the lake. That was the last traffic, and that was thirty minutes ago."

"Ok, Houlton. I copied your traffic and I'll turn around and head that way."

Ian forgot about being tired or yawning and headed for Umcolcus Lake. As fast as he was traveling, he hoped he didn't meet anyone, particularly a log truck. When he made the turn onto the Umcolcus Road from the I.P. Road, there was a rooster tail of gravel. This was a rough road that hadn't been used by lumbermen or maintained for years.

He had to pull the truck into four wheel drive at the bottom of Deadman's Pitch. The hill was muddy with deep ruts. Halfway up the hill the transmission or cross member hit a big rock sticking up. There was a loud clang, but he couldn't stop now. The ole pickup was taking a beating.

Towards the crest of the hill the mud was gone, but the tire ruts were deeper. Across the flat top, the road was better but on the back side of Deadman's Pitch, the road center had washed out and now his pickup was sliding so much, he didn't know but he might roll over. He forced himself to slow down or he wouldn't make it.

The old bridge at Wadliegh Crossing was gone and he had to ease the truck across. Once on the other side, the road was better all the way to the lake. As he drove through a soft wood forest down in the low land, he thought he would like to trap here some day. But there was a move in Augusta to ban game wardens from trapping. He had even gone to Augusta with Dan Glidden, the warden in Ashland to testify before the Fish and Game Committee why wardens should be allowed to trap.

Five minutes after leaving the softwoods behind he was making his way around a turn and saw the wrecked plane in the road. It wasn't looking good. There was no one around. There was the top of a beech tree that had been hit and broken off and then the plane had hit around the beech tree.

Both occupants were still in the cockpit, or what was left of it. Ian felt for a pulse in both men, and found none. "2256, Houlton."

"Go ahead '56," Scotty answered.

"I'm at the scene and both occupants are DOA."

"Okay '56. You know what this means. I'll contact the Medical Examiner and get him started to your location. What's the best way in?"

"It would be easier and quicker to fly into Umcolcus Lake and I could pick him up there."

"I have the M.E. on line now and the state police pilot will fly him to Houlton, and I'll contact your pilot Jack McPhee and he can pick him up there and fly him to Umcolcus."

"I copy that Houlton. And I suppose you'll want me to secure the area."

"Well, you are the first officer on the scene. I know you have been out now for. . .what, 40 hours? But you don't have a choice, do you?"

Ian looked at his watch; 2:30 P.M. "They should be here before dark."

Ian pushed his seat all the way back and with the radio on, he leaned over on the seat and was instantly asleep. At 5:40 P.M. the radio started blaring. It was pilot Jack McPhee on the Warden Service Clear Lake channel. Jack called twice more before Ian answered, "2256, go ahead, Jack."

"We're circling the lake now. Pick us up at Lucian Shaw's camp?"

"10-4. On my way." The road was still rough, but he was there before the plane. Ian waded out and stopped the plane from hitting the rock pier and then he pulled it in on the sandy shore. Jack jumped out and tied it off to a tree and then he helped Dr. Ryan and Trooper Atfield exit the plane with their gear.

"Hello, Ian."

"Hi Jack, Bob, Dr. Ryan."

"What's Roscoe Patch's story Ian? He doesn't work, except he traps a little, but he's busy building his cabin bigger and it looks like a grand estate."

"I don't know, Jack. I've laid awake many nights and days across the channel from his cabin. I have never known him to do anything illegal. He's a mystery."

"I take it the plane isn't far off?" Jack asked.

"No, about a half mile."

"He almost made the lake then."

Dr. Ryan rode in front with Ian, and Jack and Bob Atfield rode in the back. Ian drove slower so not to toss Jack and Bob out of the back.

While Dr. Ryan examined the bodies, Bob took photos to document the scene. It didn't take Dr. Ryan long to determine that both men were dead and he had all the information he needed. While he was busy writing notes in his notepad, Ian, Jack and Bob put both bodies into body bags and then put them in the back of the truck.

It was a tight squeeze when all were aboard the plane, with the two bodies. Ian pushed the plane out and Jack started the engine. He waited until they were in the air and then he radioed

Houton again. "2256, Houlton."

"Go ahead, '56."

"Houlton, I'll be 10-7 tonight at Lucian Shaw's camp at Umcolcus. I'm too tired to drive out."

"Okay, '56. I'll call Ashland."

Years ago, Lucian had shown Ian where he had a key hidden, and he had told him to use the cabin whenever he wanted. There was still enough daylight left so he didn't need to light a lamp. He opened a can of beans and ate the beans cold and had a drink of water. He removed his wet clothes and hung them on nails on the cross logs. He found a sleeping bag and crawled in and didn't awaken until loons began calling out front after the sun had risen the next morning.

He crawled out of bed and fixed a cup of black coffee. After he finished that, he put the sleeping bag back, locked up the camp and started for home. "2256, Houlton, I'm 10-8."

"2256, an FAA inspector called and he is now on his way to the scene. He needs your escort from Rt. 11 in, so if you would meet him at the mouth of the I.P. road, that would be good."

"10-4, Houlton. I only hope they have a four wheel drive vehicle or they'll never make it in."

"I think they'll come prepared, '56."

Ian saw no need to hurry across the rough road until he was on the I.P. road. The FAA team was at the mouth of the road when Ian arrived. From what he saw of their vehicle, they wouldn't be having any problems. It was a Dodge power wagon, set up with larger tires and more clearance, and towing a special trailer with its own boom and hoist; for lifting the plane onto the trailer.

Ian stopped his truck and got out. He knew he wasn't very presentable. He hadn't shaved now in two days, his uniform was wrinkled and covered with mud, but he doesn't sit behind a desk for a living.

"You must be Ian Randall. I'm Ansel Peobody. This is David Newcomb and this is Dan Alfred," Ansel introduced his team.

Ian shook their hands and said, "I guess you won't have any

15

problems with your rig, but the road is rough. Follow me."

Ansel, who seemed to be the lead man, road with Ian and while Ian was driving, he told Ansel everything he could about the accident.

"This is a rough road," they were going up the muddy side of Deadman's Pitch.

"Wait until you see the other side."

Ten minutes later Ansel asked, "Is there another way out of here?"

"Yeah, but the bridge is out over the east branch of Umcolcus Stream on the Camp Violette Road and a beaver flowage between Umcolcus Lake and the Camp Violette Road."

"Is there room to turn the trailer around at the crash sight?"

"Not right at the sight, but there is an old log yard at the top of the hill."

While Dave was turning the truck and trailer around, Ansel and Dan went right to work unbolting the engine and disconnecting all the wires and tubing. "While we're doing this, Ian, would you look for the prop?"

Dave was a while before he returned and he didn't have to be told what to do. He went to work and hoisted the engine into the back of the Dodge Powerwagon and then he swung the boom around for the wings. "There's still plenty of fuel in the wing tanks, so fuel wasn't the problem."

The FAA Team had the plane dismantled and loaded onto the trailer and truck before Ian found the propeller. He found it about fifty feet in front and another hundred feet off to the right. Both blades were bent pretty bad.

The load was secured and Ansel said, "I guess we have everything. Thank you for your help, Ian."

*   *   *   *

Ian parked his pickup behind his house so people would think he wasn't home. Then he ate a big breakfast, showered and

16

went to bed after pulling the plug on the telephone.

His Uncle Jim Randall knew about the lost boyscouts and the plane crash from watching the local news on tv and he wanted to call his nephew to see what he would have to say about it. But he also knew he had been going straight for two and a half days, and he didn't want to bother him now.

His wife, Nancy, poured him another cup of coffee so he could soak his cookies in it. "I'll never understand how you wardens can spend so much of your life working. Your nephew, Ian, is never home; no wonder he can't keep a wife."

"I use to be just like him," Jim said.

"And I'm glad we never met until you had retired, although I think if you had had a couple of kids at home, you might have spent more time at home.

"You know, Jim," she continued, "Ian could retire any time and he better start thinking about slowing down and finding a good wife or he'll be an old lonesome man."

Jim laughed and sipped his coffee and winked at his wife. She smiled.

* * * *

When Ian awoke the next morning, he telephoned the Ashland office and requested two weeks off. The first four days he and his Uncle Jim worked up next winter's firewood for both of them, and threw it in and stacked it in the basements. As they were finishing the last of Jim's wood, Nancy said, "Ian, we're having pot roast tonight. Why don't you plan to stay for supper?"

"Okay, sounds like a good idea. I hate cooking."

When the wood was finished, Jim and Ian sat out on the back porch sipping a drink. Jim had worked just as hard as Ian had for four days and he didn't seem to be any more tired than Ian. Ian thought him an enigma. He knew he was at least 72 years—and maybe 75—but he didn't want to embarrass himself by asking. The skin on his face and around his neck was still taut, and no wrinkles about his hands and arms. And he wasn't bothered by all the chainsawing and bending over, either. His wife Nancy was fifteen years younger and she still had a supple figure.

When they all had had their fill of pot roast, Jim asked, "What are you going to do for the rest of your vacation?"

"I'm going to take off on my motorcycle and explore New Brunswick. I like the country over there and the people are friendly."

* * * *

Ian left on his motorcycle to explore the interior of New Brunswick. His first stop would be in Kedgwick. He parked the state truck in plain view between the house and garage, locked all the doors and mounted his motorcycle and never looked back.

The telephone rang at Jim and Nancy's house and Nancy was taking a shower. "Would you get that, Jim? I just stepped out of the shower."

"Hello?"

"Good morning, Jim. This is Oceana. Coffee is hot and I just made some fresh donuts. Why don't you and Nancy come down? Tilly would like to talk with you."

"Sure, Oceana, as soon as Nancy dries off. She just stepped out of the shower."

Thirty minutes later they were all sipping coffee and dunking fresh donuts. "Jim, the two Murckle brothers are back and the last three nights at about 10 to 10:30, someone goes by here on a 3-wheeler and rides around the old fields and apple trees across the road at the MacDonald place. I think it is the one that ran over his own leg with a snowsled and broke it last winter. He went by here yesterday afternoon and turned into the MacDonald place."

"Ian is on vacation for the next ten days and he is traveling through New Brunswick on his motorcycle. I'll take a walk over

18

and have a look." He finished his coffee and got up. "I'll only be a few minutes."

There were definitely 3-wheeler tracks in and out of the old driveway. The buildings had fallen in and the driveway was only a pathway now, and only wide enough for a 3-wheeler. Jim followed the trail in and around the apple trees and old fields. It was obvious what they were looking for. He wished, just for one night, he could bring himself out of retirement. He chuckled and said, "Yes sirree, this here is just like money in the bank." And Ian would be gone for the next ten days.

"I sure wish there was something I could do about this. He'll surely be back tonight." Then as an answer to the problem, his toe kicked up a narrow board with three 8-penny nails sticking through. One at each end and one in the center. Jim picked it up and realized it was just the right length to lay in the 3-wheeler track. Then he started laughing uncontrollably, as he tucked the board under the grass and across the track, with the nails sticking up.

He went back to the house and decided not to say anything about what he had done.

"Have another cup of coffee and a donut, Jim," Oceana said.

"Someone has been looking the farm over, all right. But I couldn't see where anything had been killed. Have you heard any shooting?"

"No. All we have heard is the 3-wheeler going by."

That night, some time after midnight and Jim and Nancy were sound asleep, the telephone rang. After the fourth ring Jim picked up and was able to mumble, "Hello?"

There was a long silence and then someone said, "You old bastard, you."

Jim roared with laughter and whoever was on the other end got mad and hung up. Jim roared with laughter for five minutes before he could compose himself enough to tell Nancy all about what he had done. And then she too began to laugh. "I wonder how far he had to walk?" and she laughed some more.

19

"I don't know now, but what it might have been fun married to you when you were a game warden." They both began laughing again.

They sat up in bed for a long time laughing about that and some of the antics Jim and Uncle Royal used to play on each other. In between laughing, Jim said, "Yes sirree, it was a great game."

"Won't this Murckle guy be mad?" Nancy asked.

"Oh yeah, he'll be mad as hell for a while. But when he gets over it, even he himself will see the humor in it."

"Who are these Murckle brothers?" Nancy asked.

"Fred and Ralph. Fred is a year older. Right out of high school they both went to driving log trucks in the woods for Merle York. They both were good drivers and could see there was more money hauling cross-country. They'll work hard every day, for a while. They're a driving team, so they can drive 24 hours a day. They make pretty good money, but when they come home for a week or two. . .well, they both like to fish and hunt and really are not too fussy if it's legal or not."

"Have they ever been caught?"

"Several small charges, but nothing where either one of them would have to spend three days in jail."

*   *   *   *

"Damn that old man to hell!" Fred Murckle screamed as he slammed the phone down.

"So it was Jim that laid out that board with nails?" Ralph asked.

"Yeah, it was him all right. I wasn't positive though until he started laughing."

"He was laughing?" Ralph asked.

"Yeah, that no-good has-been. I'll show him."

"What are you talking about, Fred?"

"We take a pot plant and plant it on his property and then wait until the morning. We leave and call the Sheriff Department."

"That's mean, Fred."

"What the hell do you think he did to me? I had five miles to walk."

"We planned on leaving Friday morning. That gives us three days," Ralph said.

"Then we do it tonight. After midnight."

They drank another can of beer and began laughing about the prank. For supper they fried up some fresh deer tenderloin and another beer each. By midnight, they each had drank a six pack.

"We can leave our truck at the old Hall place between Hall's Corner and old man Jim's."

The moon wasn't in full phase but there was enough light for the two to make their way through the trees. Fred had brought only a small pen flashlight. He didn't want Jim seeing a beam of light shining through the trees. Their progress was still slow and occasionally Fred had to use his pen light.

"Where are we going to plant it?" Ralph asked.

"Close to the brook that runs behind the house."

They found the brook and waded into some soft black muck. Ralph found a grassy spot close to the brook and they could see the outline of the house roof. "Here," Fred whispered.

Ralph used a trenching tool he had brought and when they had finished, they worked their way back to their truck. Laughing all the way.

"I sure would like to be here when Sheriff Darel Campbell finds the plant."

They stayed up until almost daylight drinking more beer and laughing.

*   *   *   *

Both Fred and Ralph were up at daylight Friday morning. While Ralph was inspecting the truck and trailer and getting it started, Fred made an anonymous call to the Sheriff's office in Houlton. He gave the dispatcher a description of the property and where to look for the marijuana.

"Come on Fred, you ready?"

"Yeah yeah, I'm coming."

"I'm driving first today," Ralph said. They had a load to pick up in Presque Isle for upstate New York.

* * * *

At 8 A.M. Friday morning, Darel Campbell, a deputy, Shaun, and his tracking dog Dude arrived at the Randall house. Dude was left in the vehicle and Darel and Shaun went to the kitchen door and before they could knock, Jim opened the door and said, "Just in time for coffee. Come in."

While Nancy poured two more cups, Jim asked, "What brings you two out here so early?"

"I don't know how to say this Jim. Early this morning my office received information that you have marijuana growing behind your house. I don't believe this for a moment, but. . .you understand I hope?"

"Sure. Finish your coffee and then we'll go take a look," Jim said and looked at his wife and winked.

Nancy turned away to hide her surprise. She wasn't sure what all this was about, but it was apparent her husband might.

As they sipped coffee, Jim said, "You know Darel, neither Nancy or I even smoke and we have never used any form of narcotics."

Nancy stayed to clean up the kitchen and the others went out the back door. She knew something was up but she didn't know what.

They fought their way through the bushes to the brook and started following it downstream. They hadn't gone far when Darel stopped and pointed. "There Jim."

"Well I'll be damned. You realize, Darel, this isn't ours?"

"Yeah, I came to that conclusion before leaving Houlton. We need to pull it and look around."

"Hey, Darel," the deputy said, "this is fresh dirt," and pulled the plant up. "See, the roots haven't even taken hold yet. And look at all these tracks."

"Yeah, I'm thinking the same. You and Jim stay here. I'm going to get Dude and see where these tracks take us."

Darel and Dude were back in five minutes.

Dude scented all over and began to track through the trees away from the brook and the house. The dog headed towards Rt. 11 and then turned left and the scent appeared to end in the clearing at the old Hall farm.

Sheriff Campbell pointed to fresh tire tracks. "Whoever planted that one marijuana plant parked here and walked through the woods to your house. Any idea, Jim?"

"No. . .no, not at all." He knew all right and smiled.

Sheriff Campbell saw the smile, but didn't say anything. "Let's call this a wrap, deputy, and we'll write it up as unfounded information."

"Jim," Darel asked, "has someone got a beef with you over something?"

"Gee Darel, I've been retired now longer than most of these yahoos are old."

"Well, maybe. But I think someone has it in for you. There's nothing more we can do here, so take care of yourself, Jim, and your pretty wife."

When Darel and his deputy were gone, Jim went inside. "Okay, Mr. Randall, are you going to tell me what's going on?"

Jim started laughing and then was finally able to say, "I think it was the Murckle brothers. We found one plant and tracks that led back to the Hall place. They're probably upset about that incident at the MacDonald place." He started to laugh again.

"Did you and Uncle Royal use to play like this?"

"Yeah. It was all in good fun."

Nancy just shook her head and said, "No wonder no woman

would ever stay with you until I happened along. I think I can now understand when you say it was a great game. I saw some of that game here this week."

*   *   *   *

As the Murckle brothers were leaving Presque Isle, Fred said, "Well, the Sheriff should be at the Randall's house by now," and then he began to laugh.

"Fred, I've been thinking."

"What about Ralph?"

"Well, planting that marijuana behind Jim's house. What if he is arrested and taken to jail? That was a pretty dirty trick actually."

"Well, what he did to me was pretty low, too. Besides he won't be arrested. Jim is too straight an arrow to be growing marijuana. The sheriff will figure it out."

"Then why did we do it?"

"To razz him some for those nails. Damn, he got all three tires, and it took me all night to walk home." They both laughed then. He added, "And my leg is still hurting where I broke it last winter."

CHAPTER 2

Ian filled his gas tank and then crossed into Canada at Houlton. He followed the highway to Woodstock and then turned north and began following the river road to Hartland. The scenery along the St. John River was spectacular with its high banks and gorges. There was a small diner on the corner of Main Street and he ordered a cheeseburger and fries and coffee. He drank three cups before the waitress brought him his burger.

His next stop was at Grand Falls. It was the Grand Canyon of the East. A steep gorge ran right between Grand Falls, New Brunswick and Van Buren, Maine. The St. John River was low but it still made a great show of water surging through the gorge.

From there he turned northeast and headed for the interior of New Brunswick. The scenery was beautiful and mostly forested. He reached Kedgwick just before supper. He found a motel off Main Street, showered and went to find a restaurant for dinner.

New Brunswick's time zone was an hour ahead and Ian reset his watch. "Holy cow, 7 P.M. already. I'll be lucky to find a place still open."

He closed his motel room door and almost ran down to Main Street where he had seen restaurant signs. Some were already closed or closing, but there was one still open. It was a nice restaurant and Ian hoped they didn't have a dress code.

There were people still seated and the maitre d' was at her station. She spoke to him in French and saw Ian did not understand her, so she changed to English and said, "Good evening, Monsieur. Table for one?"

"Hello, are you still serving?"

"Yes. The kitchen is open until 8 P.M."

"Thank you. Yes, a table for one, please."

She escorted him to a window seat and said, "My name is Maria. Sit down, please, and I will get you some coffee, no?"

"That would be fine, thank you."

As Maria walked away towards the coffee machine, she turned to look at Ian. He was watching her and he smiled. Maria smiled and almost forgot what she was after. For some reason she couldn't explain, this American, she was more than interested in. It was almost like seeing a friend from a long time ago.

On her way back with the coffee she posted a closing sign in the front door window. Ian was watching Maria closely. She looked to be a couple years younger. She had brown hair and eyes and a petite, shapely body. Although she was very attractive, there was something else about her. He couldn't yet describe it, but he could feel her presence whenever she was near. It was like electricity in the air and he could feel this aura that she carried with her as if it was pulling him closer.

She poured him a cup of coffee. "Thank you, Maria. My name is Ian Randall."

She reached out with her hand to shake his.

"Pleased to meet you, Mr. Randall."

"I'm happy to meet you also, and call me Ian." When he touched her hand they both could feel an electric current flowing between them. They stood there with their hands still clasped and looking into each others eyes.

"Please, won't you sit down, Maria? I mean, if you're closing and if you can. I'd like to talk with you."

Maria waved to a waiter and then sat down. "What is the special?" Ian asked.

"Monsieur, it is baked haddock with green salad and baked potato."

"I'll have that. Would you like something, Maria?"

"I am hungry. I'll have the same."

"You are alone, Ian? Do you not have a family?" she asked.

"I'm divorced. Actually twice, and I have no children. And you?"

"I, too, am divorced, only once though. I have a son, Eric. He is ten."

"Why twice divorced? You seem like a nice man."

"What I do for work really. Because of what I do, there is very little time for a home life."

"And what is it you do?"

"I'm a Maine Game Warden."

"I don't understand," she looked puzzled.

"Ahh. . .garde-chasse."

"Oh! I know this. We have garde-chasse here, also. They are married, though. In Maine, you can not be married to be this game warden?"

"Yes, we can be married. My two wives had a very difficult time being alone so much while I was working. They just had a hard time accepting me being gone so much."

"I don't understand your women. I would feel so happy to have a man to call my own who loved me, and had regular work all the time."

Their supper was served and Ian was hungrier than he had thought. Maria wasn't talking so much, either.

"This haddock is very good."

"It's fresh. How long will you be in Kedgwick?"

"I'm not sure. I have another nine days of vacation."

"Where were you going?"

"I have a motorcycle and I'm just out exploring New Brunswick. I really didn't know where I was going from here."

"If you enjoy the ocean, the trip around the Miramicihi Pennisula is a beautiful ride."

Ian surprised himself when he asked the next question. "Would you like to go with me? I know this is a little presumptuous and you don't know anything about me. But I like you."

Maria sat in silence for a few moments before answering. "Yes, I would like to go with you."

27

"What about your job here?"

"I only work four days a week. Wednesday through Saturday."

"What about Eric?" Ian asked.

"We live with my mom and dad. When I'm not working here, I help out on the farm. We have a small dairy farm, and the haying is already done.

"I would like you to meet my son and Mom and Dad tonight, before we leave in the morning."

"Okay, I'd like to meet your family. We can take the motorcycle."

"I have my Mom's car. We'll take that and then I'll bring you back here later."

Maria's family was really surprised when she walked through the door with Ian—someone she had just met. When Eric learned what Ian did for work, he became his bestest buddy. Her mom and dad, Antia and Armand, were very taken with Ian. He was so polite and thoughtful and they were amazed he wasn't already taken.

At 10 P.M., Maria drove Ian back to his motel. "I don't suppose you have a helmet somewhere on the farm, do you?"

"Eric has one I can use."

Maria walked with him to his motel door and as much as he wanted to kiss her on her lips. . .he kissed her cheek. After all, they had just met.

"I'll pick you up at 8 A.M., okay?"

"Make it 6 A.M. and you can have breakfast with us."

* * * *

Ian was a long time going to sleep that night. He was totally shocked. Never in all of his life had he met a woman so easily. It was just like falling off a log. He had never felt so excited even when he had first met his two wives. They had been good women, but they were never comfortable with Ian being the kind of warden he was. But Maria. . .he already knew she was special.

He was up at 5 A.M. the next morning. Primping and loading his motorcycle. He thought about buying a road map, but with Maria, he wouldn't need one.

At exactly 6 A.M., Ian pulled into the Bechard Farm driveway. Armand was coming out of the barn; the morning milking done. He would feed the cows after breakfast.

Maria, Ian noticed, had come out from the kitchen door and she was running to greet him with the prettiest smile he had ever seen. She ran, almost right into him, and put her arms around him and he held her in his arms, also. Armand was smiling, too, and he walked on by them without disturbing them.

"How did you sleep, Ian?" she asked.

"Not much," and he grinned.

"Me neither." Then she took his hand and led the way into the house. "Hope you're hungry."

Bacon, eggs and pancakes and strong black coffee. "After eating all this I'm not sure if the bike will hold us up." Eric was sitting beside Ian. Ian enjoyed his company, too.

"Where are you going?" Antia asked.

"Didn't Maria tell you? She's taking us around the Miramichi Peninsula."

"Oh, you'll enjoy that ride. I used to go fishing in the Miramichi for Atlantic salmon. Now there always seems to be too much around here to do. I hope you both enjoy the trip," Armand said.

They loaded Maria's extra change of clothes and things and said goodbye and left.

"Okay navigator."

"We turn left onto Rt. 17 and follow that until it turns into Rt. 11. We'll follow Rt. 11 to Bathurst and then get onto the peninsula road and Caraquet would be a nice place to stay tonight. There're nice beaches to walk on and plenty of seafood."

Ian turned left onto Rt. 17 and when he had the bike in high gear he leaned back against Maria. She put her arms around him and held on. . .tight.

It was a beautiful day to be touring on a motorcycle. The sky was blue and the temperature in the low 70's, probably because they were close to the cold waters of the North Atlantic. There was very little traffic and there was excellent scenery from on top high hills of heavily forested countryside and mountains. An hour later Ian could smell the salty air.

Before reaching Campbellton, Maria said, "There won't be any service stations until we reach Campbellton and I really have to pee. If you would pull over in a wide spot somewhere."

"Yeah, me too. Too much coffee."

There had been very little traffic on the road this morning. At the first wide spot Ian pulled over and shut the motorcycle off. There was already a path leading up into the trees. As soon as they were out of sight of the road, Maria said, "I can't go any further. I'll stop here."

"I'll go up the path a bit more." He went just far enough so Maria would feel comfort. Instead of leaving immediately, they sat down on a log at the edge of the wide spot, enjoying the warm sunshine, each other and talking. "I have a suggestion," Ian said.

"And?"

"If we like Caraquet, like I think, you think we will, instead of moving on the next day to another motel, let's stay there the next night also and we can explore the peninsula from Caraquet, or just stay put and enjoy the area and or beach."

"I'll go along with that idea."

They were needing gas for the bike and they were both hungry. They fueled up at an Irving station between Campbellton and Bathurst and there was a sandwich counter and picnic tables outside. "We should reach Caraquet early enough so we can look around some," Maria said. "It's only another twenty miles to Bathurst and maybe thirty from there to Caraquet."

In Bertrand they turned left onto the Saint Pierre Boulevard. There was some vehicle traffic here but not much. But the scenery along the boulevard was beautiful. They found a quaint little motel close to the shore line before the actual center of the village. "We would like to see the room first," Maria said.

It was not fancy, but clean and adequate and access from the room to the shore. The price was right and both Ian and Maria agreed. They paid for two nights and unloaded the motorcycle. When they were alone in their room, Ian hugged and kissed Maria tenderly and then with passion.

She whispered in his ear, "I need a shower. I'm all sticky."

"Me, too." That's all Ian could say.

And then she whispered in his ear again, "And then I'm going to jump your bones, Ian Randall. I have been so horny all day. It has been a long time since I have shared a bed with a lover."

"I know what you're saying. Me, too."

Ian watched as Maria took her clothes off. He was relishing the moment. Maria knew Ian was watching her and she was enjoying pleasing him and relishing this moment, also. Her skin was a light tawny, smooth and her breasts were small but firm. There was only a small patch of pubic hair and it was as brown as her hair.

"Well, are you going to take off your clothes? Here, let me help you." He was still speechless.

They stayed in the shower for a long time soaping and resoaping each other and playing, touching, caressing each other. When they had finished they hurriedly dried off and Maria pulled the bed covers back and Ian picked her up in his strong arms and gently laid her on the bed and he beside her.

They had already kissed so much that their inner lips were becoming sensitive. But this didn't stop them. Ian cupped her cheek in his hand and pulled back, looking into her eyes. And enjoying what he saw. Maria smiled as if to say she understood.

He kissed her ears, her neck and each breast. He laid his head on her flat belly and caressing her inner thighs and tugged playfully at her pubic hair. He moved down and relished in her womanly essence. She couldn't take any more. She clasped her hands around his head and gently pulled him up and she moved just right so he could enter her. They both experienced a moment of tremendous happiness, joy, excitement and sexual yearning.

They made love over and over. She sat on top of him; moved just right and screamed with sexual ecstasy and fulfillment. Finally from exhaustion they lay in each others embrace. "How long have you been alone, Ian?"

"Five years. And you?"

"Almost four. Don't you ever get lonely? I mean, I have my son and my folks to come home to every day. You have no one."

"When I'm busy with warden work, I don't have time to feel lonely. I do get lonely some when I go somewhere and I don't have a companion with me."

"Do you like married life?" she dared to ask.

"Actually, I do. But my wives would never have been able to feel comfortable with me being a game warden and gone so much."

"When can you retire?" she asked.

"I would like to retire in two more years. Before I could feel comfortable with giving it all up, there are two brothers I need to catch," and he told her all about the Murckle brothers.

"I'm hungry. How about you?" he asked.

"Yes."

They got up, dressed and decided to walk to a restaurant. They found the Dixilee about a quarter mile from the motel. They were shown to a table near the window overlooking the sea.

"May I make a suggestion?" Maria asked.

"Certainly."

"The fisherman's platter you can order for any number of people. We get a lobster each, clams and haddock served on fresh seaweed, which is also very good. It comes with biscuits and salad."

"That sounds good to me. Although I have never eaten seaweed."

"And what would you like to drink?" the waitress asked.

"I'll have coffee, black."

"I'll have Earl Gray tea please," Maria said.

While they waited for their fisherman's platter, they talked constantly. Ian was hoping the food would come soon as he was getting hungrier and hungrier. A half hour later, the waitress wheeled it in on a small table cart. By the looks and size of the platter, the wait was worth it.

Ian tried a piece of raw seaweed first and it was very good. The cooked seaweed was much like any leafy vegetable eaten with butter, but it had a different and enjoyable flavor. Everything was delicious. They had to force themselves to finish the platter.

After leaving the restaurant, they found an entrance to the beach and took their shoes off to walk in the sand. They followed the shoreline out along the peninsula and then turned in towards the village and walked back to the motel along the boulevard. The sun had set by the time they reached the motel.

They were both tired and they took their clothes off and went to bed. Ian laid on his back all night cradling Maria in his arms. She slept with her head on his chest.

* * * *

They awoke early the next morning and after their love making, showered and ate a large breakfast with a pot of coffee and spent the day touring the peninsula. There was a lot to see and at times they would park the motorcycle and explore on foot. Out near the head of Bas-Caraquet they found a secluded spot where they could lay down in the warm sunshine and listen to the surf crashing on the rocky shoreline below them.

"I have an idea, Maria. Now hear me through before you say anything, okay?"

"Okay." She wasn't sure if this was going to be a serious talk, like maybe goodbye—or what.

"I really like you Maria, and I want to continue seeing you. But there is one problem. From September 1st to December

1st, all Game Warden's regular days off are cancelled. We work every day, as this is our really busy season. There is no way I'll be able to come over here to visit. To leave my assigned district, but within my sergeant's section, I have to have his permission. To leave the division I am in, I have to have my lieutenant's permission, and there's just no way I could get permission to leave the state during those three months."

Maria really didn't know what he was trying to say.

"It'll be a long ride and a tiring day, but we could leave here early and return to my home in Moro PLT, in Maine and then the next day you take my vehicle and come back to your home, the farm. Then when you can, on your days off, you and Eric can come visit me. You keep my vehicle to use during those three months."

"You have to work every day until December?"

"Yeah. So you see, this is the only way we'll be able to see each other."

"Okay, then we leave here early tomorrow morning." Then she whispered in his ear, "I'm horny. What are you going to do about it?"

* * * *

They were awake at 5 A.M. and on the road by 5:30 A.M. They took Rt. 180 west across the province to Saint-Quentin and stopped there for breakfast and gas. From Saint-Quentin they took Rt. 17 to St. Leonard, then to Grand Falls down to Woodstock and back in Maine at the Houlton Border Crossing.

At the crossing, Ian explained that Maria would be having his Toyota pickup and driving back and forth at times and not to give her a hard time.

They were at Ian's house at Knowles Corner by 4 P.M. They both were saddle sore from riding for so many hours.

"Wow, you really do live out in the country, don't you?" she said. "I like your log house."

"Thank you. It's comfortable and there are two bedrooms upstairs."

For supper that night Ian opened a mason jar of canned moose meat, potatoes and green beans. The vegetables were from his own garden. "This meat is so good, Ian."

*   *   *   *

Before Maria left the next day, Ian took her down and introduced her to his Uncle Jim and Nancy. They were happy to think Ian had finally found a nice woman. It was a short visit however, as Maria still had to drive back to Kedgwick.

Back at Ian's house, they stood leaning against the Toyota pickup saying goodbye. "This has all happened so fast, it seems like a dream."

"Well, when you wake up tomorrow and your pickup is gone, you'll know this is no dream," she said.

He hugged her, kissed her and opened the door for her. "Come over whenever you want to. If I don't answer the phone. . .well, just come over anyhow. I never lock the door."

*   *   *   *

It was a long, lonely drive for Maria, but she was the happiest that she had ever been. She couldn't wait until she saw him again.

Ian still had one day left to his vacation. "Uncle Jim, do you want to go fishing at Umcolcus with me? Today is the last day of my vacation."

"Sure, come on down and we'll throw my canoe on your state truck." Nancy had to work.

Ian showed Jim where the plane crash occurred. "They hit those two beech trees there."

They unloaded the canoe in Shaw's camp yard and when all their fishing gear was loaded, Ian pushed off and sat down in the stern. "You go ahead, Jim, and get your line out and I'll paddle us over to the outlet and the point to the left. That's where I have always had my best luck. Even in the winter."

Jim let out his fly line trolling a warden's worry streamer. Then he paddled while Ian let out his line, trolling the same streamer. "Ian," Jim asked, "did you ever figure out Roscoe Patch's secret?"

"You mean where does his income come from?"

"Yeah."

"I have spent a lot of hours and days watching him. Once I camped for five days across the outlet from his cabin. I've determined that he doesn't poach. I have never found him with too many fish, trapping out of season, killing a moose or killing a deer in closed season. I have even watched the cabin to see if he would Sunday night. I camped across the outlet on a Saturday night, ready to catch him leaving his cabin at daylight. All he did all day was yard work and firewood. He has some money from somewhere or he couldn't afford that big new addition to his cabin. Hell, his cabin is better than my home. I don't know and I've stopped trying to figure him out."

Ian guided the canoe around the point and on the back side in the shade they both hooked into something large. Ian kept his line taut while Jim brought his in and netted it. "That's a beautiful trout. So orange," Ian said.

Then Ian brought his in and Jim netted it for him. It was almost identical to his. "Maybe four pounds each, I'd say," Jim said.

They went down the outlet and back up the other shore. Nothing. They trolled along the east shore to the inlet and back again. Not even a yellow perch. Roscoe was standing on his wharf, waving for them to come in. They brought in their lines and then Ian guided the canoe to his wharf.

"Been watching you two with my binoculars. These must have come from behind the point. That's about the only place you can catch a trout in this lake this late in the season. Come on in. Renée was about to fix us a lunch."

Jim offered him their trout. "Roscoe, would she cook these up for us if we cleaned them?"

"You sure about this?"

While Ian and Jim cleaned their fish on the wharf, Roscoe went in to tell Renée they had company. "You mean two game wardens are going to sit at our table?" Renée asked.

"Yeah, well Jim's been retired for a while now."

"I thought you said Ian used to camp out trying to catch you doing something."

"He got tired of that," Roscoe chuckled, and Renée laughed.

While Renée was frying the fish with some hash browns, Jim got up to look at the fire place. "Did you build this Roscoe?"

"Yeah."

"It's some fine work."

"It's the only one I ever made, and I have a lot of money invested in it." He looked at Renée and winked.

They had another cup of coffee and the three men sat out on the porch talking. Renée couldn't help from laughing when the living room sliding glass door was closed. "Just like two cats trying to torment the mouse, except here the mouse is tormenting the two cats."

She knew Ian had, for a long time, suspected Roscoe of poaching. But since she has been married to him, not once has he even as much as kept a short fish.

"I know the fishing isn't as good this time of the summer, Roscoe, but we never had a hit all the way to the inlet and back. Not even a yellow perch. I don't think this lake is as good fishing as it used to be," Jim said. "Is there much summer pressure?"

"Actually no, there're more people in the winter than in open water, but I don't think the fishermen are causing the slow fishing. There is only one inlet on this whole lake where the brook trout, salmon and smelts can spawn, and that's Wadleigh Brook and there are so many beaver dams on it that the fish can't get to the spawn beds any longer."

"Renée and I like to paddle around the lake shore in the evenings, but we take a trip about once a week downstream to the Umcolcus Deadwater. We keep a canoe below the dry-ky dam and the spring hole where Smith Pond outlet joins the deadwater still produces; even that is being fished hard," Roscoe said.

Renée hollered through the glass door that the hashbrowns and fish were ready. They sat in silence as they ate, and then drank another pot of coffee. When that too was gone, Jim stood up and said, "If we don't catch another trout to take home for Nancy, I'll never hear the end of it."

"Where is your wife, Jim?" Renée asked.

"She still works."

Roscoe held the canoe while Ian and Jim were seated. "Enjoyed your company, gentlemen. Come again."

"Thank you both for your hospitality."

The sun was lower in the sky and a thin bank of clouds overhead. Ian paddled back towards the point while Jim let out his line. Ian changed his streamer to a smelt and fed out the line. They each hooked into another fish about the same time. Only Jim had salmon this time, about the same size as the earlier trout. Ian had another trout a little smaller. "There, now we can go home," Jim said.

CHAPTER 3

"This was a quick run, Ralph, and the dispatcher has a load for us for Yorktown, Pennsylvania. After that we should be able to make two more short hauls and still be home for the Labor Day cookout."

"Where is the cookout this year?"

"I think I heard Scott say at Billy Andrew's camp on Alder Brook in Hersey," Fred said.

"That should be safe enough from prying eyes and the law."

"Fred, are we going to shoot any deer and moose to haul down to Baltimore when we leave home after the party?" Ralph asked.

"I'll have to call the broker dispatch in Presque Isle when we get back into Maine to see if he has a load of potatoes going that way."

Ralph started laughing then and was finally able to say, "I sure would have like to have been there when the law found that marijuana plant behind that old bastard's house. I wonder if they carted him off to jail?"

"He deserves it after what he did. That ain't right, flattening all three tires on my three wheel and making me walk five miles through the woods and me with no flashlight. My poor ole leg was hurting pretty bad by morning." But Fred began to laugh along with his brother, Ralph.

The next day as the brothers were nearing the Yorktown exit there was a sign up indicating all trucks to stop for inspection at the exit.

"What are you doing, Fred? They're just going to come and

get us and haul us back. We've tried this before," Ralph was worried.

"Yeah, but sometimes it works. Especially if the D.O.T. guys are busy with a lot of trucks waiting."

Sure enough, a mile before the exit there was a Pennsylvania State Trooper parked in the break down lane with his lights on. He got out of his cruiser and directed Fred to pull in behind him.

"Good morning, officer," Fred said as friendly as he could.

"Didn't you see that signing asking all trucks to take that exit for inspection?"

"Yes sir, we did."

"Then why did you drive by?" the trooper asked.

"Well sir, the guys won't find anything wrong with this truck, our log books, or our papers and we would waste at least four precious hours that we can't afford to waste," Fred replied.

"Let's see your bill of lading." Fred handed the officer the manila envelope.

"Paper goods from Rochester; paper towels, napkins and toilet paper. Gross weight 79,283. Hand down your licenses and logbook." They did.

"Either of you have any previous violations?"

"Yes sir, two years ago, both of us. . .log book violations."

"Falsifying your reporting?"

"No sir, we just forgot to update one day.

"As you can see, sir, we keep the truck in good working order. We have new tires all the way around, all our lights work and there are no oil leaks."

"Okay, Fred, you come with me and we'll walk around and see. I use to be one of the weight-wagon guys once for four years until I got tired of it, so I have heard every excuse there is."

Officer Brent Eldridge was quiet as he and Fred walked around the truck looking it over. He even got down on his knees and looked under it to see if there were any oil leaks. He began scratching his head and then he said, "This is the first time ever that a trucker has been completely honest with me. There are no problems with the truck or your papers. Why don't the two of you get out of here before my supervisor comes looking for me."

"Yes sir, and thank you," both Fred and Ralph said.

"Don't make it a habit of driving by. But I do understand about the delays. But you'd be surprised with what we find sometimes. Have a good day."

After they were back up to speed, Ralph said, "Who in hell are you? The Fred I know would have jumped down his throat."

"I don't know, something just came over me not to be a smart ass, that's all."

CHAPTER 4

Ian was glad to be back at work but he was missing Maria. He had telephoned her almost every day since she had returned to Kedgwick.

"Houlton, 2256."

"2256. Go ahead Houlton."

"I just received a telephone call from the North Country Hunting Lodge. A Dale Goodman is requesting that you stop by as soon as possible."

"10-4, Houlton. I'm close now. I'll be off there in two minutes."

Ian pulled into the driveway and Dale was already walking towards him. "Good morning, Dale."

"Good morning, Ian. We have a little bit of a problem. One of our hunters shot two bear yesterday afternoon. Two little cubs." Dale really sounded disgusted.

"We don't allow our hunters to shoot cubs or sows with cubs, and this guy shot two. Every Sunday after supper we explain the camp rules to everyone and how we operate. So this guy knew not to shoot cubs, let alone two. When you're done with him, he's out of camp. We won't skin it or handle it when any of our hunters break the rules."

"Where is he, Dale? I'll need to talk with him."

"He's in the dining room. I told him not to leave." Dale walked with Ian over to the dining room.

"Ian, this is Francis La Mont. Francis, this is Ian Randall, the game warden." He just sat there staring at the floor.

"Dale, would you leave us alone?"

Ian sat down at the same table and said, "Francis, I would like you to tell me about yesterday." From Francis' mannerisms, Ian knew he should not be too aggressive. When Francis didn't say anything, Ian said, "Let's go for a ride, Francis, and you can show me where you were hunting."

"Okay."

Francis followed Ian out to his pickup and got in. "We turn left on the highway."

"Okay, then you were hunting in Hersey?"

"Yes sir." Ian formed an opinion that this guy had some military in his background.

Francis was able to guide Ian from road to road right to the stand. "Where are you from, Francis?"

"Minnesota."

"You ex-military?"

"No sir. My father is a drill instructor, though." That explained a lot.

It wasn't a long hike into the stand. "Where did the cubs walk in from, when you first saw them?"

Francis pointed to a wet mossy area and said, "Over there. They looked like two hairy turtles."

"Why did you shoot Francis, after being told not to shoot cubs or sows with cubs, at supper the day before?"

"On the plane flying here, I was reading a magazine about a bear hunter being mauled by a bear. I guess I was a bit afraid, sir."

"Well, Francis, I'm going to arrest you for exceeding the bag limit on bear." Ian explained the cash-bail system, "and if you sign a guilty waiver you will not be required to appear in court. The cash-bail amount is $500. Do you have that much with you?"

"Yes sir, I do."

Back at the lodge, Francis went up to his room for his gear and when he came back down he gave Ian $500 and signed the guilty waiver.

"I'm sorry, sir, and Mr. Goodman, I am also sorry. I'll leave now."

Dale and Ian watched Francis leave and both felt a little empathy for him. "Lunch is about ready. Ian, stay for lunch?"

"I'd like to." The hunters were all coming in now and Ian sat down with Dale and his two sons, Bert and Hank.

After lunch he had an idea and returned home and telephoned Maria. A week from that day was Labor Day and September 1st, which meant there would not be any more time off until December. So he asked Maria if she could drive over that afternoon. "I'll have to be back for work Wednesday morning."

"If you don't mind the driving."

"I can do it just under six hours."

Ian worked the rest of the day but had requested the next three days off. There was no problem.

* * * *

Maria arrived at 8 P.M., just over six hours. She was tired of driving and hungry. "Eric said to say hello and can't wait until he can come with me sometime. My mom and dad also said to say hello."

"When hunting season is over, I promise to come and stay with you at the farm, okay?"

"Okay."

* * * *

As they laid in each other's arms, Ian said, "Tomorrow I want to introduce you to some friends. I have spent many hours and days trying to catch him poaching. They live year round in the woods at Umcolcus Lake."

"You have watched him for years and you say he is your friend? Does he know you used to watch him?"

"He knows but we seldom mention it."

She snuggled closer to Ian and said, "Hug me, I'm tired."

After breakfast the next morning they left to drive into see Roscoe and Renée. "Oh, I forgot to mention that we can't quite drive all they way in."

It was a nice day for a hike. The walk wasn't that far. Maria was completely surprised when she saw the cabin. She had been expecting an old dark stain hermitage. Roscoe and Renée were sitting on the porch drinking coffee. "Hello there!" Ian hollered to announce their presence.

"Oh, and you have an attractive woman with you this trip," Renée said.

"Maria, I'd like you to meet Roscoe and Renée Patch—Maria."

"Would you like some coffee?" Renée asked.

"I never turn down a cup," Ian said.

"Do you have any tea?" Maria asked.

"Yes, and I'll have some with you. Nobody around here drinks tea."

Maria followed Renée into the cabin. "Am I to understand you're not from around here, Renée?"

"Actually, no. Roscoe found me in Kedgwick."

"Kedgwick, that's where I live."

Renée and Maria talked constantly about back home. They sat in the living room talking, so not to disturb the men.

Roscoe and Ian's friendship had developed slowly over the last few years. But even now it was like a cat playing with a mouse and neither one of them fully understood which one was the cat. "Sometimes I envy you Roscoe, living out here as you do."

"It is nice, but it isn't easy during the winter months. As long as Bugbee is harvesting lumber in T7-R5 and has his crew camp yard plowed, we can leave our pickup there, traveling back and forth with snowsled. And then with the ATV during spring mud season. But all in all, we both love it in here and we are both in good health.

Renée and Maria made lunch; nothing fancy, cold chicken and stuffing sandwiches. But they were delicious and Renée had baked an apple pie the day before. Another cup of coffee was in order along with pie and an hour later Ian and Maria got up to leave.

"You come back any time when you're here visiting Ian, Maria. If he's out working, come on in. We don't have a telephone," and they all laughed. "And you, you come in any time you're around, you hear?"

"Yes ma'am. Thank you for lunch and coffee, Renée. Goodbye."

When Ian and Maria were out of sight, both Roscoe and Renée turned to look at each other and began laughing. "That was close, Roscoe."

"He'll never know it but that was the closest he has ever come to catching me. If he had been fifteen minutes earlier, I would have been in the middle of skinning that little buck. We'll be up to midnight now cutting it up and canning it. I'm sure glad I thought to make a cold storage room under the cabin when I started rebuilding. If he only knew there was a fresh deer underneath the cabin. . .well, he would have put me in cuffs and walked me to jail."

"Yeah, but Roscoe, he was not working."

"Don't spoil a good story, Renée. You know in a way I feel bad about it. You know as much time as he has spent watching me, he has never figured out how I do it. I always suspected he might camp out across the outlet to watch, so years ago, whenever I needed some fresh meat, I'd canoe down to Wadleigh Brook inlet and hang a wire snare in a deer trail. That way, nobody ever complained about hearing shots. Once, before we got together, Renée, I was canoeing across the lake with the four quarters and loins covered up with jackets and two fishermen motored over within ten feet of my canoe. Good thing I had taken the time to clean up and remove all the deer hair."

"Yeah, but Roscoe, he's your friend, isn't he? Don't you

feel bad?" Renée asked.

"I should, but I don't. It's just a game, Renée."

"Well, I like him and Maria. I don't want to lose their friendship, Roscoe. So if you don't stop, I'm going to tell him. You hear me?"

"All right, all right, no more. You know I actually do feel bad. I mean Uncle Jim and Ian have both become good friends. I tell you what. If Ian and Maria get married, as a wedding gift we'll give them a handful of precious stones."

"Okay Roscoe, but I'm going to hold you to your word," Renée had the last say.

CHAPTER 5

Fred and Ralph Murckle delivered their load to Yorktown, Pennsylvania and deadheaded to Newark, New Jersey for a load of heavy equipment for Buffalo, New York. And there they picked up a container box back to the shipping terminal in Newark, then they deadheaded to a produce dealer in Boston for a load to Bangor, Maine.

"This is going to work out just right, Fred," Ralph said as he shifted up. "We'll be home two days before Labor Day."

Fred was lying down in the sleeper, but he was listening to Ralph. "Ralph, I'll take over when we get to Kittery. I'm going to get some sleep."

There was a lot of traffic going north, probably to spend the last long holiday weekend before cold weather arrives. As Ralph drove, he kept thinking about the party at the Leonard camp on Alder Brook.

When he was clear of the toll booth in Kittery, he pulled over and woke Fred up. "Hey Fred, we're in Kittery."

"Okay, just give me a minute."

Ralph rode up front. He wasn't interested in sleeping. Neither one of them said much all the way to Bangor. They had been on the road constantly for several days.

Once at the produce dealer in Bangor, they were given an empty box trailer to haul back to the Maine Potato Grower Broker in Presque Isle. That they wouldn't drop off until they went up for a load of potatoes.

It was early evening and the sun was just beginning to dip below the tree tops. There was another big rig traveling behind them that took the Lincoln exit. There wasn't another vehicle in sight. Which wasn't uncommon on I-95 north of Old Town. Just beyond the Lincoln on-ramp north bound, laid a dead deer in the grass. Fred down-shifted and pulled over and stopped.

They got out and walked up to look at the deer. "It ain't stove up none bad Fred, but you ain't thinking about taking that to the party?"

"No. But let's throw it in the trailer. I'll explain what I'm thinking once we're back on the road."

Two hours later they backed the rig in beside the house and before exiting they updated their log books. "Don't say anything about this deer to anyone. Especially our folks."

*   *   *   *

The next day Fred and Ralph located Scott and Leonard to see if the party was still on. "Yeah. You and Ralph bringing venison again?"

"Sure thing."

"Do you have it yet?" Scott asked.

"Not yet, but don't worry."

"We're expecting a few more people this year. We have two kegs coming. You might want to bring sleeping bags."

Fred and Ralph purposely were keeping a low profile until the party, so Ian or his Uncle Jim would not know they were back in town. Saturday afternoon they greased the truck and adjusted the brakes, checked the tires and washed it. They stayed home and watched TV that night with their folks until 10 P.M. Then they grabbed a six pack of beer and drove off in Fred's pickup looking for night deer. If they wanted a deer to register, they would go out back to the back field. But one outside the law usually came from I-95 where there was very little traffic after 10 P.M.

They drove across the Moro Town Line Road slowly, checking out the old farms and hay fields. They knew this was a favorite haunt of Ian's and they knew better than to shine a light or jig the headlights into a field.

They turned onto the Clark Settlement Road in Merrill and then down Rt. 212 to Oakfield and southbound on I-95. At Battle Brook they began to see deer. A lot of does and lambs. Then at the field below the cross-over there was a huge lone buck in the ditch. Fred slowed the pickup and the deer stood there. He stopped the pickup and Ralph rolled the window down and still the buck stood. "Tomorrow night that's our deer."

They left and opened another beer and drove to the Sherman exit and saw five more deer. But the one they wanted was below the cross-over. They drove around the Happy Corner Road and the Poor Man's Retreat Road and from there up through the woods in Hersey and back to the Moro Town Line Road. It was 3 A.M. and the beer gone, they went home.

The next day they stayed around the house and helped their father bring in the last of the winter's firewood. They had a big roast beef dinner and then beer all afternoon. Their folks went to bed at 9 P.M. Sunday night and Fred and Ralph waited until 9:30 P.M. before they left. But first they put the dead deer in the back of their pickup, opened a beer and drove north to the Moro Town Line Road.

At Hall's Corner, just beyond on the south side of the road was an old field and apple trees lining the westerly side. And there was one particularly large apple tree about one hundred feet from the road that headlights from a westerly traveling vehicle would illuminate a deer standing under the tree.

Fred backed up to the tree and they pulled the dead deer out of the pickup and placed it under the tree so the white belly would be visible from the road. Then they drove back onto the Line Road, purposely leaving muddy tracks in the road. It was 10 P.M. and Ralph stood outside with a .270 Winchester rifle and pointed it straight up and a little westerly, so the bullet would not fall back on them. Ralph pulled the trigger and the silent night exploded. He waited fifteen seconds and fired another shot.

Both empties were purposely left on the road side. "There, that old bastard will have surely heard those. Let's go."

They turned south on Rt. 11 and headed for Patten.

Jim Randall had just gotten up to go to the bathroom when he heard the first shot. It was close but he wasn't sure in which direction. Then there was a second shot and he knew it was at the field by Hall's Corner; only a stone's throw away.

Jim immediately telephoned Ian and gave him the information. "Thank you, Uncle Jim." Ten minutes later, Ian called the Houlton Barracks.

"2256, Houlton. 10-8."

"10-4, 2256."

Ian drove as fast as he could towards Hall's Corner. As he slowed near the field he saw two brass shells lying in the road. His lights and brake lights were switched off and he sat there in the road looking down and across the field. There was nobody there. He waited and then got out with his flashlight to look around. He saw the muddy tracks coming out of the field and he picked up the two empty shells. He shined his light down and across the field and saw a dead deer under the apple tree.

"Why did they drive off and leave the deer?"

He scratched his head and turned his light off, standing in the middle of the road. A coyote howled not far behind him. He could probably smell the dead deer. It would be more risky trying to come back for it than if they had taken it with them.

The Moro Town Line Road ran straight west to east and he couldn't see any headlights. There was nothing else to do but go look at the deer. Before he even got close he could see the deer's belly was bloated. And it was obviously a road kill. The two shells? Probably for his benefit. But was it a prank or were they now hunting some place else, knowing he was there?

There was no sense in chasing them trying to guess where they had gone. He would bet a week's pay that this had been the work of the Murckle brothers. He slipped his pen inside the empty shells and picked them up and put them in a clean sandwich bag. Then he took his camera and photographed the tire treads and tracks in the road and then he photographed the dead deer and when he turned the deer over to look for marks, there was a pattern of square grooves, like the deer had lain on something for a while. The pattern reminded him of the floor of a trailer box. Then he began to put things together.

He decided that this was definitely the work of the Murckle brothers and they were now off some place else shooting a deer. He pulled some hair off the deer, making sure he had roots on the hair for DNA testing and then he took a small piece of meat. He also noticed that within the groove pattern, it appeared as if some hair had been pulled off when the deer had been moved.

He knew he had to see if the two brothers had a box trailer at their home and if they did, he would have to inspect the inside.

As he drove towards their house, which wasn't far, he tried to legally justify inspecting the trailer without a search warrant. He decided because it was a motor vehicle and capable of being moved and the evidence destroyed before he could possibly get a search warrant signed before Tuesday; being this was a national holiday weekend, this became an exigent circumstance and he would not have to have a warrant as long as he had articulatable suspicion.

He was satisfied as he closed his pickup door, hidden in a little hidey hole not far away. He checked his watch; 11:15 P.M. The lights in the house were off. So far so good. The truck and trailer were parked where they always parked when the boys are home. He opened the rear door quietly and climbed up into the box.

There was deer hair right by the door. He put some in another sandwich bag and hiked back to his pickup.

* * * *

Fred and Ralph opened another beer and laughing sped down Rt. 11 to Patten and then east on Rt. 159 towards Island

Falls. Fred took the I-95 north on-ramp and headed up I-95 towards Dyer Brook and Battle Brook. Driving slow now in case of a ditch deer, Ralph had his window down and loaded the 12 ga. shotgun with a slug. They never used their .270 Winchester when ditch hunting. The shotgun, they considered a throw away gun in case they saw a game warden. Besides, there were no riflings in the barrel for a ballistics comparison.

Near Battle Brook, Fred saw a set of eyes in the ditch. "Get ready Ralph, I think this is the one." Fred slowed and pulled over to the breakdown shoulder. The deer was standing there. A nice buck, but not the same one they had seen last night. Ralph finished his beer and stuck the shotgun out through the open window. Fred stopped the truck and the deer was only maybe thirty feet away, looking directly at them. Ralph put the front sight on the deer's neck and pulled the trigger. The report was deafening and the deer dropped dead.

Without wasting time, Ralph put the shotgun behind the seat with the .270 and then they both hurried down to the deer and drug it back to the pickup. They put the deer in back and then covered it with a piece of canvas. Then back inside they left the scene and decided to drive to Houlton. They needed to kill some time to let Ian sputter and finally go home. They left Houlton and drove south. There was no hurry and they just poked along. But when there were headlights coming up behind them, Fred decided he'd better drive the speed limit so not to raise any suspicions. Ten miles down the road a state trooper went by them. "I was going to drive to Sherman before getting off, but now I think we'd better get off at Island Falls exit and get to camp at Alder Brook as soon as we can."

Ralph opened them each another beer. The only other vehicle they had seen was the trooper, but Fred still wanted to stop playing around and get to camp.

As Ian was driving slowly up Rt. 11 without his lights on, he could see headlights coming up behind him. But way off. He sped up and ducked into the Pleasant Lake Road at the foot of Bates Hill to wait for the vehicle to pass by. And much to his surprise, the vehicle turned off Rt. 11 east, onto the road across from Ian. When it turned, he recognized it as the Murckle brother's pickup. He pulled out to follow them without lights through Hersey.

Fred stopped in the middle of the road after the first corner and said, "I got to make a pit stop."

"Me too," Ralph added.

But before either one of them opened a door, Ian was standing beside the driver's door and he opened it. The look on Fred and Ralph's faces was total shock and Ian could see the color draining from their faces. He would never forget that look.

Ian could smell beer although the empty cans had been thrown out. Fred finally composed himself and said, "What's this all about, Ian? You scaring the living hell out of us like that."

"Ralph, you roll your window up and shut the door." When Ralph just sat there, Ian said, "Now, damn you!" He did.

"Step out, Fred, and turn around and put your hands on the roof." When he did, Ian frisked him and removed a sharp skinning knife. His pant legs were covered with deer hair. But he didn't say anything about that just yet. "Fred, you stand in front of the pickup between the lights and keep your hands on the hood."

"You, Ralph, slide over here and get out." He did and Ian frisked him and removed another sharp skinning knife and three .12 ga. slugs. There was deer hair on his pant legs also.

"What are you looking for, Ian?" Ralph asked.

Ian reached behind the seat and removed the shotgun and laid that on the seat and then reached back again and removed the .270 Winchester Model 70. "This is what I want," and he handled it so not to destroy the fingerprints. And he put that in his pickup. "I wouldn't move if I were you. Remember, I can run faster and farther than either of you." Ian also turned on his headlights and as he walked back, he saw blood dripping out of the body onto the road. There was a pool of blood in the gravel.

"Okay, Ian, so you have our rifle, can we leave now?" Fred asked.

"I'm not done looking yet. Fred, you step over here by Ralph." He put a handcuff on Ralph and had Fred stick his arm through the open window and attached the other cuff.

"There, now I can do my job without having to worry about you two."

Ian pulled the canvas back and a cloud of steam rose from the deer. He looked it over and saw a large entry wound in the throat and no exit wound. The slug would still be inside.

Ian dug around in his wooden box in the body and removed his post-mortem kit. He put a thermometer in the deer's nose and another in one thigh. "This is going to take a while."

"I have to pee," Fred said.

"Me, too," Ralph said.

"Go right where you're standing."

Adding insult to injury, Ian said, "That's a mighty fine deer. Boy, that's going to taste good."

"What are you doing anyhow, Ian?" Ralph asked.

"I'm doing a post-mortem test to determine when this deer died."

"You can do that?"

"With great accuracy. This will probably take me until daylight. If you would be honest with me, we could get out of here earlier. Of course, that's only a suggestion. But before you say anything, I probably better advise you guys of your Miranda Rights." Ian went through the whole spiel and then asked, "Well, how about it? You want to stand there until daylight? Your choice."

"Okay, okay, about 11:45."

"Okay, that's good. But I'm going to take one reading just to see if you're telling me the truth."

Ian waited another half hour before reading the thermometer. In the mean time, he measured the deer's eye dilation. When he had all the figures on a graph, he said, "From these readings, I'd say the deer died between 11:30 P.M. and midnight. You were being truthful." Ian put away his kit and backed his pickup up to Murckle's to load the deer on his own truck.

"Fred and Ralph Murckle, I'm arresting you both for night hunting." Ian now put the shotgun in his pickup, behind his seat with the .270.

"Why are you keeping the rifle? It should be obvious that we used the shotgun," Fred said.

"Oh, the rifle has nothing to do with the night hunting charge." He left it at that.

"2256, Houlton."

"Go ahead, '56," Scotty replied.

"Hey Scotty, would you 10-21 my Uncle Jim at 528-2192 and advise when you have him on the line?"

Ten minutes later, "Houlton, 2256. Jim is on the line."

"Ask him to come to the foot of Bates Hill on Rt. 11 and take the left in Hersey. He'll see us around the first corner."

"2256, he said he'll be there in ten minutes."

"Thank you, Scotty."

When Jim arrived and saw the brothers hand-cuffed together through the window, he began laughing. "Well you got 'em after all. Good job, Ian."

Jim drove their pickup and took Ralph with him and Ian took Fred. "I thought that old man retired?"

"He did. He's doing this for fun." He knew this would give Fred something to think about. "And that old man is in better shape than you and can do a great deal more work each day than you. And you and your brother would be wise to remember that.

"How much beer have you and Ralph had tonight?"

"We killed a six pack."

"When did you start drinking?"

"When we left the house at 10 P.M."

"You don't seem drunk to me. Either one of you. If I was to administer a breathalyzer test, do you think you'd be higher than .08?"

"Might be."

"Well, so far I have seen nothing that would give me probable cause to administer a test, so don't give me one."

"No, sir." *That's better*, Ian thought.

"Now, Fred, here's the clincher. Right now I'm willing to forget an OUI charge. You need your license to earn a living. But you and your brother really pissed me and my Uncle Jim off when you staged that scene in the Hall Corner field and fired two shots. Uncle Jim is more pissed than I am. Now I expect you and your brother to plead guilty to night hunting at your arraignment, which will be Wednesday morning in Houlton. If you plead guilty, then I'm only going to explain to the judge why you staged a decoy scene. But if you don't, well, I'm confiscating your pickup and the .270 Winchester rifle tonight. And you get them back only if you two plead guilty. Are you understanding this, Fred?"

"Yeah, you have us over the barrel. We'll plead guilty even if I have to thump Ralph a little. Thanks, Ian. You know, you're not such a hard ass, after all."

* * * *

On the way home, Jim asked, "What are you going to do with this deer?"

"Clean it and eat it. You and Nancy want half?"

"Sure do. I can smell the gravy now."

They pulled into one of the gravel roads in Hersey and gutted the deer and then hung it up in Jim's garage. "I'll take care of this. You go home and get some sleep."

"Yeah, I've got a lot of report writing to do, also."

"Be here at 5 P.M. for supper. We'll have the heart and liver and Nancy made some whoopee pies yesterday."

* * * *

Scott Allery and Leonard Perks arrived at their camp shortly after daylight and expected to find the Murckle brothers already there with a deer. They unloaded the coolers and set up the two beer kegs on the sink counter. Paul Newman and his girlfriend Sandra arrived next. Then Carroll Miller and Diane Peck. Billy Andrews and his wife Alice shortly after and then Stacey and his girlfriend Beckie and at noon, while everyone was eating hamburgers and hot dogs and drinking keg beer, the only ones not there were Fred and Ralph.

Their father bailed them out of jail at 12:25 P.M. and he wasn't happy. He had to put up his house as security. So Fred and Ralph didn't make it to the party until 2:30 P.M. They came walking down the trail to the camp like two whipped dogs.

"Where have you two been? Did you get us any deer meat?" Scott asked.

"Here, have a beer," Leonard said.

"We've been in jail. Ian caught us last night." Everyone start laughing.

"I told you two, you were pushing your luck," Carroll said. "I think he has caught all of us now for one thing or another and sent us all to jail for three days."

Everyone nodded their head that they had all done three days because of Ian Randall. Being a wisenheimer, Scott said, "Here's a toast to The Three Day Club!"

Everyone laughed and said, "The Three Day Club!"

Ralph said, "He took our pickup, .12 ga. shotgun and our .270 Winchester, even though we told him we used the shotgun."

"Better shut up, Ralph," Fred said.

"He's a no good son of a bitch," Ralph said. "He never sleeps."

"When he caught me, he laughed and rubbed my nose in it. I didn't like that done. Yeah, I agree with Ralph, he is a son of a bitch," Leonard said.

"He's good. He's damn good," Fred said and this surprised everyone there. "I ain't playing no more games as long as he's around or his Uncle Jim."

Paul said, "What bothers me is that he gets so much fun out of throwing someone in jail. I hope he gets done soon."

They went on and on telling stories about getting caught by Ian and having to do three days in jail. "He's just like his Uncle Jim," Bill Andrews said. "He caught my old man more than once and a few of my uncles, too."

Sammy Wilbur and his girlfriend, Lynda, had been sitting quietly in the corner, listening. "All Ian needs to keep him home and entertained is a good woman. Maybe we could hook him up with someone," Sammy said.

"He's been married twice and those wives couldn't keep him home," Beckie said.

"Maybe they weren't womanly enough," Bill said. "If you know what I mean."

Carroll Miller took another drink of his beer and said, "How many of us here today didn't get what we deserved? He's only doing his job and because he is damn good at it, doesn't excuse any of us from paying our dues. When he caught me with three moose hindquarters, I was mad as hell at first, but Diane reminded me I didn't have to go out that night or shoot two moose."

"Yeah, I told you not to go that night, didn't I? I said I had a bad feeling about it."

"Yeah, I had a choice, and it put me in jail. He's good, damn good at what he does and damn it, there's not one of us here that can say he isn't fair. He could have taken me for more than he did, but he didn't." Carroll looked at Fred and Ralph, then said, "Well, how about it, Fred? My guess is Ian probably could have charged you both with one or more violations."

Ralph sat silent. He was still mad. "That's right, Ian ain't all that bad." He didn't want to tell them about the two breaks Ian had given them and certainly not about razzing ole Jim.

"That morning when Ian drove into my dooryard my heart stopped. I didn't know what to do. My pickup body still had blood and hair in it. I hadn't had time yet to wash it out or my truck. It was covered with mud," Carroll said.

"How in hell did he know you had shot a moose the night before?" Bill asked.

"Well, according to his report—I was given a copy—someone had seen where two moose had been shot the night before next to the road near Tilly Palmer's house that goes south into Hersey." Carroll stopped and looked at Scott. He looked away.

"Well, this guy stopped and told Tilly about the moose remains and Tilly telephoned Ian. Ian stated in his report that when he went by our place—we were living at Bob Levesque's house in Moro PLT. then, he noticed that I had driven my truck up to the garage, where as I always back it in. He said he noticed my truck was covered with mud and dirt and he knew I always kept it clean. He drove right down to the scene and said he found empty beer bottles and the same kind I drink."

"That's right ain't it, Scott? Can you imagine how dumb-founded I was when I read that in his report? Especially when I had shot my two moose behind the Sherman Lumber Company. What was I supposed to do, say, "No, Scott shot those moose. I shot mine behind the Sherman Lumber Company."

Everybody started laughing, even Ralph.

"He had me fair and square and there was no way I could argue that. There was no sense in hiring an attorney. He would have just charged me more than the fine. No, Ian is okay in my book. He gave me a break and then again a couple of years later. I was just dumping old pastries, wrappers and all in the woods for bear bait and one day he stopped me and suggested I take the wrappers off first. He could have charged me for that, but he didn't."

Carroll started laughing then, and was finally able to say, "With Ian's help, Diane was able to straighten me out." He looked at Diane and she was smiling.

Billy and Paul tapped the second keg and to everyone's surprise, Beckie said, "I can tell about another side of Ian."

They all were silent and looking at Beckie.

"When my first husband and I got a divorce, Ian and his wife were there for a divorce, also. Ian and his wife sat together and every other couple sat on separate sides with their attorney. They didn't have an attorney and the judge, Julian Werner called their case first and Ian took the stand. The judge read the complaint and said, "...for irreconcilable differences. What's so irreconcilable, that it can't be fixed?"

"Ian said he loved his job more than his wife. He was never home and didn't even know what color the sheets were on their bed, and that wasn't fair to his wife."

"The judge looked at Mrs. Randall and asked, 'Is this so, Mrs. Randall?' She said in a weak voice that it was. The judge signed the request for divorce and said, 'I grant this divorce because of irreconcilable differences. You're free to go and I wish you both good luck.'"

"Ian walked up the isle and stopped, waited for Mrs. Randall to get up and then they walked out of the courtroom together. The judge said, 'If that doesn't beat all.'"

"I learned that day that he cares about people."

"Maybe we should have invited him to this party," Leonard said.

Beckie said, "I have another story about Ian. This involved me when I was thirteen. One day, while I was in school at Southern Aroostook, my dad shot two doe deer and then bought me a hunting license. I was in school all day and then cheerleader practice until 4 P.M. Just before supper that evening, the phone rang and I answered it. It was Ian wanting to speak to my dad. When my dad put the phone down, I could tell he wasn't happy. I asked him, 'What did he want, Dad?'"

"He said he wanted to come over after supper and talk with my dad. I knew this was about the deer I had tagged after I got home. I was so afraid I'd go to jail, I started crying. I mean, I was really crying. My dad said, 'Don't worry Beckie, you won't go to jail.'"

"I couldn't eat and I ran upstairs to my room. True to his word, as soon as supper was over, he knocked at the door and my dad met him on the porch. My dad had time to think it over and I think this is why Ian called and said he'd be down after supper. To give my dad time to think about it. Before Ian could say anything, my dad said, 'I shot both deer, Ian. My daughter Beckie had nothing to do with it. I even had to talk her into tagging it. Take me, not her, or I'll fight you in court.'"

"Ian told my dad he didn't want me, he wanted my dad for shooting two deer. After he left, I was still afraid he'd come back for me. I have never been so scared. But he was true to his word, he only wanted my dad."

Leonard stood up and said, "I propose a toast to Ian Randall and his Uncle Jim."

Paul said, "Let's change the name of this cabin to The Three Day Club. And anyone who wants to join has to do his or her three days first." It was unanimous.

CHAPTER 6

At the Murckle brother's arraignment, Judge Julian Werner read off the charge and asked the two how they pled. And true to their word they both pled guilty. When the judge asked for the circumstances, Ian told him the full story.

"Did you stop them?"

"No, Your Honor, I was following without lights when they stopped on their own."

"Did they give you any problems?"

"After they understood how much evidence I had, they cooperated."

"Fred and Ralph Murckle, I find you both guilty of night hunting. I see this is your first night hunting offense, so you'll only have the three days in jail, and this will qualify you both for the Three Day Club. Because of how you went about decoying the game warden so you would feel free to hunt I-95, I fine you both $1,200."

When the two brothers had left the courtroom, Judge Werner said, "Nice job, Ian."

When Ian walked out to the hall, the two brothers were waiting for him. He was surprised.

"We asked the bailiff if we could wait until you came out. No hard feelings, Ian. You're better than what we thought. And thank you, and you know what I am saying, I think," Fred said.

"Yeah, I know. You two take care of yourselves. . .those three days. People are in jail for a reason."

"We will."

Ian wrote up a prosecution report for headquarters and decided to check out the St. Croix Lake area and Parnell Purchase. He poked around some of the old back roads and didn't find much of interest. He waited until evening before going in to see Parnell for a purpose—to see if he'd be at camp or out committing some dastardly deed.

He was at camp and graciously invited Ian in. "Tea or coffee?"

"Coffee, if you have it."

They sipped coffee and talked until after sunset and Ian stood up to leave. "Thank you for the coffee, Parnell."

Parnell sat at the table long after Ian left, wondering what had brought the visit. He had intended to go up the tracks for a deer when he saw Ian drive through the siding. He picked up his rifle and unloaded it. "Maybe another night, but not as long as I know he is around."

For two hours Ian drove around the roads between St. Croix and the siding at Masardis, hoping to run into the Lindley brothers, Elbert and Elmo. He had seen them in here before, late in the evening, about this same time of year.

Before going home, he drove through Bugbee's crew camps and followed the Bugbee Road down along the west branch of Hasting Brook to the I.P. Road. There were no new tire tracks in the road and all seemed to be quiet.

Not wanting to go home yet, he drove across the Mill Brook Road in Moro PLT and stopped in the road on top of the hill by the Gallagher farm.

He had a good view. He sat on top of his pickup hood where it was warm. There was a chill in the air. About 11 P.M. he heard a rifle shot from the south. He could just hear it, it was so far away. He waited for another shot that never came.

He had been there parked off the Moro Town Line Road near the Gallagher farm for more than an hour without seeing a vehicle or headlights. And he could see six miles east, as the road went east and west and he was on high ground. He decided to drive across the Clark Settlement Road to Rt. 212 and home. He signed off at home with Houlton at 12:30 A.M. He was so tired he couldn't even remember lying down and he slept good all night.

Every night that he worked after that he would hear a rifle shot, always between 10:30 and 11:30 P.M. Always to the south of him but always in a different area. It wasn't his patrol, but he knew sooner or later he'd go poaching in the other warden's district. This is what he always called it, when he went after someone in another district without telling that warden.

One day he telephoned Terry Hunter in Ashland and asked, "Terry, do you want to catch a night hunter tonight?"

"Sure, what have you got in mind?"

"Be at my house at 4:30 P.M. and I'll fill you in."

When Terry arrived, Ian had him leave his pickup between the house and garage where it would be visible from the road. "Why are we starting so early?" Terry asked.

Ian showed him his pickup that he had parked out back. There was a ladder tied onto the boatrack, a sawhorse, planks and a wheel barrow in back, green Vermont license plates and magnetic company signs on both doors. "I figure we should be able to drive through Patten around supper time and no one will take a second look at a Vermont construction pickup. For the last two weeks, I have heard almost nightly rifle shots from around Patten. I picked out one old farm and if anyone is out hunting tonight, they'll eventually end up at the Hatt farm, only a mile out of town; green hay fields."

"Hope you brought a lunch and hot coffee. This may be a long night."

They both pulled on camouflage shirts over their uniforms and a camouflage hat. "Let's go."

Just before they reached downtown Patten, Ian recognized the pickup coming up the hill towards them. He kept looking straight ahead. When the other vehicle was by, Ian said, "That vehicle? That was Dan Glidden's brother, Brian; he never recognized us with green Vermont plates and this construction material." They drove through town and no one stopped to look. No one cared about a pickup with green Vermont plates.

There was a small field on the right about half way in. There were a few tire tracks in the grass but they decided the field at the end of the road would be a better bet. They found a good place to hide their pickup and unloaded the construction gear. They removed the company signs and Vermont plates. They broke off a couple of spruce boughs and brushed out their tire tracks in the road and where they had turned off. Then they walked around the perimeter of the field. Ian wanted to know what was there—roads, apple trees, hunting stands. "This looks like a sure thing, Ian."

"Yeah, it's like money in the bank."

They ate a lunch before it got dark and a cup of hot coffee. "Do you have any idea who might be hunting this field?"

"I know Roger Atwood has been looking this over, but I really don't know more than that."

There was nothing more to do than sit there and talk and listen. At 9:30 P.M. they both were standing outside and heard one high powered rifle shot, a little north of town. "Where did that come from, Ian?"

"My guess would be out at the end of the Clark Road just north of town. There's some old farm land out at the end of the road and pretty good deer country."

"Are we going to check it out?"

"No, it doesn't pay to chase shots. I still think whoever has been checking out these fields will be in tonight."

Fifteen minutes later they were back inside the pickup and Ian saw a bright light descend in the sky in the area of Mount Katahdin. "You see that, Terry?"

"Yeah." They were both now watching the light through their binoculars, as the light appeared to hover in place. "It's moving north now," Ian said.

They both got out of the pickup and were watching the light as it was passing overhead and a little to the east. There were five amber lights in a V pattern and there was no sound at all.

"That was interesting," Terry said.

"I don't have a clue what it was," Ian replied.

They sat back in the pickup and Ian poured another cup of coffee. It was now about 10:30 P.M. and Ian said, "Lights coming, Terry." Ian threw his coffee out the window. The lights disappeared for a few moments and then reappeared. "They probably checked out the first field."

The lights were coming closer. "How do you want to work this, Ian?"

"We sit here and see what they do."

It seemed like forever before the vehicle came out into the field. It was a car. They drove into the field and jigged left and right, illuminating the entire field. Then they just sat there momentarily and then they turned around to leave.

"Okay, Terry, now we stop them." They pulled in behind the car and then Ian turned on the siren and blue lights and then the headlights. The driver in the car punched it and took off. "Damn it, that's a Z-28, Terry. If they reach the hot top, we'll never see them again."

"They aren't going to stop," Terry said.

"I'll bump him and he'll stop."

There was no way they were going to stop and once on the hot top, Ian knew he'd never be able to overtake a Z-28. There was a slightly wide place in the road, but not wide enough to pass, so Ian worked the nose of his pickup beside the Z-28 and very slightly bumped the rear quarter panel. That's all it took and the Z-28 stopped. Terry jumped out to secure the passenger with the rifle, the shooter, if a deer had been seen. Ian jumped out and ran into a dead pine limb almost putting his eye out. It hurt and he had to hold his right hand over his right eye.

But this did little to stop him. He rushed to the driver's side and pulled open the door and helped the driver to get out. He frisked him and removed a knife. Terry had the rifle secured in Ian's truck and was talking with the passenger, Sammy Holmes. The driver, Roger Atwood, was trying to make a fuss and Ian knew he had to do something quick or he would lose control of the situation. He opened the Z-28 door and with one arm forcibly put Mr. Atwood back inside.

"How long do I have to sit in here?" Atwood asked.

"You can get out when you behave yourself."

"Okay, I'll behave myself."

Roger Atwood's attitude did change. "I'm cold," he said.

Ian took off his jacket and gave it to Atwood.

The rifle, a Belgium made Ithica .243 and clip and shells were secured in Ian's pickup.

"Terry, you drive the Z-28 and take one of them and I'll take the other. Follow me."

As soon as Ian was in his vehicle he called the State Police Barracks, "2256, Houlton."

"Go ahead, '56."

"Would you 10-21 (telephone call) Warden Carroll Bates and have him bring a camera to take photos and meet me at the Hunter's club house on the Cow Team Road.

A few moments later, Houlton called back, "Houlton, 2256, your traffic was delivered and he'll be driving time."

Carroll was already there by the time Ian and Terry arrived. "What's up, Ian?"

"I had to bump his left rear quarter panel. I need photos in case he takes a sledge hammer to it later and claims I did it." Carroll laughed and took the photos. There wasn't much damage.

About that time, Roger's father arrived madder than all get-out. Not that we had arrested his son for night hunting, but because his son had taken his favorite rifle without asking. "I want that rifle. He took it without my permission!"

"Maybe so, but I have confiscated it as an instrumentality of the crime. If he is found guilty, then it becomes the property of I.F.W. And that's a state law. If you continue to make a scene, you'll be arrested for interfering." Carroll Bates was well acquainted with Mr. Atwood and was instrumental in quieting him down and sending him on his way.

"Thanks, Carroll."

"What happened to you?"

"I jumped out of the truck into a pine limb."

The Z-28 was left there and Mr. Atwood could take it home later. Ian, Terry and the two night hunters all got into Ian's truck. Terry had to drive as Ian's eye was really hurting. Before approaching the I-95 Houlton exit, Ian said, "Terry, maybe you better drop me off at the hospital. My eye is really beginning to hurt. Can you handle these two all right?"

"Sure, no problem. You boys aren't going to give me any problems, are you?"

"No, sir."

"If you do, I'll handcuff you in back," Terry said.

* * * *

Terry was waiting for Ian when the doctors finally discharged him. He walked out with a patch over his right eye. "How serious is it, Ian?"

"A puncture wound into the white of the eye. The stick missed the iris."

Outside, "You want to drive, Terry? We still have to go back to the Hatt Farm and pick up the construction gear."

It was about 3 A.M. Friday before Ian called it a night and went to bed. Terry still had to drive to Ashland.

Ian was on sick leave for the next four days, allowing the eye to heal, and much to his surprise, Maria arrived at 9 P.M. Sunday night. She was shocked when she saw the patch over Ian's eye. "My word, Ian, what happened?"

"I jumped out of my truck and ran into a dead pine limb. It'll be okay. It only punctured the white part of the eye."

69

Then she wanted to know all about that night and about catching the Murckle brothers, too.

He remembered what he had said to Maria earlier about not retiring until he caught the brothers, and now that he had, he hoped she wasn't going to hold him to it. He knew he was falling in love with Maria, but he just wasn't ready yet to give up the game.

"Canada celebrates Thanskgiving Day on the second Monday in October, but it has only been optional in New Brunswick for a few years, but the province has always celebrated it the same as the rest of the nation. I would like to bring Eric with me for a few days. I can also make arrangements for him to miss a day or two of school.

"Maybe we could get together with Roscoe and Renée and have a Canadian Thanksgiving at Umcolcus Lake?"

"I would like you to bring Eric with you."

On Tuesday, Maria drove Ian to the hospital and the doctor examined his eye. "I don't think you'll need to wear this patch any longer and there shouldn't be any change with your vision."

For the rest of Maria's visit, they stayed at home enjoying each other. "Sometimes you talk as if what you do for work is a game, I don't understand this. You carry a gun. You chase people who have guns and knives and sometimes you go without sleep for days. How can this be a game?"

"I take what I do very seriously, but I enjoy it as much as if I was playing a game of baseball. Sometimes poachers will try to pull a prank on me and there have been times when I have done the same to them. Nothing mean spirited or hateful. The best prank I guess you'd have to say I kind of pulled on myself. Of course, I had a little help.

"The second deer season that I had this district, I was young and new. It was the last day of the season and there was eight inches of new snow on the ground. I was patrolling in the woods in Smyrna. There weren't any good gravel roads then; not like there is today. The existing roads were narrow, bushes had grown in and up the middle of the roads. Well, I found a pickup parked along the side of one of these roads and from the tracks in the snow I decided it was just the one hunter. I recognized the pickup belonging to Jerry Collier, who lived on the same road I did in Oakfield about 400 feet up the road. I'd known Jerry to be a trapper and hunter and wondered if he was hunting after having already tagged one deer. So I decided to follow his tracks. Always watching to see if his tracks were following deer tracks.

"I had to hike right along trying to catch up with him and I was soon hot and my clothes were wet with sweat. Sometime after twelve noon I found where he had taken off his jacket and hung it on a tree limb. I stood there for quite some time trying to decide if he knew I was behind him and he had left his jacket there thinking I'd sit on it, while he went off hunting. I stood there so long now I was getting cold because I was wet and my feet were like icicles."

"After a while, I decided to continue following his tracks. I had to. . .I was so cold. He turned off that old road onto another and after a while more hunter tracks had come out of either side of the road and now I didn't know which tracks were his. I picked one and followed that to a camp on Duck Pond. There was smoke in the chimney and I knocked on the door. 'Come in!' someone hollered.

"I walked in and introduced myself and he said his name was Nate Churchill. He fixed me a cup of hot tea and we talked while I warmed up by the stove.

"I had no idea where I was or now how to get back to my pickup. He asked where I came in from and I told him the old Brown Farm. He gave me directions to get to my pickup. When I got there, Jerry's was still there. I was tired and wet and the day was about over. I went home.

"As I was eating supper, I received a telephone call from Nate Churchill; he had to come out to use the phone. One of his hunters was lost where I had been following Jerry earlier. I told him I'd get right on it."

"I went up to see Jerry at his house. He answered the door with a bewildered look on his face when he saw me. I told him there was a lost hunter from Churchill's camp on Duck Pond and I needed some help. I said, 'I know you know that area a whole lot better than I do.' Then I told him about following him and waiting at his jacket. He roared with laughter. Said he had no idea I had been following him, although he said when he started back out he did see someone's boot tracks along with his, but at the time hadn't thought much about it.

"He had shot a nice doe. Probably while I was inside of Churchill's camp and I didn't hear the shot.

"We spent pretty much the entire night in there looking for him. We'd fired a signal shot and never heard an answer. We were about ready to give up when we heard him hollering down hill by the east branch of the Mattawamkeag River. Then we had to walk him back to Churchill's camp and then we finally walked out of there."

"If it hadn't been for Jerry, I don't think I would have found him that night and as cold and wet as the hunter was, he might not have survived the cold night."

"So, this Jerry Collier never knew you had been following him? Then why did he leave his jacket?" Maria asked.

"He was hot and sweaty like me and that's why he took it off. The only prank was me thinking Jerry had left his jacket as a decoy."

"Okay, I guess I can understand that, but when you go out to work night hunters, this is serious business and no game. They have guns."

"It is serious business. But you have to look at it like this: I like to hunt and there's nothing more enjoyable than trying to out-smart and out-fox a poacher. It's fun. If I catch the poacher and get him into court, that's icing on the cake."

"You're terrible. You know that?" she said jokingly.

"Yeah, but is it fun to look for a lost hunter or how about a small child?" Maria asked, trying to understand Ian.

"Some people don't feel comfortable in the woods at night. I do and I'm good with a compass. When I find someone it is really gratifying.

"Last year I received a call that a bear hunter was lost. He was hunting out of the Driftwood Lodge on Upper Shin Pond. I found the area where this hunter's stand was and figured he probably had gotten turned around in the dark coming out and headed in the opposite direction. I knew of another road that would take me close if he had gone in the opposite direction.

"I fired a signal shot and got an answer, and I took a compass heading and went in. He was about a half mile away. When I got to him, he was real glad, he didn't want to spend all night in the woods. But he asked, 'Do you know which way to go to get back where you started from?'

"I said, 'just 180° in the opposite direction.' And when we came out to within fifty feet of my truck, he couldn't believe it. This guy was a federal judge from Baltimore, Maryland. The next day, when I got home, there was a half gallon of Canadian Hardwood Whiskey sitting on my step."

"I would be very nervous if I had to go out into the woods alone at night," Maria said.

"Many people are."

"I don't like looking for drowned bodies. I've pulled a few up and into the boot. One was the eighteen year-old daughter of a friend at a graduation party at Cary Lake in Littleton. She was a very pretty girl and my friend lost it when the divers brought her to the surface and I pulled her in to the boat.

"Enough talk for now." He turned the light out and held Maria against his chest and kissed her passionately. After their love making they laid on their backs and Ian had his arm around her and under her head. They fell asleep like that, Ian dreaming about chasing poachers in the Astral World and Maria of building a new house and moving.

*   *   *   *

Every time Maria and Ian were together, it was becoming more difficult to say goodbye. "In December I would like to spend some time with you on the farm with your family."

Not long after Maria had left, Jim arrived with a box of cut and wrapped deer meat, thanks to the Murckle brothers. "I see Maria has left already."

"Yeah."

"I was hoping to see her before she had to leave."

"Any special reason?" Ian asked.

"Just to see her beautiful smile and to say goodbye. She's a beautiful woman, that one. You asked her to marry you yet?"

Ian looked at his uncle with surprise.

"Don't look at me like that. If you haven't, then you're a big idiot! What are you waiting for? Women like Maria don't come into a man's life often. You miss out on Maria, and another one won't be coming. Just believe me, Ian, married life is a lot better than I ever remember it being. If not for Nancy, I'd be a lonesome old man. You don't have but a few years left and you'll be forced to retire."

"I know. I've been thinking along some of those lines. I've always wanted to put in thirty years before I retired. I have one left. And damn it, I'm still having fun. And I can't risk marrying her now before I do retire, because I'm afraid of losing her because of my job."

"Have you said anything to Maria about all this?"

"Not exactly."

"Well, damn it boy, don't you think it is about time?" *Boy?* Ian was 51 and Uncle Jim was calling him 'boy'. *Well considering Jim's age, maybe.*

Jim left and returned home and Ian put the deer meat down stairs in the chest freezer.

All the rest of that day he couldn't stop thinking about he and Maria and what his Uncle Jim had said, but before he could make any plans, he wanted to spend some time with Maria and her son, Eric, and with her mom and dad on the farm. Get to know them first. His mind was made up now and no changing it. He would be back at work tomorrow. The soreness around his eye was almost gone.

The Hatt Farm night hunters, Atwood and Holmes, instead of pleading guilty at their arraignment, opted for a district court trial where there would be no jury. The final decision would be Judge Julian Werner's alone, after hearing all of the evidence.

Since Ian and Terry Hunter had arrested those two, the shots at night stopped and so did any information leaking out from around the area. But Ian was still out there looking and listening for a shot in the darkness.

Dan Glidden, from Garfield, teamed up with Ian the last Wednesday night in September. Ian had parked his pickup behind the tractor shed on the north side of the Moro Town Line Road on the Gallagher farm. Whenever a vehicle came through, Dan would run down to the road and lay in the tall grass so he could watch as the vehicle passed by. The opposite side of the road was the old Irving Bates farm. The old farmhouse had fallen in on itself and the fields on that side of the farm had grown up with apple trees, and that year everyone of them were loaded with apples.

"I can remember as a kid going for a ride around the Moro Town Line Road, the Clark Settlement Road to Rt. 212 and then back on Rt. 11, just to look at all of the deer. We'd count as many as forty deer around the loop," Dan said.

"The first year I was on when Virgil Grant came out of retirement that fall to work with me, there'd be twenty or so deer in this field here every night. When the St. Regis Paper Company started harvesting lumber so fast across the road in Hersey, the deer disappeared. Now, you'd be lucky to see one deer making the loop. But there are still people looking for an easy kill," Ian said.

At about 9 P.M., after an east bound vehicle had gone by, a huge bear climbed down out of one tree and started crossing the Town Line Road towards Dan. He didn't see the bear until the bear started clicking his teeth together and blowing. He must have scented him.

Ian was puzzled why Dan was still staying by the roadside unless there was another vehicle. But he couldn't see any lights.

Dan just stood there thinking the bear would go around him. But the big brute was still clicking his teeth and this wasn't a good sign. He took a couple fast steps in Dan's direction, probably trying a bluff. Dan stayed low in the grass and picked up two rocks about the size of baseballs and then to the bear's surprise, Dan jumped up and hollered and threw one of the rocks at the bear and then he ran at the bear and threw his other rock. The bear turned tail and ran back across the road and Dan ran out onto the road hoping his bluff had worked. That ole bear had had enough of Dan Glidden.

When Dan walked back to the pickup, Ian asked, "What was all that hollering about?"

"A bear came across the road from the apple trees and tried to put the run to me." Then he told Ian all about the encounter. Ian laughed so hard people down over the hill by the river could have heard him.

That was all the excitement until 10:30 P.M. when another vehicle was driving easterly, very slowly. Dan ran down to the tall grass at the side of the road and waited. It was taking so long, Ian wondered if the vehicle had stopped somewhere, but he could still see the illumination in the tree tops.

It came through eventually, but you could have walked faster. They were sure looking for a deer. There was no doubt in Ian's mind. As soon as the car had driven beyond Dan, he came running back. "That's my Uncle Jack and Merle York. There's no doubt what those two are looking for."

Without lights and the brake switch off, Ian drove out on to the road. There were no vehicles in either direction, except for Merle and Jack. Ian pulled in behind them, staying about forty feet back so not to be visible in the mirrors. They were still driving slow. Across the bridge on the west branch of the

Mattawamkeag River and up York Hill, Merle, whose car it was, turned into the old yard where he once lived. There was a large field out back that bordered the road and several apple trees. The headlights were put out across the field and a flashlight beam from the passenger window. This was enough for Ian to arrest them for night hunting and he started to speed up.

"No, no, Ian, that's my Uncle Jack and we'd better wait until he has blood on his hands, or as sure as I'm sitting here, we'll lose the case."

"Okay." They were both shaking so much with excitement, the pickup was rocking back and forth.

Merle backed onto the road again and continued traveling in the same direction and still at a slow pace. "Merle once lived here, so he'll be very familiar with the good deer spots."

They followed Merle and Uncle Jack by Gerald Mitchell's farm, the Don Mitchell farm and through the Merrill woods and as Merle started up Mitchell Hill, he turned and jigged the lights to the right, where there were numerous apple trees. Ian stopped the pickup and he and Dan were looking through their binoculars. But they were still shaking so much from the excitement, the pickup was shaking and rattling. Dan said, "I can't see anything, I'm shaking so much."

Both he and Ian got out and stood on the road and watched through binoculars. A flashlight beam came out of the passenger window again. And then Merle backed up and continued on up Mitchell Hill. When they got to the top, they turned left onto the Clark Settlement Road. "This is good," Ian said, "there's always deer through here." The first two night hunters Ian caught were on this road, and using a 50,000 watt spotlight.

There were a collection of old, gone-by farms along this road, growing back to nature and apple trees. Always a good place to find deer. But not tonight. Merle drove by the old Porter fields and never put out a light. He made the sharp turn by the Lawler Farm and east now towards Rt. 212. But along this stretch were numerous green fields. But as luck would have it, there were no deer tonight. "Well, maybe they'll get onto I-95 and head south. There's always deer feeding on the grassy shoulders."

They followed Merle's car eastward on Rt. 212 towards Smyrna Mills. Ian couldn't drive through Smyrna and Oakfield without lights, so he turned them on and dropped back further so not to spook them. "They're turning south on I-95."

Before taking the on ramp, Ian once again turned his lights off. They were about a mile ahead now, but still driving slow for I-95. "They're looking for a ditch deer," Dan said.

Merle drove under the Island Falls overpass and continued southerly towards the Sherman exit. "If they don't see anything before reaching the Sherman exit, they may take a median crossover and head back towards Oakfield," Dan said.

But they didn't. Merle exited I-95 at Sherman and turned right towards Patten. Again, Ian had to drop back so he could turn his headlights on. But they could still see Merle's tail lights, as his car was the only one on the road. They followed Merle and Jack through Sherman, Stacyville, Patten and then turned left or west onto the Clark Road. "This road deadends in about two miles at an old farm. The fields are still mowed and I've known my uncle to hunt out here some in the past," Dan said.

But somehow, somewhere Dan and Ian lost sight of Merle's car. They checked the old farm at the end of the road and nothing. Dan knew of another field road that circles back onto Rt. 11 just above town. So Ian turned onto this. There were fields on both sides of the dirt field road, but no sign of Merle and Jack. The field road led them almost through Leroy Giles' dooryard.

"Where in hell did we lose them?" Ian asked.

"They had to have pulled into someone's driveway that we missed."

"Do you think they knew we were behind them all this time?" Ian asked.

"I don't know. But if they did, my brother Brian will call and ask what was going on. If I don't hear from him, then we can assume they were just lucky tonight."

It was now going on 2 A.M. so Ian drove back to his house and Dan still had forty miles to drive. As Ian laid in bed, he kept going over the night's events. Where had they lost them? "Or did Merle and Jack know all the time that we were behind them, and they were just playing with us?"

Ian rolled over and went to sleep.

* * * *

The next day, Ian went to Umcolcus Lake to visit Roscoe and Renée. They were happy to see him and offered a late breakfast of pancakes and bacon with real maple syrup. "We make our own syrup. There are only a few rock maples near, so we don't boil down much."

"What brings you out here, Ian? You didn't come out just to have breakfast with Renée and me?"

"No, I didn't. Canada's Thanksgiving Day is the second Monday in October." Renée nodded her head that it was.

"I thought it would be nice, since both Renée and Maria are from Kedgwick, that we all get together that day for a Thanksgiving dinner. Maria's son, Eric, will be with us for a couple of days then, also."

"That would be a grand idea, Ian. We can have Thanksgiving dinner right here. That's okay with you, isn't Roscoe?" Renée asked.

"Absolutely. I think it would be nice." Then Roscoe began to laugh. "You'd better get used to Maria making the decisions around the house, Ian. That is, I presume, you two will be getting married some day."

"Yes, I hope to, but we really haven't talked too much about it."

Plans were made, for it was only nine days away.

"We had to go into Patten two days ago to do some shopping. The word is you have really quelled the night hunting around Patten, after catching the Murckle brothers and then Atwood and

Holmes. The talk is that Patten really ain't your patrol and you have people there, especially the poachers, a little scared and paranoid about you.

"I used to see them knucklehead Murckle brothers in here some, until I ran them the hell out of here. I think that kinda relieved me too, cause I ain't seen 'em in here since."

He wanted to ask Roscoe if he had heard anything about Merle York and Jack Craig, but decided it would be best to let that one alone. He didn't want to embarrass himself. But he was more sure now than before that Merle and Jack had known all the time that he and Dan had been behind them all the way to the Sherman exit. They had played their own sort of game this time.

Partridge season opened on Monday and Ian was out in the woods after his four birds. He actually enjoyed partridge meat better than deer or moose steaks. But canned venison was the ultimate food. Fit for kings. He brought home three or four birds every day. He made a big kettle of partridge stew and everyday he would add another partridge breast and vegetables. The legal limit to possess at home was only eight birds, so when he had too many, he would give some to Miss Pearl in Oxbow, Tilly and Oceana Palmer and Gerald and Geraldine Mitchell.

* * * *

The restaurant where Maria worked closed early on Sunday, the day before Thanksgiving and she and her son, Eric, were on their way to Moro PLT., Maine by 4 P.M. She had been able now to reduce the driving time to four hours, by knowing which highway to take.

Eric had never been to Maine before, but he was more excited about seeing Ian again.

When they arrived at Ian's house, he wasn't home. Maria explained to him about Ian's job and how he wouldn't have any days off until December. It was simply the nature of the job.

Maria fixed them something to eat. While she was doing

that, Eric found a note that had blown onto the floor. "Hey Mom, here's a note from Ian."

"He's looking for moose hunter in the St. Croix area and will try to be home early."

Ian was tucked away in a hidey hole watching the Blackwater Road out of Masardis. He figured on a Sunday evening, a moose poacher might feel a little safer. If a vehicle drove by, he would pull in behind it and follow without lights.

Then a pickup went by and Ian could see two people in the cab. He had to hurry to catch up and when he did he thought they were driving a little fast to be looking for a moose to kill. But then they might have a favorite spot or they might have one down already.

He followed them to the turn off for the old Levesque City. The city had been abandoned a few years and only the garage and the office building remained. There were nice roads that stretched out behind where the city used to be and it was awfully fine moose country. It was darker now and Ian was following closer when the vehicle pulled into the old yard. There was a camper set up in the yard. The pickup pulled up beside the camper and Ian stopped and got out and walked over. Ian recognized both men. They had worked for Levesque and stayed at the camps during the week. Paul Courtiere and Raymond LaRoche. "Good evening gentlemen." Until he had spoken, neither of the two men knew Ian or anyone else was around. "You coming in to bird hunt tomorrow or are you working in here again?"

Courtiere said, "We going to hunt birds tomorrow. What you doing here?"

"I followed you in from Blackwater. Didn't know you might be a after a moose. Before I leave, I'd like to see your hunting licenses and any firearms you have in your pickup."

Niether shotgun was in a case, which was the law on Sunday in an unorganized township. "Open the actions for me?"

They were both empty. "Ay, next time fellas you might want to put your shotguns in a case on Sunday."

"We forget me, sorry," LaRoche said.

"Enjoy your hunt tomorrow." Ian got in his pickup and drove off with his lights still off. LaRoche and Courtiere watched in disbelief as Ian drove out of sight. Ian headed for home and turned his lights back on once he was away from Levesque City. He knew Maria and Eric would be home by now and he drove a bit faster than he normally would.

Ian drove in his driveway at 9:30 P.M. and signed off with the police barracks. Maria and Eric came outside to greet him. Eric ran over to Ian and hugged him. Ian liked that. Maria stood back on the steps and smiled as she watched the two of them together.

"Did you see anything?" Maria asked.

"I followed two guys in a pickup from Masardis to the old Levesque City. But they had a camper trailer set up there. They were going to spend the night in and hunt tomorrow. It was a good check and I think it'll keep them honest or looking over their shoulders for awhile." He had to explain what Levesque City was.

"Are you hungry? I fixed a sandwich and some cheese macaroni for Eric and me."

"That sounds good."

While Maria made a lunch, Ian took his uniform off and took a shower. When he finished eating, he showed Eric and Maria where he hung up his gunbelt in the closet. "Eric, this gun is always loaded, and it's nothing more than a tool I use. Sometimes to signal a lost person or shoot a sick or wounded animal. Sometimes I have to leave here in a hurry and wouldn't have time to load it first. So that's why it stays loaded. You are not to handle this gun. Is that understood?"

"Yes sir."

"When you're old enough, I'll teach you how to shoot a handgun and you are old enough now to go hunting with me."

Maria heard what he wasn't saying and this made her happy, and she was smiling.

*   *   *   *

The next morning before loading the pickup with Maria's cooking for the dinner, Ian took Eric down to Lougee's store, just down the road, to get him a junior hunting license. "There now, if we see a partridge, I'll let you shoot it." Ted Lougee always acted like a grouch, but secretly he enjoyed children. "Here young Mr. Eric, you'll be needing an orange hat. On the house."

Eric put the hat on and said, "Gee, thanks Mr. Lougee." Instead of taking the faster route through Bugbee's camp yard, Ian drove down to West Hasting Brook and then up the Bugbee Road to Friel's Road. Near the bridge, across West Hasting Brook, sat three partridges on the roadside. Ian stopped the pickup and got out with the shotgun, a .20 guage, and said, "Eric, slide over and get out and stay behind this door." Ian loaded the shotgun and showed Eric how to move the safety. "Pick out one bird and aim for its head and pull the trigger."

Eric stepped around the door and pulled the shotgun to his shoulder, picked out a bird and pulled the trigger. Two birds went down and the third flew off. Eric gave the gun to Ian and ran up to claim his prize. "Two birds with one shot! Holy cow, Mom, kids at school will never believe this."

Ian put the two birds in the back of his pickup. And they saw no more partridge. There was a short walk into their camp and all three had their arms loaded with food for dinner. Ian had signed off, 10-7, with the police barracks at Umcolcus Lake in T8-R5 for most of the day.

Inside and their arms unloaded, Ian introduced Eric to Roscoe and Renée. "Are you from back home, Ma'am?" Eric asked.

"Yes, I am, Eric. Your mother and I know some of the same people."

"Ian, how about a drink?"

Ian took his gunbelt and uniform shirt off and said, "I just went off duty. I'd love a drink."

Eric looked at Ian with surprise etched all over his face. "You can do that? Just go off duty?"

"I have worn this uniform long enough, Eric, so I can do that."

Ian told Roscoe about the two birds with one shot Eric got on the way in.

"Ian, before I forget it, Renée and me, we've been hearing some shooting around 8 P.M. in the evenings out towards Bugbee's camps. Might be some of his French help. I'm surprised he still hires the French loggers, especially after the trouble he had just a few years ago. I'll admit, they work like dogs, but any lumbering contractor in Maine should hire Maine workers first."

Eric wandered around outside for a while then he sat and listened to Roscoe and Ian telling stories.

When dinner was served, there was a good deal more food on the table than the five of them could possibly eat. Renée asked, "Ian, would you say grace?"

"In the name of the Father,
The Son, and the Holy Spirit,
I would like to thank
The turkey and all the vegetables
That gave their life, so that
We may take sustenance.
May the Blessings be."

"That was a little unusual, Ian, but very appropriate," Roscoe said.

Everyone was hungry and they at in silence until the meal was almost eaten. "My, I can't remember a better tasting meal," Ian said. "You ladies have surely outdone yourselves."

When the meal was finished, they all sat out on the porch sipping coffee. Eric had tea. The sound of gun shots from across the lake reminded Ian that he was supposed to be working. "Where will you three go when you leave here?"

"I think we'll take the Camp Violette Road west to the Snowshoe Road and maybe back across the I.P. Road."

Roscoe could see Ian was itching to go. Those shots across the lake were calling to him like a sweet woman's voice. He thought he would make it easy for him and he said, "Well, are you going to go to work today or waste my hard earned tax dollars?" Then he laughed.

Back in Ian's pickup, they rode through Bugbee's camp yard. "I'll have to come back here Thursday afternoon. One of these crews are shooting moose. Bugbee's crews all leave and go home on Thursday, so if they have any meat to take with them, they'll wait until they re about to leave."

There was no one in the yard when they drove through, so word won't get out that the game warden was about and spook them. Ian drove north up Rt. 11 from there to the Camp Violette Road. "This road gets a little rough about eight miles in. But you'll see a lot of country."

Just then, the State Police Dispatcher in Houlton was calling Ian. "Houlton, 2256."

"Go ahead, Scotty."

"Your Uncle Jim just called and advised that a tractor-trailer heading south on Rt. 11 hit a moose in Game Warden Curve. The moose has a broken front leg, but managed to run off. The trucker left the road. He was empty though."

"10-4 Houlton. I just turned onto the Camp Violette Road but will turn around and head in that direction.

"See how your day and plans can change in a heartbeat?"

For Eric's benefit, he turned the blue light on when he was back on Rt. 11. "Okay Eric, you see that toggle switch there?"

"Yes sir."

"That's the siren. When I say to, turn it on."

"You bet." Maria looked at Ian and smiled.

They were traveling fast and came up behind a loaded log truck. "Okay, Eric."

"Gee, that's loud."

"It's supposed to be, to get the attention of drivers."

The truck driver pulled over to the right as far as he could and waved his arm motioning that it was okay to pass.

As they passed the truck, Ian said, "Okay, Eric, turn it off, then on again and then off."

He did and asked, "Why?"

"To say thank you to the truck driver for motioning us on by."

"Okay, we're coming close to Knowles Corner and Rt. 212, so turn it on."

There was one car that stopped at the junction and waited for Ian to pass. "There are more houses down through here, and traveling this fast we'd better keep the siren on, okay?"

"Okay."

When they passed the Katahdin Lodge, he slowed up.

"Okay, you can turn it off now." The truck was on its side in the right ditch. The state trooper was with the driver and Uncle Jim was there, as well. They were waiting for the wrecker coming out of Houlton. Mac gave Ian a copy of his report so Ian could make out his own.

"Do you want the moose, if I can find it?" Ian asked the driver.

"You've got to be kidding, right? After this? No, you keep it."

"Eric, do you want to go moose hunting?"

"Yeah! I mean yes, sir!"

"How about you, Maria?"

"No, I'm fine. I'll visit with Nancy."

"Okay, we'll put this pickup in Jim's yard." Then he hollered, "Yeah, Uncle Jim, do you want to go with Eric and me?"

"No, you two go ahead. I've tracked down and shot my share of moose."

The driver said, "It's a cow moose and her left front leg is badly broken. She won't get too far. She's on that side of the road," and he pointed to the left side.

He picked up the tracks and blood trail and he and Eric began to follow. It soon became obvious that the moose was having a hard time of it, and it was losing a lot of blood. The trail was going directly east, never varying. About a hundred yards below Rt. 11, Ian got his first glimpse of the hind quarters. The moose was hobbling pretty bad.

"Come, we need to get ahead of it and let it come to us, Eric." Ian circled high to the left and as fast as he could. After ten minutes he found where he hoped the moose would come.

They stopped and waited. They couldn't see it yet, but they could hear it crashing through the bushes. Ian took his .357 pistol out to be ready. They were still above the moose which would give Ian a good broadside shot. "Okay, here it comes."

The moose was about fifty feet away in a little clearing. Ian aimed where the heart would be and he squeezed the trigger. The loud noise jumped Eric. The moose went down but it wasn't dead. Ian ran over before the moose was able to stand again and he put a round in the head behind the ear. "It's okay, Eric. She's dead now." Eric walked over. . .feeling a little uneasy about seeing such a big animal suffer with a broken leg and then hunt it down and kill it.

"Now what do you do with it, sir?"

"Well, we'll leave it. It won't be any good eating. There was a whole bunch of adrenaline hormones cruising through the body because of the crash and then trying to escape. The adrenaline would make the meat so tough you couldn't chew it. I've tried.

"Can you guide us back to the road?"

"Gosh, I don't know, but I'll try."

Ian was surprised how well he had done. He didn't try to correct him when he swung too far to the right to go around a thick stand at the top of the hill. "Not bad, Eric, for your first hike and no compass."

The big wrecker was there righting the truck and trailer. They walked on by to Uncle Jim's. It was too late now to think about doing something else and being a Monday, he decided to stay home with Maria and Eric. But first he showed Eric how to pull the breast out of his two partridges. He didn't like that, especially when he heard sinew ripping.

"After you wash these up, we'll put them in the freezer so you can take them with you, when you and your Mom leave."

"Okay."

After supper, Eric went to bed early. He had had an eventful day. "Is every day as busy or interesting as this has been?" Maria asked.

"Some days are real boring. Some days are so exciting the time passes without noticing."

"I think I can understand some, why you have been a game warden for so long."

They were on the porch even though the night was cool. Ian heard the southbound train as the engineer backed off the throttles approaching the down grade at Dudley Siding.

"What's that noise, Ian?"

"That's the southbound train out of Ashland as the engineer uses the engines to slow his approach to Dudley Siding. From there to Smyrna the track is down hill."

"To answer your question Maria, I'll be retiring next summer. That'll give me thirty years, like my Uncle Jim."

* * * *

Maria and Eric left the next morning and that evening as Ian sat on the porch sipping a brandy, his thoughts were all about Maria and Eric. He felt the same towards Eric as he would his own son. And he wished he had met Maria twenty years ago. She was more understanding, friendly and personable than any woman he had ever known. His loving thoughts and dreams of Maria were keeping him warm, although the temperature had dropped to 35°. At midnight he yawned, stood up and stretched and went to bed.

But his dreams that night in the Astral world were not of

Maria. Instead, even in this inner world he found himself chasing poachers.

Thursday morning about 10:30 A.M., Ian hid his truck and walked into Bugbee's camps. He waited in the bushes for a while to see if there was any activity at the garage or the camps. When he was satisfied there was no one around, he began searching behind each camp.

Behind the middle camp he found a black plastic bag full of meat scraps. It looked as if they had already butchered the moose. Then the meat may be in plastic bags set in a cold brook somewhere, or in ice coolers in the camp.

He found a comfortable spot where he could lean back against a tree and he sat down to wait for the occupants of the camp to come back. He hoped they would leave early like they usually did on Thursdays. The mosquitoes and minges were terrible and he didn't have any fly dope.

Harry Bugbee came flying into the yard hell bent for election and skidded to a stop in front of the garage and a few minutes later came back out and put something into the back of his pickup and then stormed out of there again. Some machinery had probably broken down.

At noon everyone came back for lunch, even the two using the camp Ian was watching. One by one they all loaded up their pickups for the drive home. Except for the two Ian was watching. Harry put some more parts into his pickup and went back into the woods. The only ones there now were the two Ian was watching.

After Harry left, the two came out and loaded bags of dirty clothes, their suitcases and then they hauled out an enormous igloo ice cooler. It was heavy as it took both boys to carry it and slide it up into the body of their truck. And lastly, the heavy-set fellow brought what looked like a new rifle, and put that in the cab. Then he went back to lock the camp door and the other fellow started the pickup. Ian chose this moment to step out and up to the driver's door.

"Hello there," Ian said to the driver.

The driver jumped and hollered, "Jesus Christ! You jumped the hell out of me."

Ian looked at the heavy-set fellow. At first he was afraid he might run off. But he just stood between the tailgate of the pickup and the camp steps staring at Ian. He knew his world was turning upside down in a hell-basket.

"Isn't this awful early to be going home when the weather is so nice?" Ian asked.

"We live in Caribou, mister, and we spend all week living in this camp and come Thursday afternoon we can't wait to leave."

"You must have some pretty good wood if you can afford a three and a half day weekend."

"It's not bad. Look mister, we'd really like to be on our way."

"Well, I'm not done here yet. We'll start with that rifle. Pass it out to me, butt first."

Ian pulled the bolt back and ejected an empty shell. He picked it up and put it in his pocket. "Any handguns?"

The driver said, "No."

"If you have any, you'd do yourself a favor and hand it out the window, because you know I'll find it when I search."

The driver reached under the seat and pulled out a holster with a Blackhawk .44 Magnum gun. It was loaded. Ian emptied that and put the shells in his other pocket and for now put the gun on the roof.

He looked at the heavy-set fellow and said, "You step over here."

He did and Ian frisked him, and asked, "What is your name?"

"Francis Sirois."

"Okay, Francis, you go back and stand by the tailgate. You step out."

Ian frisked the driver and was surprised he had not found any knives. "Your name?"

"Arron Skidgell."

"Are you both from Caribou?"

"Yes."

"Arron, you go stand with Francis while I search your cab."

He did.

Ian was looking for the knives they used to cut up the moose. When he didn't find them, he suspected they might be in the camp.

"Okay, Francis, jump up in the body and open this cooler for me."

Regretably he did, and just like Ian thought, it was filled with deboned moose meat. "Is this all of it or did you leave some in the woods?"

"This is all. We ate the heart and liver."

"Francis, Arron, you both are under arrest for illegal possession of moose meat. Is the rifle yours, Francis?"

"Yes."

"New?"

"Yes."

It was a Remington .30 06 and a Vari X 3 Leupold scope. "Open the camp door, Francis."

He did, and then all three went inside. In the back, leaning up against the wall, was a piece of plywood they had used as a cutting board. It didn't take Ian long to find the knives. He decided to leave the plywood and the knives. "Okay fellas, now I want you to take me out where you shot the moose. Only I'll be driving."

They drove out of the camp yard and onto the Dow Road heading south. About a mile and a half down, Arron said, "We were about here and the moose came out of the left and stood in the road."

"How many shots?"

"One with the rifle and one with the .44 to finish it off."

"What did you do with the rest of the remains?"

"We dropped them off in the woods." They got out and the

boys showed Ian where the remains were. Coyotes and bear had already cleaned up a lot of it.

They turned around and drove out where Ian had his pickup hidden. "Arron, I'll let you follow me to jail so you'll have transportation when you make bail. "Francis, you and the .44 and .30-06 will go with me. Drop the tailgate and I'll back up to it and we'll put the cooler on my truck."

Fransic was pretty quiet all the way to Houlton.

Ian put ice on the meat to keep it until morning when he would take it down to his Uncle Jim's and the two could cut and wrap it.

"My freezer is getting pretty full, Ian. I hope you have some room in yours?"

"We'll be all right, Uncle Jim. I plan to give some of it to other folks."

Two weeks later Atwood and Holmes went to trial in District Court and no jury. Judge Julian Werner was presiding and he alone would determine guilt or innocence. They had hired a well known attorney who in the past had had a lot of experience defending night hunters.

Ian was called first to testify and in cross-examination their attorney, Bud Salmon, asked, "Mr. Warden, are you acquainted with Mr. Atwood and Mr. Holmes?"

"I know who they are."

"Do you know if they have hunting dogs?"

"I have no idea if they have hunting dogs or not."

"Isn't it true, Mr. Warden, that the two were only there at the Hatt Farm looking for their dogs?"

"No sir, it isn't." There was no hesitation with Ian's reply. Their attorney was getting flustered and his face was turning red.

"How can you be so sure, Mr. Warden?"

"When they drove into the field, the car was jigged to the left first, illuminating that section of the field and then jigged to the right. At no time did either occupant exit the car and call for a dog."

The attorney handed Ian the clip he had retrieved from the vehicle. "Mr. Warden, what caliber clip is this?" He handed it to Ian.

"Stamped on the clip is .308."

"And what caliber was the rifle you confiscated?"

"It was a .243."

"Then there was no way that this .308 clip could be inserted in that .243 rifle, is there?"

"Actually, it fits very good."

"But they are two different calibers, are they not!?" Ole Bud was getting excited.

Very calmly, Ian said, "A .243 shell is the same shell as a .308, only necked down to a .243."

"No more questions for this witness," Attorney Bud Salmon said and sat down.

It was the prosecutor's turn for redirect questioning. "Mr. Randall, you seem to be quite sure that the two defendants were not looking for a dog. Would you explain this?"

"Yes. Myself and Warden Terry Hunter arrived at the Hatt Farm field about 5 P.M." He glanced towards the two and this too surprised them both. "The first thing we did was to walk around the circumference of the field and across it and then we brushed out our tire tracks in the gravel road. There was no sign of dog tracks in the mud or loose sand and gravel. Nothing to indicate that dogs were running loose there and there was no barking."

That night, once they were on I-95 heading towards the county jail in Houlton, Ian had told them about the UFO they had seen only 45 minutes before they came in to the field. During Terry Hunter's cross-examination, the attorney said, "Isn't it true you and the other warden were seeing UFO's that night?"

"We saw something fly right overhead."

"So were there any green men in the field that night or just UFO's? Actually, you aren't sure if there was a vehicle in that field that night, or spaceships."

"We saw something 45 minutes before Atwood and Holmes drove into the field."

Ian looked at Judge Werner. He was smiling.

"No further questions."

"The state rests, Your Honor."

It didn't take the judge long to make his determination. "I find you both guilty of night hunting and fine you $1,000 each, plus cost of court and you both will join the Three Day Club."

Attorney Bud Salmon was so upset, he left the courtroom immediately.

* * * *

Trapping season was only three days away and although the department had decided that game wardens would not be allowed to trap at all, the department had issued Ian a current trapping license. He figured what he did on his own time was his business. He had never tended traps while on duty.

Maria had his good vehicle, but he kept an old rattletrap of a Datsun pickup that he used only in the woods and not his good pickup. The body was just large enough to carry his three wheeler ATV. The day before trapping season, he loaded up the old rattletrap with ATV, traps and bait.

Night hunting in the area had really slowed. He was home at 11 P.M. and up the next morning at 4 A.M. He first wanted to set up an old road behind Rockabema Lake and north of Mud Lake near Huntly Pond. During the summer, he had found where someone had set up a temporary plastic tent and over the bulldozed bank he had found the remains of a doe deer, which had probably been camp meat. He didn't know whose camp it had been, but this year he would be a trapper and work them undercover at the same time.

He set up four traps on that road and two more on an even older road that had at one time extended all the way to Pleasant Lake. From there, there was just enough time left before he would put on his uniform and go to work, to set a coyote trap and one fisher trap in the hardwoods near his house. The next day he set up near Sholler Mountain. The third day he checked traps in behind Rockabema Lake and then set up around Hale Pond and Frost Adam Ridge. He lost a coyote near his house and had a nice fisher in his other trap. He reset both. The Sunday before open deer season for non-residents, he was once again behind Rockabema Lake and found his plastic tent hunters. There were four men all 40-45 years old. One of them heard his ATV coming and walked out to see who was coming. "Hello there," Ian said. "I didn't know there was anyone else around here." His traps and equipment were visible in his pack, so there would be no doubt what he was doing.

"Hello, my name is Bob. We came in yesterday and set up."

"If you're going to be here for a few days, I'll pull my traps I have sets in beyond you. My name is Lee Gordon."

"After you have pulled your traps, stop in and have a cup of coffee."

"Sure thing. I won't be long." Ian left on his ATV, grinning to himself. This posing as a trapper is going to work. In his last set, he had a large fisher. He put everything in his pack basket and returned to the plastic tent.

Bob Huntly came over to greet Ian, or maybe to inspect his gear. "I see you had some luck. What are fisher worth today?"

"A male like this one about $125, a female would be worth about $175."

"Why so much for the female?" An honest question.

"The hair is finer and softer."

"Come in, I'll introduce you to the other guys." Ian noticed there were two Massachusetts registered pickups.

"This is Lee Gordon, and this is John Smith, Fred Bear, and Al Simon. How do you like your coffee?"

"Black would be fine."

They all talked for a long time. Bob and John, however, were doing most of the talking. At one point, Fred went outside and Ian supposed to look through his gear. He came back and when he looked towards Al, Ian noticed the slightest movement of his head, meaning a no or negative. For Ian's sake, this was a good thing.

Ian also noticed that each man carried a 9mm automatic in a shoulder holster. This could mean cops or someone on the other end of the spectrum.

Bob poured Ian a second cup of coffee and Ian thought everyone was satisfied that he was as he looked to be.

"Do you trap all season or do you take some time to hunt, Lee?" Bob asked.

"Well, my brother and me aren't in any need of any meat right now, but I'll probably shoot another, the last week."

"Do you live around here?" John asked.

"Oh, God forbid! Live in this hell hole. I come up only at the start of trapping and leave after deer season. I live just outside of Skowhegan. Me and my brother, we rent us a camp somewhere tucked back in the woods, where folks won't be bothered if we target shoot some."

"Does your brother trap, also?" John asked.

"Nah, he likes the ladies too much. He spends a lot of his time in a bar in Ashland. He does guide, though, for the Bear Mountain Lodge. He isn't prone to do much physical labor."

When Ian's second cup of coffee was gone, Bob offered him something a bit stronger.

"How about something stronger to drink, Lee?"

"You got any whiskey?" Ian asked.

Little by little the four men seemed to be feeling more comfortable with Ian. Then John said, "I shot me one of those black animals last year. One like the one you have in your basket. What did you call it? A fisher?"

"Either that or a black cat."

"I saw something last year," John continued, "that looked like a super large red squirrel. What was it?"

"Pine martin."

"How much are they worth?"

"A male will bring $35 and female $17 or $20."

Apparently Bob owned a heating company, so he wasn't a cop. And Ian was beginning to doubt if the others were either.

Fred was the quiet one and then he said, out of the blue, "A game warden would have to be crazy to go poking his nose around here."

"Well if you see one, don't tell him you have seen me, all right?"

After four hours of coffee and whiskey, and telling lies, Ian stood up and said, "If I don't get the rest of my trap line tended today, I'll be in an awful fix," and he left it at that.

"Will you be back in this way tomorrow?" Bob asked.

"Yeah, in the morning. I have a few traps out on some of the other roads in here."

"Well, stop in for another cup of coffee," John offered.

"I'll do that. Thanks for the coffee and such."

They had plied him with whiskey, probably to keep him talking, to see if he would reveal something about himself that he was not portraying. He had had more whiskey than he wanted and he was certainly feeling the affects. He loaded his ATV and started for home. It was 1:30 P.M. already, and he was expecting his folks and Uncle John. They were going to spend a few days hunting.

When he got home, his folks and Uncle John were already there and unloading his father's scout. He still was feeling the whiskey and his father said, "I thought you had to work today. We weren't expecting you until later." He could smell the whiskey on his son's breath. So could his Uncle John. "I've been working a group of four non-resident hunters undercover. They plied me with whiskey, to get me talking. Earlier I set out a few traps where they're camped, to give me an excuse to keep coming back. I'm supposed to be a trapper and poacher from the Skowhegan area and my brother and I are staying in an isolated camp."

"You working this alone, Ian?" Uncle John asked.

"Yeah, I don't think my supervisor would approve. Especially my trapping."

"When will you see them again?"

"Tomorrow morning. I've gotten some pretty good information already. Oh, by the way, I'm trapper Lee Gordon."

His mother was pleased to see him, "When are you going to get married, Ian? You shouldn't be living alone."

"Well, I am seeing someone from Kedgwick, New Brunswick. Maria. And Mom, please don't say anything to her about us getting married."

Ian stayed home on-call the rest of the day, except when he took all three for a ride on the I.P. Road to show them a good place to hunt. When they returned, Maria was there. Ian made all the introductions and everyone was happy to meet her.

After supper that evening, all were sitting in the living room when Uncle John Kenoyer said, "You working an undercover detail reminds me of a story. One in which you were there, Ian." Everyone's attention was now riveted on John. He continued, "Do you remember when you were working on the Filopalus camp on the Taylor Hill Road in New Vineyard?"

"Yes, but how do you know I was working there?" Ian was baffled and so too were his folks. Maria was just interested.

John started laughing and after a while, he was able to continue. "When you and your helper drew out your hammers and threatened those five men, if they didn't stop shooting towards the Filopalus camp. I was across the road on stake out. I was undercover."

Maria said, "Stake out, undercover?"

"Maria, my Uncle John is an FBI Special Agent."

"Oh."

"You probably never told your folks, did you?"

"No."

"Well, I'll tell the rest of the story.

"Did it ever occur to you why these five men each had

shoulder holsters with 9mm's, or that there were two AR-15 rifles and an automatic .44 rifle? They were mafia. And they were all there for a meeting with the owner of the second camp down the road. He owned a night club on Washington Street in Boston and he was wanted by the FBI. There were other agents not far away, but I was across the road in the bushes."

"You must have called the sheriff when they wouldn't stop shooting?"

"Yeah, I did."

"When that sheriff arrived, all hopes of our man showing went out the window."

"I couldn't help but laugh. The audacity of you two threatening to do bodily harm with your hammers, when they had so many firearms.

"I guess after watching you then, I know you'll take care of yourself with your present detail." He looked at Toby and his sister, Alice, and said, "You should be proud of him."

"They were using a piece of paper for a target without any backstop and the bullets were hitting the trees around us at the Filopalus camp."

Ian's dad couldn't believe it. He sat there shaking his head in disbelief.

That night, as Ian and Maria laid in bed, he had a lot of explaining to do. She didn't complain until he got up at 4 A.M. to tend traps. e kissed her and said, "Bye. I may be back by noon, but not sure."

He tended traps first on Sholler Mountain and picked up three martin and a fox. It was still dark so he tended just north of Knowles Corner, off a deadend woods road. There he picked up a fisher and a martin. Then he headed for Rockabema. He tended first the two other old roads and met a hunter he knew. He didn't want anyone in the area knowing the game warden was about, particularly the plastic campers. Instead of stopping, he drove on and pulled the last trap on that old road.

With those traps all tended, he headed for the plastic

campers. He had all of the animals he had caught that morning to showboat the crew.

He stopped and it was beginning to rain. Not just a sprinkle. Bob invited him inside the plastic tent and pulled up a lawn chair for him. "Looks like you have had a good moring."

"Indeed, about $350. and I still have a couple of more traps to tend."

He was given a cup of coffee and a glass of whiskey.

This visit, John told him about shooting a small doe last year and no one having a doe permit, so it became camp meat. That explained the doe remains he had found earlier. He was beginning to believe the poaching stories they were telling him. It was still raining and it wasn't acting like it would stop anytime soon.

*   *   *   *

Ian had already left to tend his traps when everyone else got up. Ian's mother, Alice, instead of hunting, also decided to spend the day with Maria at the house. "Let them hunt and get wet today," she said.

Ian's dad and Uncle drove west on the I.P. Road and then turned north on Bugbee's Road and parked the scout next to West Hasting Brook and hunted west of the road. They split up on different sides on the west branch of Hasting Brook. It was excellent deer habitat and they each actually jumped and saw deer.

But at 9 A.M. it started to rain heavier and the two men came back to the scout. "You as wet as I am, Toby?" John asked.

"Wet like a drowned rat. What do you say we just drive the roads and ditch hunt?"

"That's okay with me."

*   *   *   *

Ian drank more whiskey than he had the first visit. He put

away his equipment, skun the animals and rolled the hides up and put them in the freezer.

"Have you been drinking, Ian?" Maria asked.

"Yeah. This group that I'm working undercover ply me with whiskey. I think to see if I will make a slip and say something I don't want them to know. If you are going to town, I need a half gallon of vanilla ice cream. Oh, and don't go to Patten, go to Oakfield."

"Why do you need ice cream?" his mother asked.

"The leader of this group said if I come back tomorrow, they'll have apple pie. So I said I would bring some vanilla ice cream."

"You're almost drunk, Ian. Before you go to work, you better have some black coffee and something to eat. I'll make you a sandwich."

His Mom fixed the coffee.

"Are you making any headway with this group?" Maria asked.

"Well, I have them trusting me now, and I've learned enough to keep going."

*   *   *   *

Toby and John followed Bugbee's Road north where the road ended near the Umcolcus Deadwater. They had seen four bull moose and two large bucks that ran off through a thicket of second growth spruce and fir. "You interested in chasing after him, Toby?" John asked.

"I'll wait here and let you chase him back close to the road and then I'll shoot it." The second deer they just watched as it, too, ran off through the wet thicket. "What we need is a couple of deer to stand in the road," Toby said.

John just laughed. He couldn't respond to that.

They eventually found the Camp Violette Road and followed that to the Snowshoe Road. "Are you getting hungry, Toby?"

"Yeah, I could eat a couple of burgers alright."

"Well, according to this gazetteer, this road will take us to the paved road between Shin Pond and Matagamon. I know there's a couple of restaurants in Patten. I've stopped there before while investigating a situation in Fort Kent."

*   *   *   *

For the rest of that day, Ian worked hunters east of Rt. 11. He didn't want to be anywhere near Rockabema or the plastic tent group. He stopped to see Parnell Purchaser and had another cup of strong coffee. Parnell's coffee was always strong. He knew Parnell would wait until the weather got cold before he would hunt, so the meat would not spoil.

He left Parnell's and decided to look around the Beaver Brook country, in T8-R4. It was still raining and most hunters had called it a day or were road hunting. He had only driven about a half mile in on the lower road and when he turned a corner, he saw a shotgun stick out through the passenger window and then the smoke and then heard the report.

No one knew Ian was around. The passenger got out and ran up to the bird that was flopping around in the road and Ian walked up to the passenger door and said, "Gentlemen, nice day, huh?

"Before we do anything, I want to check your firearms to see if they are loaded." There was one passenger in back and the driver. Both hunters had their 30-06's loaded, plus the driver had a loaded handgun. The passenger who had shot the partridge was back now, and Ian picked his .30-06 rifle up and pulled the bolt back. It, too, was loaded. He wrote three summonses for loaded firearms in a motor vehicle and a second summons for the shooter for hunting from a motor vehicle. He cash bailed them for the four charges for $400. "Have a nice day, gentlemen, and do not carry loaded firearms in your vehicles."

The Massachusetts vehicle turned around and headed back

for camp. Ian decided to work his way through the Beaver Brook country to the Blackwater Road out of Masardis.

* * * *

Toby and John's clothing had dried by now, as Toby had turned the heater and blower on high. "Toby, I think you can turn the heat off now. This feels like a sweat lodge in here."

"How about this place. The Shin Pond Cafe? I'm hungry and I don't want to wait any longer," Toby said.

"Okay." It looked like the noon crowd had left. There were only two vehicles in the yard. They chose a table in the corner and a young woman asked them, "Would you like something to drink first?"

"Yes, two beers please, draft," John replied.

When she came back with the beer, they both ordered a cheeseburger and onion rings. As they were sipping their beer, a man approached them and asked, "Are you two hunters?"

"Well, not in this weather."

"Did you see anything?"

Toby started to answer and John interrupted him. "We saw a moose and a partridge. We're not so sure there are any deer in this country."

"Well, if you get discouraged, I might know where you could buy yourselves a nice buck to take home with you."

"Well, that sounds pretty tempting. Let us talk it over and come back after we have finished our burgers."

"Okay."

When he had left, Toby whispered to John, "What in hell are you doing, John? If he finds out my son is Ian Randall, we'll be in big trouble."

"Relax, Toby. Oh yeah, we'd better change your name, also. Ian said he was using Lee Gordon; you'll be Al Gordon. Let's play along and see what he has to offer."

"You're going to get us in a lot of trouble."

"Relax, Al. Remember, this is what I do for a living."

"Yeah, but you always have a badge and a gun when you're working."

"I have my identification. Besides, I don't think it'll come to that. Loosen up, Al, or he'll suspect something is wrong."

"Okay, but you do all the talking. I'm no good at this sort of thing."

"Take a drink of your beer and try not to look so scared."

"Easy enough for you to say," Toby said.

Their burgers and onion rings came and Al asked for another beer for each. "That was a delicious burger," Al said.

"And the onion rings. Here comes our friend, Al, so let me do the talking. You're still too nervous."

"How was your meal, gentlemen? By the way, my name is Jason Campbell and I own this café-restaurant."

"Everything was delicious, Jason, and I have never tasted onion rings with that particular flavoring."

"I'm glad you noticed and enjoyed the difference. We cook pieces of smoked bacon at the same time as the onion rings for that special flavoring.

"Now how about that earlier proposition?"

"If we don't have any luck come Thursday evening, then maybe. I would like at least a ten pointer, so I can have the head mounted."

"A ten pointer will cost you $600. And another $100 for each additional point."

"That's a lot of money."

"Well, I'm taking all the risks, and how much have you spent already for this trip?" Jason asked.

"Good point.

"I don't know. What do you think, Al? Would a nice ten point rack be worth $600?"

"It sounds too much. But I'll make a deal with you, John. If we do, you keep the head and rack and I keep the meat."

"Okay, Jason. If we don't have any luck come Thursday

afternoon, we'll stop in for supper. My name is John Kenoyer and this is my friend, Al Gordon."

"Pleased to meet you," Jason said. Just then, a tall, slim, dark-haired man walked into the room and Jason excused himself to go over and talk with this newcomer.

Not wanting to go back to Ian's house so early in the afternoon, they rode the roads in Hersey Township. They saw two moose and flags of three deer before disappearing out of sight in the wet second growth. It was still raining and neither of them felt like chasing deer through the thicket and wet second growth. "What's the matter with those deer? I'd like for just one to stand in the road so we could get a shot at it," John said.

Sunset would soon be on them, so John said, "How about it, Al, let's call it a day," John was laughing.

"Fair enough with me."

*   *   *   *

Ian worked his way back through the woods to the St. Croix bridge crossing and then out along the 3A Road to Rt. 11 just north of the Camp Violette Road, looking for a late hunter to work. But it was still raining and he didn't find anyone still out, so he headed for home, also.

Everyone was surprised to see Ian home so early; but then again, it was still raining. Maria was especially happy to see him. "Your Mom and I had a nice day together. She told me all about you." All he could do was smile.

After supper, and the dishes and kitchen had been cleaned, they sat in the living room sipping a highball. "Your father and I were approached today to buy a deer," Uncle John said. Then he continued and told Ian all about the proposition.

"For $600, hey?" Ian asked.

"For a ten point rack."

"Would you be willing to continue the charade and make

the buy? You might have to appear in court to testify, but similar cases have never required the buyer to be there," Ian said.

"It would be fun," John replied.

Ian telephoned his sergeant and advised him of his Uncle's willingness to make the buy and appear in court later.

"It all sounds good, Ian, but I'll have to run this by the lieutenant, and I'm not sure what Bill will say. I'll call you in the morning."

"Ah, be better if I call you and it probably won't be until the afternoon." He didn't want to say anything about trapping and his undercover work.

Ian told them he wouldn't know until he called his sergeant tomorrow. He then told them about his day with the plastic tent group. "I'm getting a lot of useful information that I might be able to use for an undercover operation."

"How's your supervisor going to react when they learn about your work undercover with this group?"

"Well, if I had to guess, I'd say they won't like it. But then again, all I'm doing is gathering information."

"I'll say one thing, I think you're wrong not keeping your supervisors informed, but there may be a reason for that. But you have plenty of guts and fortitude going there alone, particularly since no one knows where you are. Except us, of course," John said.

"Are you going in tomorrow?" his dad asked.

"Yes, I promised to bring a half gallon of vanilla ice cream for apple pie." Uncle John and Toby both started laughing and choked on their drinks.

That night, as he and Maria were laying in each other's embrace, Maria asked, "Aren't you getting tired? I mean, you've been working every day for nine weeks and there's still three weeks to go."

"About the middle of the third week of deer season, I get tired and wish it was over."

"You said earlier that you would be back in the afternoon

to call your sergeant. I'll have to leave in the afternoon, but I'll wait until you're back."

*　　*　　*　　*

Ian was up at 4 A.M. the next morning, and put the half gallon of vanilla ice cream in his pack. He didn't want to forget that. He actually had six hours of sleep. He had a cup of coffee and a muffin and left to check traps on Sholler Mountain. There he picked up another female fisher and one martin. At his sets just north of Knowles Corner, he had the largest martin he had ever seen. It was in a leg hold trap and Ian always used a .22 short bullet. He would wait until the martin started screeching and then he would put the barrel of his .22 pistol in the martin's mouth and pull the trigger, killing the martin instantly without damaging the fur. Only this time, the martin wasn't at the end of the chain securing the trap and when Ian reached down to place the gun barrel in its mouth, the martin lunged forward and latched onto Ian's middle finger. He had the entire finger in his mouth when he was jerked back when he came to the end of the chain and the martin bit down and its teeth gouged Ian's finger along the entire finger. His finger was bleeding profusely. He tore his handkerchief in half and wrapped it around his finger and tied it off. That would have to do.

Then he turned his attention back to the martin and after he pulled the martin from the trap, he decided to pull that trap. He still had two more sets at the end of that short road.

He checked and pulled the rest of his traps at Rockobema and had one fox. The ice cream was getting soft, so he headed for the plastic tent goup.

They were actually glad to see him and decided to have the apple pie now, instead of waiting, as the ice cream was getting really soft. But with the pie, it was good. And instead of coffee, they filled his cup with whiskey. "We stop hunting before sunset on Wednesdays. We drive to Ashland and get a motel room and shower and eat out that night. On the way up, there's a field we like to hunt. The field on the left is planted to spruce trees, but there are apple trees at the back end of the field and in the past we have killed deer there and then tagged them the next day in Ashland. There's a green field on the right and although we have seen deer there, we were never able to kill one. Too bad you couldn't go up with us," Bob said.

"Nice offer, but I've pulled all of my traps today around here and above Knowles Corner, and tomorrow I'll set traps over by Skitacook Lake, east of Oakfield.

"Have you guys had any luck here?" Ian asked.

"I think I had a buck coming into my stand late yesterday afternoon, and I tried rattling antlers for it, and I never heard it again," John said.

"How about you?" John asked.

"Hope you guys aren't cops or anything. My brother and I got a nice one last night. He tagged it this morning."

"What exactly do you mean last night?" John asked.

"Oh, 6 P.M. or so, about the same time a game warden would be sitting down to supper."

"Do you know who the warden is here?" Bob asked.

"I have no idea. I have never met him. You mean, you guys have never been checked in here?"

"Never seen one. Like we said on Sunday, a game warden would have to be crazy to come into our camp," Al Simon said and then he laughed.

"We see only an occasional deer in here. Where do you and your brother hunt, Lee?"

"Well, I'm usually too busy tending traps to do much hunting during daylight. So twice a week my brother and I ditch hunt in the woods after midnight."

"Where do you go?" John asked.

"Our favorite place is the wood roads in Hersey Township. Those woods are full of deer but they don't come out until after dark. Usually after midnight."

"There are really that many deer?" Bob asked.

"Yeah. The second growth is so thick, hunters can't walk through it and deer go in there and spend the day and rest. Then come out at night to feed."

The pie and ice cream gone, only two whiskeys today, and a pot of coffee, and now 11:30 A.M., Ian had a phone call to make. "I do have to be leaving. I want to set up around Skitacook before dark."

He stood and shook hands with all. On his way out, he was thinking he'd have to call Terry to see if he would work night hunters tomorrow night at the McMannus fields.

As he drove home he was satisfied now that the plastic hunters had no more suspicions about being anything but what he wanted them to believe.

His Mom and Maria were just sitting down to lunch when Ian walked in. "You're home earlier than I thought you'd be. Everything go okay?"

"Yeah, I don't think I'll be going back."

"I'll make you a lunch while you're talking with your boss."

Ian called the Ashland office and waited for his sergeant to pick up. "Sorry Ian, it's no go. Bill doesn't want to involve the FBI." It was useless to argue with him, but he wanted to wring someone's neck.

When Ian turned around, both his Mom and Maria knew the news wasn't good. "The Lieutenant doesn't want to involve the FBI."

"So what will you do now?" his Mom asked.

"Not much. You see, Patten isn't even in my district; not even my Division. My sergeant said he would pass along the information to the sergeant of that area, Dave Sewall."

After he had eaten, he called Terry Hunter and he was surprised to find him home. He told Terry what he expected to happen tomorrow night at the McMannus field and Terry said he would meet him there. "No Terry, not there, they drive out back in the field on the left and I don't want them to see a pickup.

109

Meet me down the road on the left. The old Levesque Road. I'll be in there around the first corner."

Ian's dad and Uncle John came back early for lunch before going out again.

"My lieutenant said he didn't want to involve the FBI. That really irritates the hell out of me. You're an official law enforcement officer."

"It sounds to me, Ian, like your lieutenant doesn't want to have to explain to the chief why he employed the FBI. It would have been fun. But maybe you'll be able to use this information to send a covert buyer in there."

"We saw two more deer today where you told us to hunt. We like that spot and will go back again," Toby said.

Maria said she had to leave and said goodbye to everyone and gave Ian's Mom, Alice, a hug. "Nice to have met you."

*   *   *   *

Toby, John and Ian's Mom went back out hunting and Ian decided to work the St. Croix area and come in from the old Smokey Hauler's Road. It would be a rough ride until he got to Smith Brook. Because of the clear weather, hunters were everywhere and he didn't run into any non-residents until he was north of Smith Brook.

He had thought about working his way out through to Harvey Siding. That was Warden Rodney Small's district but he was off. But he decided to work his way to the St. Croix Siding and then out through Bugbee's Road to T7-R5, and then in behind the Bugbee camps. There was a new RV camper near the bridge and no one around. Ian got out and walked around, just to see what was there. It looked like a husband and wife team and the area was clean.

He continued on out through Bugbee's Road to Rt. 11. This was excellent moose country, and no deer and no hunters. Legal hunting would be over shortly and he drove out through

Bugbee's camp yard, slowing down so all would see him. The two young fellas he had arrested earlier for moose had been fired and their arraignment would be in two days.

He followed the Dow Road down to the I.P. Road and then back to Rt. 11 and home. As they were all eating supper, John said, "I still think we should have bought that deer, Toby. That way we would have something to take back."

"Well, I have plenty of moose meat downstairs in the freezer and you can have what you want."

"Are you going out tonight, Ian?" Alice asked.

"Not unless I get a lost hunter. Terry Hunter, from Ashland, and I are planning to work night hunters tomorrow night. Maybe we'll get that plastic tent group. Bob told me they always go to Ashland and stay in a motel Wednesday nights and check out the old set of fields at the McMannus farm. Terry and I will be there."

"You have done well trapping," Toby said. "How much are they worth?"

"There's probably a $1,000 or so there."

"Where do you sell them?" John asked.

"Dad's, fur buyer in Brownville. He takes them to the Hudson Bay Fur Auctions in Ontario. You have to wait for your money selling in the auction, but you can usually about double your money."

"This moose meat you said you'd give us some—I take it was confiscated?" his father asked.

"Yes, about five weeks ago from two young French wood cutters staying at the Bugbee camps. They had de-boned the meat there in their camp."

"Since we have been here," John said, "you've been working sixteen hours a day, trapping for four hours a day and that only leaves about four hours of sleep. Is it normal?"

"Well, from September 1st to December 1st, our days off are cancelled. This has been a busy fall and trapping helps me to unwind some. Besides, it's fun."

The next morning, Ian was up again at 4 A.M. and since he didn't have but only a few traps to tend now, he was home before his dad and Uncle John left to go hunting. This morning, Sirois and Skidgell were due for arraignment. They had asked Ian at the jail if he would give them some time to put some money together before court.

"Warden Randall," Judge Werner asked, "were these two cooperative, or did they give you some trouble?"

"They both were very cooperative, Your Honor."

"The minimum I can fine you is $1,000 and three days in jail. Are you prepared to pay that today?"

"Yes sir," they both replied.

"Warden Randall, what about the .44 and rifle you confiscated? They do not fall under the statutory law."

"I have them with me, Your Honor, and I'll go out with the two and return them."

"Thank you."

Ian waited while they paid the clerk and then walked out with them and gave them their firearms. "Come on, Francis, you heard the judge. We get to put ourselves in jail. Just think, Francis, we now belong to The Three Day Club."

"Big deal."

Ian returned home and started catching up with reports. He knew it would be a late night so he had no qualms about being home on call. He had a good visit with his mother while his dad and Uncle John were hunting. "I hope they get something today, because I think we'll probably be leaving sometime tomorrow."

While they talked, Ian ate two sandwiches and black coffee. At 3:30 P.M. he had all of his gear and thermos of coffee and said goodbye and drove up to the old Levesque Road, just below the McMannus farm. He hid his truck and found a good spot to watch the road for the plastic group and wait for Terry.

When Terry arrived, they had to make a hidey hole in the

alders on the left at the edge of the fields. Terry was going to be the chase vehicle and Ian would be in the lower field on the right with a set of hand held deer eyes. It was two old railroad crossing reflectors that he had set into wood. Illuminated in vehicle headlights and they would look exactly like deer eyes. The trick was not to give the approaching vehicles too much of a look-see. He didn't want to get shot.

There was surprisingly very little traffic on the road tonight and Ian was afraid that the plastic group might have gone to Ashland earlier. At 8:30 P.M. a northbound vehicle was coming north very slow. Ian gave them a blink of the eyes from the shoulder of the road. A blink only and then he ran behind a small spruce tree and held the eyes up and around the tree and the vehicle stopped and a flashlight came out of the passenger window, but the batteries must have been low because the light beam was weak. The driver gigged the vehicle and then drove by slowly and then turned around and came north again. And this time the vehicle gigged almost squarely in the road, shining the headlights down across the field. Then it squared around and drove up the road. "Okay, Terry, that was enough. Come on out," he whispered into his portable radio.

He jumped in and Terry tore off after the vehicle without lights. Just before catching up to the vehicle, it had started to turn around and make another pass. Terry turned on the blue light and pulled up almost to the driver's door. Ian jumped out and ran to the passenger side and to the one who would have been the shooter. He pulled open the door and shined his flashlight inside and said, "You both are under arrest for night hunting."

Just then, a northbound vehicle drove by and Ian recognized it as Bob Huntley's vehicle that he used for his heating and plumbing business.

The passenger was holding a .308 Remmington rifle and Ian took possession of it and unloaded it. They were two brothers from Patten, Michael and Kevin Nemore. They were caught fair and square and didn't give them any trouble. Ian had the eyes in his pocket and hoped they didn't fall out. Ian drove Michael's pickup and took him with him, and Terry took Kevin. They had to go to Presque Isle, which is only a temporary holding facility. If they couldn't make bail, they would be transported to Caribou. The two were more worried about their parents than they were about going to jail.

At the jail, and after the paperwork was done, Ian and Terry escorted the two downstairs to the temporary holding cell. "Just think, fellas. After you do your time, you'll be able to join The Three Day Club." They didn't think that was funny at all. They wouldn't appear in court until the middle of December.

Terry drove Ian back to his pickup on the Old Levesque Road. "I wish it had been the group that I wanted and now I think they probably can smell a rat, so it would be useless to try and catch 'em here. They may have even figured it out that it was a game warden that they have been entertaining. Thanks for your help, Terry. Good night."

It was only midnight when Ian returned home.

In the morning he pulled the rest of his traps and returned home. His dad and uncle were still there, just getting ready to go hunting. "Any luck last night?" his dad asked.

"Yeah, we arrested two, but it wasn't the ones I wanted. They drove by as we were frisking the ones we did catch. I don't think they'll be back again now."

They left and Ian and his Mom had breakfast and then he had to write up a report for the D.A. and take the paperwork to the D.A.'s office in the Superior Courthouse. It started to drizzle before he got back to his house. "This will keep many hunters sitting beside the woodstoves today." He figured his dad and uncle were probably road hunting and not in the woods.

Ian called his Uncle Jim, and he and his wife, Nancy, came up for lunch with the family. Toby and John were back at the house by noon and their rifles put away. Alice had roasted a chicken that morning and Nancy had brought potatoes already cooked and mashed, and a pie.

"Isn't your sergeant going to say something about you spending so much time at home during the day this week?" his dad asked.

"With the fall that I have had, he shouldn't. If he does, I'll threaten to retire," he said in jest. But Uncle Jim and Nancy knew he was serious.

At 3 P.M. they all left and suddenly Ian found himself in an empty, quiet house. And he had decided to stay at home that night. Then at 6 P.M. he received a telephone call from Scotty at the State Police Barracks. "Hello, Ian. I just received a call from Larry Bottle Sr. and he is reporting an overdue hunter in Dyer Brook off the Moro Town Line Road, across the road, he said, from the old Searles farm. He said he would wait for you by the garage across the road."

"Okay, Scotty."

It was still drizzling and he packed his rain gear in his pack and drove down to the Searles farm. Larry Sr. always was an excitable fellow. Ian seemed to think he always acted as though he had just been caught with his hand in the cookie jar.

"Ian, this guy is 65 years old and can't walk very far or fast because of an old war wound. I had him in a tree seat at the bottom end of this here field. He was seen at 4 P.M. climbing down from the tree seat, but nobody has seen him since. I mean, how far could he have gotten? I mean, he can't walk but a little."

More help was arriving and Ian took them down to the tree seat and made a sweep in the woods, staying parallel to the edge of the field. Then they dropped down some, and made another sweep, then another and another, and it was raining now. Ian fired signal shots and no answers. Searchers all up and down the line were hollering his name. Still no answer. Ian was beginning to think the hunter might have gone in the wrong direction, maybe suffering from a heart attack, and was now down somewhere.

There was no more anyone could do tonight, so he told everyone to go home, that they would start searching again in the morning at daylight when the airplane could fly.

Ian brought his pickup down by the tree stand and he sat in that, out of the rain, with the window down. Every hour he would get out and walk down into the woods a ways and holler. Then he'd go back and sit in his pickup. There wasn't much more he could do until daylight.

Just as the eastern horizon was beginning to lighten, Ian's sergeant and lieutenant showed up and Dan Glidden. Ian brought them all up to speed on what he had done so far and the condition of the hunter. The warden pilot, Gary Dumond, radioed that he had left the plane base at Eagle Lake and his ETA was travel time.

While everyone waited for Gary Dumond to arrive, Ian and Dan started walking along the edge of the field, away from the others. They had gone about a hundred yards when suddenly Dan said, "There he goes!" and Dan took off running like a gazelle down through the old choppings. Ian saw the lost hunter now, running away from them deeper into the woods. He sure wasn't having any trouble running through the thick regeneration. But Dan was running faster and he soon caught up with the old guy. Ian wasn't far behind.

The old guy then turned around, "Oh my God, friendly faces at last." Then he breathed a sigh of relief.

Dan took his rifle and handed it to Ian. Ian checked the action and it was loaded with four more in the magazine. He hadn't fired a shot at all.

Dan said, "Come on, walk with us back to the field."

The old guy didn't resist at all. "Boy am I ever glad to see you guys. What infantry are you two with?"

"We aren't with any infantry. We are game wardens looking for you," Ian said.

"Son, I'm glad for that. I spent one hell of a night. There were Germans all over and I think they were looking for me. I'd pull my rifle up and just get a bead on one of them and he would slip behind a tree or something."

Ian realized the old guy thought the searchers last night were Germans and they were after him. He suddenly realized how close he and the others had come to being shot last night.

"I finally found a hollow log and I crawled inside that. All night I could hear them walking by me, inside the log. I've never been so scared in all my life."

When they were back with the others, the rest of the old guy's hunting party was there, as was Larry Bottle, Sr. and Jr. One of them in the party was the old guy's son, and he immediately took charge of his dad. He cancelled the last two days at the Hillside Lodge and instead of he and his father driving back to Pennsylvania, his friend would drop them off at the Portland Airport and then drive back. The son wanted to get his father to a Veteran's Hospital at home in Pennsylvania as soon as possible.

No one there knew for sure what had happened. Had the old guy had a stroke and then didn't know where he was and in his mind he was back fighting in WWII? Or had he gotten confused when he stepped into the woods and panicked, and lost his mind? Either way, the search was over.

"What are you going to do now, Ian?" Dan asked.

"Go home, eat, shower and go to bed. I was out here all night. If I wake up in time, maybe I'll look for a twilight hunter. Thanks for coming down, Dan."

*　　*　　*　　*

The needed sleep didn't last for long. At 1:20 P.M. the phone rang, then twice and a third time before Ian answered. "Ian, I have a strange one for you. A hunter from Portland has a camp on the Smyrna Center Road about one half mile from the junction of Rt. 2 near I-95. It seems while he was lost, he found what he thinks was an old body."

"Okay, Scotty, I'll get geared up and head that way."

"Thanks, Ian. I know you were out all night."

A half hour later, Ian drove into the camp yard owned by Kermit Braley. Mr. Braley came outside to greet Ian. Ian had the feeling Mr. Braley didn't want Ian inside his camp.

"Mr. Braley, I'm Ian Randall. Can you start at the beginning and tell me what you found."

"I left camp here about 7 A.M. this morning and drove to the end of the Hemore Road in Hammond PLT, near B Lake. I hunted around a hardwood ridge and eventually came to Mill Brook. I was hunting upstream and parallel to the brook. I remember seeing an old stove and then an old rusty fifty gallon drum and then I think I was close to the brook and I saw some clothes lying on the ground."

"Can you describe what you saw?"

"Old grey flannel shirt, sneakers, jeans and I think there was a bra."

"What did you do then, Mr. Braley?"

"I was really upset and I began to run. I didn't know then where I was going, but I eventually came out to a camp on Mill Brook and I recognized the road as the Smokey Haulers Road that goes out to Smyrna Center, just up the road from here."

"Will you go with me back to the camp on the brook and see if we can work from there back where you found the clothes?" He thought it might be better to say clothes than a dead body. This might get him upset again.

Mr. Braley was awful quiet as they drove out to Mill Brook. The road was seldom used now and it was very rough. Ian left his pickup in the camp yard and said, "Okay, Mr. Braley, you go ahead and see if you can find your way back to the clothes."

"Okay, but I don't know."

Ian kept trying to find his tracks in the mud along the brook bank or in any loose soil. His boot track was unmistakable. He wore a big winter boot with a deep tread design. Ian couldn't find any tracks at all.

"I just can't remember where I ran after I saw. . .saw the body."

It was getting late and it was useless trying to have Mr. Braley do any more that day. He would have to start over in the morning.

Back at his camp, Ian said, "We'll start again in the morning, so don't go anywhere. I'll be here early. I'll see if I can get a state police tracking dog tomorrow."

Ian talked with his sergeant. He was no longer a lost hunter or missing person complaint. But a possible homicide. His sergeant gave him two days to work the case. After all, it was still the first of the deer hunting season; and so far it was proving to be a busy one.

The next morning Ian met Roland Pelletier at the end of the Hemore Road at sunrise. They waited for Mr. Braley, and two state troopers, one being a K 9 handler. When everyone finally arrived, Ian told Mr. Braley, "As best you can, try to duplicate everything you did yesterday. The K 9 and trooper will be out ahead of everyone else, so as to eliminate as much contamination as possible. Al will be with you, and the other warden and I will flank the K 9 and his handler. Now which direction did you go from here?"

Mr. Braley pointed off towards the northwest and the K 9 picked up Mr. Braley's scent immediately. Mr. Braley's large boot track was seen in many muddy locations.

During the evening before, Ian made some inquiries of some of the older citizens in the area and he discovered that back in the late 50's, Kermit Brannen had had a lumber camp near Mill Brook and there was a woman in her mid thirties from across the border in New Brunswick who worked at the camps; helping the cookee and cleaning. Two men got to fighting over her and one weekend when the crew had gone back to their homes for the weekend, she disappeared. Mr. Brannen and the cookee figured she had gone back to New Brunswick without saying a word.

But her disappearance was 22 years earlier and it would be very doubtful if there could be enough left of her clothing to identify.

For the most part, the team was able to follow Mr. Braley's path he had taken the day before. At times, they would lose his trail and then Ian and Roland would make a circle and one or the other of them would find a clue.

They went up and around a hardwood ridge and to Mill Brook where Mr. Braley said he had seen an old rusted drum and an old wood stove shortly before discovering the body. The dog stopped near the Brook and was not able to pick up the scent again. Ian and Roland made circle after circle and they could not find anything. It appeared Mr. Braley had stopped there. But the day before he had told Ian he had walked out of the Smokey Hauler's Road and followed that to the Smyrna Center Road. But there was no indication that he had done this.

It was obviously not a lost person. It was either a missing person or a homicide complaint. Ian couldn't afford to work on this case any longer.[1]

After supper that evening, Ian wrote up the report while it was still fresh in his mind. He then made a drive down the Mill Brook Road in Moro PLT and up to the Gallagher farm where he sat for a while watching and listening. He was tired, so he didn't stay there for long. He made his way across the Clark Settlement Road in Merrill and sat for a while on a high knoll in the field on the old Porter farm. There was no traffic there either, so he went home and to bed.

* * * *

He was up at 7 A.M. the next morning feeling refreshed. After a hearty breakfast, he took a hot shower. While he was shaving, the telephone rang. "Hello."

"Ian, this is Carroll Gerow at Bear Mountain Lodge."

"Good morning, Carroll, what can I do for you?"

"Could you stop by this morning?"

"Sure, I'll be there about 10 A.M."

Ian finished his weekly reports, which in this case were extensive. But at exactly 10 A.M., Ian drove into the Bear Mountain Lodge. All of last weeks guests had left and now new guests were arriving.

---

1 See notes on page 249

In the main dining room, Deanna Gerow gave Ian a cup of black coffee. "Sit down, Ian; Carroll is out back. He'll only be a few minutes."

Ian had finished his coffee and Carroll came in from the kitchen. "Morning, Ian. Some of our guests—they have all gone now—complained about someone riding around the Rockabema area shooting, and probably out the window. This went on all Friday afternoon and again yesterday around noon. I know you have been busy looking for that missing woman in Smyrna, but I wanted to let you know."

"Thanks. I'll be in and around that area more this week. How was your week?"

"Not bad actually. We had twenty guests and eight bucks. Two nice ones—and one bear."

While Carroll and Ian were talking, the plastic group arrived with a small buck to tag.

Apparently, the deer was John Smith's, and Ian heard him say he had shot it yesterday afternoon about 4 P.M. Knowing these guys, Ian decided this would be a good case for a post mortem test. He chuckled to himself. This was going to be a surprise to the entire group.

Deanna had finished and was about to take the tag out and attach it. "Ah, Deanna. Ah, hold off attaching that tag for a while."

"Okay."

John turned around to see who was talking and almost fell over backward when he recognized Ian or Lee Gordon.

"Hello, John. Before Deanna attaches that tag, I'm going to do a post-mortem test to determine time of death."

"You son of a bitch," John said.

Ian snapped around and said rather firmly, "Mr. Smith, as long as you are on these premises, you'll conduct yourself accordingly and no foul language, is that clear? Because if it isn't, I'll forget about the test for now and transport you to jail. Now do you understand me?"

John nodded his head that he did. "Okay, let's go look at this deer."

The other three of the plastic group were standing around the pickup. They saw a game warden walking with John, but had not yet recognized him.

When they did, they were all speechless. "I'm going to do a post mortem test on the deer to determine the time of death. But before I get started, I want to check your handguns. Are any of you carrying?"

"I am," Bob said rather disgruntled. He wasn't happy.

"I am, also," Fred Bear said.

"Okay, take out your handguns and hand them to me." Ian stood there with his hands on his hips waiting.

They handed them to Ian and Bob said, "What do we call you? It obviously isn't Lee Gordon."

"Ian Randall."

"We've heard of you," Al Simon said.

Carroll and Deanna were watching all this from inside the dining room. "Maybe Ian has found those yahoos that were doing all that shooting."

Ian put the handguns inside his pickup for now and dug out his test kit. The four plastic hunters watched as Ian inserted a thermometer into the nose and another one in the thigh and then measure the pupils.

Ian recorded all this information on a graph and while he waited he wrote out summons and cash bails for Bob Huntly and Fred Bear for a loaded gun and they were all too happy to sign a guilty waver so they would not have to come back for trial.

"How long is this going to take, Warden?" John asked.

"To do a thorough test, it'll take me four hours." He left it there. Later he would offer him a deal.

After the first hour had passed, Ian recorded the readings on his graph, and just took an estimated time of death: 16 to 17 hours ago. That would make it between 5:30 P.M. and 6:30 P.M. yesterday. But he couldn't calculate the time of death with only one reading. That's why it would take him four hours to complete the test.

Bob was getting impatient as was John, but he wasn't going to make too many waves. He was worried. "You come into our camp posing as a trapper. You drink our coffee and whiskey, eat our pie. For what? Are you just a hard ass?" Bob asked.

"This spring, while walking around where you guys had camped the year before, I found the remains of a camp deer. A doe, which was never registered. And I found all that plastic you dumped over the bank. When I leave here today, I'm going out to your campsite and if you have left any garbage behind, you'll be hearing from me again."

"When can we leave?" Bob asked.

"I have to take three more readings to complete the graph. That's another three hours."

Ian took the pupil dilation measurement and put that on another graph. That time added another hour and a half. Or about 4:00 or 4:30 P.M.

Another hour had passed and Ian recorded the readings again. "Okay warden, what are your findings telling you?" John asked.

"According to these figures, this deer died between 4:30 and 5:30 P.M. But I'll have to do two more sets of readings to be absolutely sure."

"If you fellows really want to be on your way, tell me when you shot this deer. Or we sit here another two hours. That would make 2:30 P.M. How long does it take to drive home from here?"

There was noticeable sweat on John's forehead. And he was as nervous as all-get-out. Ian had 'em over a barrel and he was enjoying it.

The four men discussed things away from Ian. He knew they were about to propose a deal.

"What can we do to make this go away?" Bob asked.

"Well, depending on what the next two hour readings say, which I'm certain they'll indicate that the deer probably died closer to 6:00 or 6:30 P.M., then I will arrest you for possessing a deer killed at night, confiscate the deer, your rifles, and take you to jail. Then you'd have to return for the arraignment and if you wanted a trial, you'd probably have to return in another two months. I have no idea what you would lose in wages, but I'd bet it would be more than the fine.

"How much is the fine?" John asked.

"The fine is $1,000. But don't forget, there's a statutory jail sentence also of three days. Just think, you'd belong to The Three Day Club then."

John wasn't happy. "Could I plead to a lesser charge now and pay you another cash bail?"

"I could charge you with twilight hunting and the usual fine is $200. But under these circumstances, I think you can see I'd have to keep the deer."

"Do it, John," Al Simon said. "We'll all chip in for the cash bail."

"Let the son of a bitch have the deer, John," Fred said.

"Well, John, the choice is yours. I don't have any qualms going to superior court with this case."

"What about my rifle?"

"You get to keep it."

"Okay, damn it! You have me over a barrel. Do your paperwork," John submitted.

"While I'm doing this, you can put this deer in the back of my pickup."

Ian recorded the figures one last time. He was sure the deer had died probably closer to 6:30 or 7:00 P.M., and a jury just might not find him guilty. He figured they both were getting a good deal.

Ian gave the hand guns back and gave John his summons and cash bail receipt. He had the deer, and three summons and $400.

"Do you remember what I said to you that first day when you came in to our camp? '. . .that a warden would have to be

124

crazy to come here alone?' Well, you are crazy. You're one tough son of a bitch and you have balls," John said.

"Oh, one last thing," Ian said, "don't come back here hunting again."

"You can count on it," John said.

They got in their pickup and drove off. Ian went back inside to explain.

"I think I owe you two an explanation. I was working that group undercover the first half of this week. I knew about the concealed handguns they wore and obtained some useful information. Then when they showed up here this morning with a deer to register, and knowing what goes on with that group and what you said about the shots, I figured it would be a good idea to run a post-mortem test on that deer. And it proved my suspicions were correct."

He had a cup of coffee with Carroll and Deanna and then he took that deer down to the senior citizen apartments in Oakfield. He knew one of the residents there who would enjoy taking care of the meat and that he would see to it that everyone got some. Then he went home to write up the reports on this group and left the $400 on his desk.

He had forgotten in all the excitement the last few days that he still had two traps out in T7-R5 on the Bugbee Road. They were both 220 Conibear traps set on leaning poles, which required tending once a week. He was still within the law in that regard. There had been some strong wind gusts last night and he half expected to find his traps on the ground and sprung.

He was in uniform and he was in the state vehicle. But after the week he had just had, he could justify what he was doing. At the first leaning tree set, it was indeed on the ground with a nice pine martin dead in the trap. He pulled the nails out of the dead pole and laid the trap and martin together on the ground.

The next trap was on the same hillside, but further in, away from the road. This set was also lying on the ground and nothing in the trap. He laid his hammer down and walked over and pulled the pole up and at the same time he grabbed the 220 Conibear trap by the jaws without thinking what he was doing. The jaws on this trap were not sprung. But when he hit the trigger, the trap jaws slammed shut around his hand, just behind the knuckles.

The leaning tree was still attached to the roots, so he couldn't move the tree enough to reach his hammer. He might be able to force the jaws apart with the hammer claws or pull the nails and drive home with the trap still on his hand and get his Uncle Jim to help him, but he couldn't reach the hammer.

He was really in a fix, and he could see the tissue around his knuckles beginning to swell. Not only that, he wasn't supposed to be trapping or using the state vehicle, but he was and now he was caught like a rat in his own trap. "Boy, would the plastic guys laugh if they knew what kind of a fix I'm in."

He could compress one spring with his free hand, but he couldn't set the safety and both springs needed to be compressed before the jaws would open. There was only one choice; he had to forcibly pull his hand out between the two jaws.

As he was pulling, he was surprised to see how much his knuckles and hand could be squeezed together. One last pull and his hand was free, but now the thumb on his other hand was stuck in between the jaws. His left hand was really hurting. He couldn't spring the jaws apart; not even a little, so he forcibly pulled his thumb out. Now both hands were hurting. He gathered up his traps and pine martin and put those away in the green box in back and beat-foot it for home.

At home, he put the traps in the garage and the martin downstairs to skin later, then he soaked his hands in cold water. The swelling had stopped and had almost reduced. He began to laugh at himself.

With both his hands swollen and hurting, there was no way he was going to be able to skin the martin, so he put it in the freezer. He hoped he could stay away from his sergeant until his hands were not so swollen.

In the early afternoon, Uncle Jim and Nancy showed up

with a box of moose meat. "I shot a deer Saturday afternoon right off the back porch and we don't have room enough in our freezer. Hope you have room for this moose meat."

"My, what did you do to your hands, Ian?" Nancy asked.

"I got them caught in a 220 Conibear trap."

"Okay," Uncle Jim said, "now how about the rest of the story."

So Ian did. He told them how the department has said game wardens couldn't trap, how he was trapping while undercover with the plastic tent people and having to get up every morning at 4 A.M. to tend traps before he put on his uniform and started game wardening.

"I have never heard of anything so preposterous. If the department is going to sell you a trapping license, then there is no way in hell they can prevent you from trapping, legally. The department cancels all days off for three months in the fall but won't pay the men for 24 hour service. Then I'd say they have no legal grounds to prevent you from trapping. Besides, you were out there trapping and aware of what was happening."

Just then, Ian's telephone rang. "Hello."

It was Ian's sergeant.

"Ian, I need you to write a report about the owner of the Pub offering your father and uncle to buy a deer. Be sure to include that your uncle is an FBI agent and get this to me by 0800 tomorrow. I have been talking with Dave Sewall and he was saying that Warden Carroll Bates has information about deer being sold there, also. With your report corroborating the information Carroll has, we may be able to get some outside undercover help."

"If you stop here on your way to Ashland in the morning, I'll have the report for you."

"Are you sure you can write?" Uncle Jim asked.

"It'll be slow work, but I should be able to get it written."

"Okay, we'll leave so you can get started."

Yes, he started to write, he kept thinking maybe something

will come of his dad's and Uncle John's visit. He had to stop once in a while to run cold water over his right hand to reduce the swelling in the thumb and down to the wrist. But eventually he had the report complete. He remained home on call for the rest of the afternoon.

The swelling in both hands had gone down during the night. His right hand was black and blue around the knuckles. He'd keep that hand in his pocket if he saw his sergeant.

*   *   *   *

With Monday morning, came a new populace of deer hunters. Some experienced, some surely would be neophytes. He left the report for his sergeant on the kitchen counter and he drove across the Moro Town Line Road to see the hunter concentration. There weren't as many hunters as he would have thought. He drove back across the Town Line Road and made the loop around Rockabema and saw only two vehicles. One had two elderly men from Patten who were road hunting partridges. The second vehicle was one of the miners near Pickett Mountain Lake in T6-R6. They weren't mining, only prospecting.

He next drove up to the I.P. Road and headed west towards the Snowshoe Road in T7-R6. He found a lot of hunters parked along the I.P. Road, some taking a morning break and drinking hot coffee.

There were fresh tracks headed up the Green Mountain Road and he decided to follow them. Just before he reached the Green Pond outlet brook, he found two vehicles parked. One belonged to Carroll Miller. *He probably had deer hunters up here*, he thought. He stopped and got out and Carroll came walking out of an old twitch trail that goes back towards Lane Pond.

"Hello, Ian. I'm glad to see you. I came up here to pick up my bear stands and haul them out of here before it snows. But the hunter that has this pickup with Massachusetts plates is using

128

my stand without permission and he won't come down. I felt like hauling his ass down out of there, but figured it would be best to get a hold of you. That's where I was going from here."

"You probably don't know his name by any chance, do you?" Ian asked.

"No."

"Ah, Carroll, you wait here. I'll go in and haul him out of there. How far in, Carroll?"

"About 200 yards you'll come to a fork and take the left. The stand is only a short distance from there."

Ian disappeared into the forest. Carroll had noticed that Ian was wearing his blue uniform and no hunter orange. He thought he was taking an awful risk. The path was free of leaves and debris and Ian was able to walk along in silence.

When he came to the fork, he turned left and slowed his pace. If the hunter was wearing his orange, then Ian should be able to see him long before the hunter saw him. He was just placing one foot ahead of the other; stopping often to listen and scan the woods ahead of him. If he was lucky, this path would bring him in behind the stand and hunter.

He continued on, one foot at a time. He could now see the stand legs but he still wasn't sure in which direction it was facing. He bent down low to get a better view. But still all he could see was the bottom portion of the legs. He stood up again and parted the branches. He could see now he was coming in at an angle to the hunter and he was dressed in camouflage and no orange. Not wanting to get shot, he picked up a small rock and threw it at the hunter; hitting the stand. He had his attention now and the first thing the hunter did was pull on his orange hat that had probably been in his pocket.

Ian whistled and the hunter whistled back. "Game Warden, I'm coming in." The hunter climbed down out of the stand. He was considerably taller than Ian.

"Do you have your name tag and address on your stand?" Ian asked.

"Yes, sir, it's right here on the 2x4 leg." Ian looked at it and said nothing.

"I'd like to see your hunting license."

When he handed his license to Ian, Ian looked at the name. Henry Osgood from Danbury, Massachusetts. "When did you bring your stand in, Mr. Osgood?"

"I guess you noticed my name is not the same as on the tag."

"Yeah, I noticed. I'm going to summons you for a violation of rule, using another hunter's tree stand without permission. Mr. Miller told me you refused to leave his stand when you were asked. But that isn't your biggest problem. I was observing you before I threw the rock and you were not wearing any hunter orange at all. Then when you thought I was watching, you slipped your hat on. You are required to wear a vest or jacket and a hat. You were hunting entirely in camouflage. Unload your rifle and come with me."

Carroll was still there when Ian returned with the hunter. "Put your rifle in your Jeep, Henry." Ian pulled out his summons book and cash bail bonds.

He wrote a summons for violation of rule; using another's observation stand without permission. And another for no hunter orange.

"If you don't want to return to Maine for court, or you can't, I can cash bail you here and now. And if you sign a guilty waver, the bail will be used for the fines and no appearance is needed."

"How much money are you talking?"

"$100 for using another's stand and $200 for no orange."

"This really stinks. You have me over a barrel and there's nothing I can do about it."

"Well, Henry, if you had left the stand when Carroll asked you to, you probably wouldn't be here now under arrest."

Carroll knew enough not to get involved, but Mr. Osgood just didn't know when to shut up. He started in on Carroll, "What fucking harm was I doing to your frigging stand? You had to go and complain to the damn warden!"

Ian took two steps closer to Osgood and in a much deeper toned voice he said, "Mr. Osgood, I've had enough of your bellyaching. You are under arrest because of you and only you. Unless you want me to handcuff you and transport you to jail, and impound your pickup, I suggest you keep your mouth shut. Now, if you have $300, I'll sign your cash bail and then you're free to leave."

Without saying a word, he counted out $300 and handed it to Ian, and then he signed a guilty waiver. "Am I free to leave now?"

"Yes, you are."

Ian put the summons, cash bail and money in his pickup and he and Carroll watched as Mr. Osgood left.

"He wasn't happy," Ian said, with a little smile.

"He towered over you, Ian, and probably out-weighed you by 30 pounds, yet you never backed down. I have a new respect for you. And then you went walking in there all dressed in blue and no blaze orange. You must have a lucky star on your shoulder."

"Something like that. Do you want me to help you carry the stand out?"

"It would be easier with two people and I'd much appreciate it."

The wooden stand was heavy and Ian began wondering how Carroll could have gotten it out of there by himself. "How were the bear up here this year, Carroll?"

"This corner of T6-R6 has always produced some of the largest bear my hunters have shot."

"I used to deer hunt up here until the regeneration grew so thick. And there again those hills and swamps have produced big bucks."

"You know, Ian, me and a lot of the guys around are glad you finally caught the Murckle brothers. They never knew when to quit. And they had it coming."

"Well, it took a while, but as my Uncle Jim said once, that when I did catch them, it would be like falling off a log. Their mistake that night was trying to be too clever and harassing my Uncle Jim. He didn't take too kindly to that. I hope they learn a lesson and quit."

"Well, if they don't, I think people around will be more willing to talk with you."

They were quiet for a few minutes, carrying the heavy stand through the woods. Carroll stopped and put his end down for a break. "You know when I first moved up here and met you, Ian, I didn't like you much. I listened too much to what my friends were saying about you and I formed my opinion of you from what they were saying. They said you were a bastard, and so much so, you couldn't keep a wife. I now know the difference there, too. When you caught me, you used me pretty good. I know you could have charged me with more and charged my lady friend, Diane, and I think you know what I'm talking about. There was more and I never thanked you for that. Thanks, Ian."

When the tree stand was loaded onto Carroll's pickup, Ian left to patrol across the Cyr Road to the Camp Violette Road. Then west to the Snowshoe Road and he turned north towards T8-R7 and ridges east of the north end of Grand Lake Sebois. These hills were known for big deer. There were many winter roads which even 4x4 pickups couldn't travel, but were excellent hunting. It was the middle of the afternoon and he had only seen a few hunters.

He found the old winter road he was thinking about that went between the Wadliegh Deadwater and the ridge to the north. Sometimes hunters had walked into the area from the Oxbow end. He needed to stretch his legs, so he grabbed his gear and locked his pickup. This time he was in full hunter orange.

About one and a half miles from his pickup, he found two hunters that had just come out onto the winter road from blinds. They were certainly surprised to see him on foot and so far away from everything. They were all legal and they seemed to like being checked by a game warden, particularly so far back from everything. They were all legal and it was a good check.

Ian left the two hunters and headed back for his pickup. He knew it would be after sunset when he got back, but he didn't care. The walking was good and the air fresh and clean.

After he was back in his pickup, he decided to drive out the Camp Violette Road and stop and talk with hunters camped along the way. It would be a good check to let them know there was a game warden around in the dark. It just might help keep them honest.

He found three parties camped along the road and in all cases they were glad that Ian had stopped for a visit. At each campsite he was offered a bite to eat and coffee. When he would finally get back to his house, there would be no need for supper.

As he was on his way, he received a radio call from the State Police Barracks.

"Houlton, 2256."

"Go ahead, Houlton."

"Ian, I have an attempt to locate to deliver a message. Ruth Stanley from Biddeford called and asked that we. . .you get a message to her husband at Tracey Brook. She didn't know which township. Mrs. Stanley said she had to take her mother to the hospital and the doctors don't expect her to last the night."

"I copy that, Houlton, and I'm on my way."

He just pulled onto Rt. 11 at Camp Violette. He turned on his blue light and drove like the devil was after him all they way to the Tracey Brook Road in T7-R5 on top of Dunbar Hill at the old Lower McMannus Farm. He turned the blue light off and slowed almost to a crawl in places. The road had not been graded for two years. He could see in the mud where a couple of vehicles had been in and one of them towing a camper.

There was a beaver flowage on the right side of the road just before Maple Ridge and it looked as if someone had gotten stuck there, maybe two days ago. As he made the corner just before the Tracey Brook Bridge, he saw firelight through the bushes.

Two men and two teenage boys were sitting around the fire.

Ian got out and walked over. "Is this the Stanley party?"

"Yes, I'm Ralph Stanley."

"I have a message from your wife, Ruth."

Before he could continue, Ralph interrupted and said, "Her mother must have died."

"Your wife has taken her mother to the hospital and the doctors don't expect her to last the night."

"What the hell does she expect me to do about it?"

"Message delivered," and Ian got back in his pickup and left; swearing under his breath. The trip back to Rt. 11 was a little slower and he wasn't bumped around as much. As he drove into his dooryard, he called the Barracks, "2256, Houlton, message delivered and I'll be 10-7."

"One moment, 2256. Stand by for traffic." In a few moments the Barracks came back. "Houlton , 2256, you have a lost hunter from the Bear Camp at the Upper McMannus Farm. The caller said you would know where to find the camp."

"10-4, Houlton. I'll leave now."

As he drove towards the McMannus Farm, he was thinking about what he had found there during the summer two years ago. He had pulled up into the upper field and was dog tired. He dug out his sleeping bag and unrolled it in the shade of a tall spruce tree. The ground was covered with a thick layer of moss. He laid down and slept for two hours. When he awoke, he was refreshed. He started exploring the old farm and near the end of the field where there were several apple trees growing, he found a well used trail and started following it.

It led back to the Bear and Moose Camps, owned by two men from Connecticut. Behind the two camps he found another hunting trail. That fall, while the owners were up during the second week of the deer season, he had hidden his pickup down on the old Levesque Road and walked up to the old farm and in, so he could watch the camp and the trail that led back to the apple trees. He stayed there in the cold, watching until the lights went out and the hunters had gone to sleep. The next day he had returned at 3:30 P.M. and hid where he could see the camp yard and the apple trees. There was one hunter watching the trees. Sunset came and the hunter was still there. A half hour after sunset, the hunter finally gave it up and started walking back to camp. When he had walked by Ian, he stepped out and followed him back to the camp yard. As the hunter was unloading his rifle, Ian had made his presence known. The hunter, James Bowman, was not upset. He knew he had been hunting beyond twilight heading into night hunting and Ian had only charged him with twilight hunting.

The lost hunter this night was James Bowman. "I'm concerned because he knows this country behind the camp and he should have been back before dark."

"Have you heard any signal shots?"

"No sir, none."

Ian knew the hunting trail to the west came real close to one of Bugbee's clear cuts. So he drove around and found the road he wanted and then he came to the clear cut he had in mind. He stopped and got out and fired a signal shot. Seconds later he could hear someone hollering just beyond the edge of the clear cut. He took a compass reading and left his truck running and the lights on and hiked down across the clear cut and James was so happy to see him he almost hugged Ian.

"This time, I am certainly happy to see you, Ian," James said.

"Are you okay? Can you hike up out of here?"

"As long as I know where I'm going."

James was tired and he was slow hiking up across the clear cut. Ian drove him back around to the camp and said, "Good night."

"2256, Houlton, I'm 10-7."

"10-4, 2256." It was now 2 A.M.

*   *   *   *

The Murckle brothers were on their way back from Montana after delivering a load of French fries and picked up a load of steel beams for Newark, New Jersey. Since getting out of jail, they had been on the road constantly, sometimes falsifying their log books. "I'm tired, Fred, of being on the road every day. I want to take a couple of days and go home and hunt. We still have our licenses. We won't be able to hunt legally next year," Ralph said.

"Look Ralph, it took every cent we had in our trucking account to pay our fine. We need an oil change but the money isn't there. If we blow a tire or if we break down, we're screwed. So we keep trucking until we have money in the account again."

"Damn Ian and his Uncle Jim!" Ralph exclaimed. "We need to get even with those two, Fred."

"Have you forgotton, Ralph—we tried that with the marijuana remember? It backfired on us, didn't it? You keep fooling around with those two and you'll end up in jail again, and for more than three days. Or worse yet, you could get the living hell beaten out of you."

"What, from those two old men? Jim is over 70, and Ian has to be over 50. They're both old men," Ralph said.

Fred started laughing and this irritated Ralph even more. "What are you laughing about, anyhow?"

"I'm laughing at you, Ralph. We together couldn't whoop either one of them. Not even that 70 year old man. He's all raw bone and muscle. And there's something about Ian that makes me believe that just underneath that friendly disposition is a volcano waiting to erupt. Besides, after what he did for us, Ralph, I have a new respect for Ian Randall."

"What are you talking about, Fred? What did he ever do for us?"

"We were drunk that night and he could have taken both of us for operating under the influence, and he could have charged us with interfering with the duties of a game warden, when we set up that scene with that dead deer. And he could have charged us with harassment. I'd say he did us a big favor by taking us only for night hunting. Think about it, Ralph."

"Well. . .maybe. But I miss hunting."

*   *   *   *

After breakfast, Ian took the summons, cash bail and the money to the Clerk of Courts in Houlton. Then he drove to Harvey Siding, north of Monticello and out through to St. Croix Siding and to Rt. 11. He found several hunters, but no one had shot a deer. He decided to go see Roscoe and Renée and have a cup of coffee. As he was going through Bugbee's camp yard, Harry Bugbee stopped him. "Hello, Ian. I had to fire those two young men from Caribou. I didn't want to. . .they were the best crew I had. But my ole man said he wouldn't tolerate any poaching going on in his camps. Twenty years ago we used to do a lot of that, but Maurice Gordon in Masardis caught a few of the men and told the ole man that if it didn't stop, he was going to arrest him."

Harry got in his truck and drove down the Dow Road. Ian left his pickup at the turn off for the Patch Camp.

"Well hello, Ian. What brings you out when I've heard you're so busy?" Roscoe asked.

"I came for a cup of coffee. Hope you haven't forgotten how to make it," he replied good naturedly.

"Come in and sit. Between lost hunters and poachers, you must be worn to a frazzle. That was quite a feather in your cap nabbing that crew behind Rockabema. Me and Renée heard some shooting one night coming from the Upper McMannus Farm. I guess that was the Hermo brothers."

Ian told Roscoe, and Renée was just as interested, about the plastic tent crew. "I don't think they'll be back this way again."

"How's Maria, Ian?" Renée asked.

"She's good."

"Roscoe, you better tell Ian what you heard two days ago," Renée said.

Roscoe hemmed and hawed, trying to find the correct way to tell Ian.

"Two days ago I overheard two fellows from Smyrna talking. One of them was telling the other about Tommie Trout going to Washington Avenue in Boston, looking to hire someone to take care of you. All he had was $10,000 and he couldn't get anyone.

"What in holy tar-nation did you do, Ian?" Roscoe asked.

"A few years ago, I arrested his son twice in eleven days for illegal possession of moose meat. I didn't have enough information the first time for a warrant, so Terry Hunter came down and was on foot behind his house. When he was ready, Dan Glidden telephoned his son and told him to get rid of his moose meat. The game warden was coming. Well, it didn't take him but a minute to empty his house and start to leave and I pulled up. Then eleven days later, I received more information from the same informant that he had more moose meat. This time, the previous informant was good and I didn't have to disclose his name on the affidavit and the judge signed the warrant. The information was good and I charged him a second time. At the trial, he had asked for a court appointed attorney and he was given one at arraignment, but when he was found guilty of both charges, the judge said if he had enough free time to have two moose in his possession in eleven days, then he could afford to get a job and pay for his own attorney."

"Then some time after that, he was convicted of armed robbery. He did his time; of course this now made him a felon and he could not possess a firearm. Right after he was paroled, I had him twice in five days for driving after suspension and then later for a felon possessing a firearm. I haven't seen much of him since then.

"I haven't heard anything about his father trying to hire a hit man."

"I don't know if it is true or not. This is all I heard. But you'd better be careful. I'm glad I don't have your job," Roscoe said.

"And you call this fun?" Renée asked.

"Well, most of the time it is."

They drank coffee and sampled Renée's peanut butter cookies that she just pulled from the oven.

"The next time I come in, I'll bring some of that moose meat I confiscated from the Caribou crew. After all, it was you who put me on to them."

"How was your trapping this year, Ian?"

"I ended up with 3 fisher, 3 fox and 15 pine martin. I had to pull everything; there just wasn't time to tend them anymore. How about you?"

"We both trap and we have 4 bobcats, 4 fisher, 20 martin, 2 coyotes and 2 foxes."

Ian stood up to leave. "Thank you for the coffee and cookies, Renée."

"Anytime, Ian. And bring that pretty Maria and her son by again."

Ian was getting tired. Partly because he had been on the go for the last three weeks, between night hunters, lost hunters, a missing woman, his undercover work and trapping, and partly because he was 51 and his body was actually calling out and telling him to slow down.

He drove home, forgetting working twilight hunters. He decided to have a good supper of canned moose meat, a boiled potato and dandelion greens. His mouth began watering just thinking about it. As his meal was cooking, he made a thermos of coffee.

When he had finished eating, he sat down to watch the evening news. He wanted to close his eyes and lean his head back for a few minutes, but he knew if he closed his eyes, he would fall asleep. He got up and fixed a cup of coffee and watched the rest of the evening news.

Just as he was about to fall asleep, the phone rang and it was Maria. "My, I'm surprised to find you home."

"Hi, Maria. I was having a coffee and watching the news before heading out."

"Where you going tonight?"

"Something different. Instead of watching the fields, I'm going out in the big woods and see if anyone is riding around and looking."

After he said goodbye to Maria, he got in his pickup and drove to the I.P. Road and turned his lights off. The moon wasn't full, but what little there was helped him to see the tree tops. That is what he used to guide him when he drove without lights. That, and feeling the tires on the road via the steering wheel.

He wanted to find a hidey hole at the Hot Pond round about road. There he would be concealed from traffic in either direction. He had decided to follow the first vehicle that came through traveling north on the Snowshoe Road.

The night air was getting colder each night and soon, some morning he would wake up to snow on the ground. Sometimes to wake up, he would get out and walk back and forth near the pickup. He had a cup of coffee and poured another. The hot cup felt good in his hands.

Coyotes started howling on the other shore of Hot Pond. Then another and then a lone male with a much deeper voice howled once and the others were quiet.

He drank the last of his coffee and a little past 10 P.M., he saw the illumination of headlights coming towards him from the south. He started his pickup to be ready to pull out behind them. He checked all his switches to be sure they were all off. The vehicle was coming very slow, and then it stopped right in front of the hidey hole road he was parked on. He immediately turned his truck off. Lights came on inside their vehicle meaning one or both doors had opened. He could hear talking now and a beer can being tossed into the bushes. He decided they must be taking a pee break. And then he decided that was a good idea also, and suddenly he had to pee.

He heard the beer cans pop as they each opened a new can. Then they got back in and started moving again. Not wanting to be too close, he waited momentarily before pulling onto the gravel road. Not wanting the reflections of the chrome and his windshield to be seen in their rearview mirror, he stayed back quite aways. More so than if there were no moon.

They were driving so slow, Ian knew he could walk faster. There was no doubt in his mind that the two were looking for a deer to shoot. Or maybe a moose? But when they came to an opening, these guys didn't turn wide to shine the headlights across the opening.

Maybe they were just out riding and drinking? Or being super cautious? He was learning to be cautious also. He knew in his gut they were after a deer. But ditch hunters are usually on hot top, not in the woods. But as they came to clear cuts beside the road, they still didn't put out any light or gig the headlights out across the cut. They stayed away from roads that were dead ends. *Then maybe they were very familiar with the area.*

They stopped at the mouth of the I.P. Road, and Ian stopped behind a corner and was shadowed by bushes along the road side. The two were taking another pee break and they tossed the empty cans into the bushes. Ian could hear the flip tops open. They sat in the pickup for a few minutes before continuing. He wasn't sure now if they were hunting or just out drinking beer. He wished he had some coffee left.

They drove by every road, and when there were clear cuts beside the road, they made no attempt to gig the headlights or put out a spotlight. They turned east on the Camp Violette Road. The Snowshoe Road would dead end at Flying Hill and all spur roads off that also were dead ends. They had gone a short distance and they stopped for another pee break. There was a huge clear cut on the left in T8-R6 and a long twisting road winding its way north from the Camp Violette Road, but in the end it would dead end.

They stopped on the bridge over Cut Stream and threw their empties in the brook and opened two more cans. Instead of following the Camp Violette Road to Rt. 11, they turned south on the Cyr Road, that went by the east side of Cut Lake.

On top of the first hill, beyond Cut Brook, a huge bull moose walked out onto the road and stood there. The vehicle stopped and Ian was sure they would shoot it. But they sat there and watched it. When the moose moved on, they continued. They stopped on the bridge over Weeks Brooks for another pee break and another can of beer. They sat there for ten minutes before moving on. Clouds had covered up the moon and Ian could now follow closer.

When they reached the I.P. Road, they turned to the right back towards the Snowshoe Road. The driver made a wide turn and drove partially off the road onto the soft shoulder. They were stuck and they only had a two wheel drive. This was going to be Ian's best chance for a surprise check. He turned his pickup off and with flashlight in hand he ran up to the passenger's door and yanked it open and hollered, "Game Warden! Don't move!"

They both responded, "Holy shit! Where in hell did you come from? We didn't see any lights."

Ian could smell the strong odor of beer, "Before we do anything, I want you to pass your rifle out so I can check it. Butt first."

The passenger had the rifle between his legs. He could see the driver was wearing a holster and handgun. "It's loaded, sir, so be careful."

.308 Winchester automatic. Ian removed the loaded clip and ejected a live round from the chamber. He put those in his pocket and the rifle he put on the roof. "Okay, you," and he was talking to the driver, "pass me your handgun. Butt first."

He had a Smith & Wesson .357 Magnum. He emptied it and put the bullets in his pocket and the handgun on the roof. "How much beer have you each had?"

"Well, we left camp with two 12 packs. There ain't but four cans left. Can you pull us out of this ditch? We're stuck."

"I don't have a chain."

"Shit," the passenger said.

"What are your names?"

The passenger said, "Devin Albert."

"Roy Adams," the driver said.

"What are you two yah-hoos doing out here at midnight?"

Devin said, "We ain't seen nothing this week. We're just riding around drinking beer to see what we could see. Anything wrong with that?"

"And why the loaded firearms, if you're just drinking and looking?"

"You know man! Just in case, man," Roy said.

Ian had a problem and he knew it. Although they both had admitted to looking for deer with two loaded firearms, they had not committed an illegal act other than loaded weapons in a motor vehicle, and driving under the influence. "Let me see your hunting licenses."

They both were from Burlington, Vermont. "What do you two do for a living?"

"We work on a dairy farm."

"Where are you staying up here?"

"We rented this nice camp on Shin Pond."

"Upper or Lower Shin Pond?" Ian asked.

Roy and Devin looked at each other and Roy said, "How the hell should we know?"

"Do you have more ammunition than what was in your handgun and rifle?"

"Yeah, we have a box of each in the glove box."

"Okay, hand them to me." Devin did.

He gave them back their rifle and handgun. "Okay, Roy. Rock it and see if you can get out."

Roy put it in reverse and floored it. It didn't move. Then he put it in forward gear and floored it again. It still didn't move. "I guess you are stuck. That's lucky for you, because I think if a deer had stepped out, you wouldn't have thought twice about killing it. But now you sure as hell ain't going anywhere and you're both too drunk to drive anyhow. This is what I am going to do. I'm charging you both with having a loaded gun in a motor vehicle. And to insure your presence in court, you are both under arrest. If you don't want to come back for court, you can sign a guilty waver and there will be no appearance needed. I'll need $200 for cash bail. Do you have that?"

"Yes sir, Mr. Warden."

Ian wrote out the summons and cash bails and said, "I'm leaving and I have all of your ammunition, so I feel pretty safe you aren't going to shoot anything. And I'm also going to leave you two here stuck in the ditch. Someone will be along after sunrise that'll probably have a tow chain. If you want your ammunition, I live at Knowles Corner on top of the hill on Rt. 212. I'll leave your shells on the deck next to the kitchen. I suggest you get some sleep and sober up before driving."

Ian got in his pickup and put the two boxes of ammunition on the seat. Then he drove out the I.P. Road to Rt. 11 and home.

He put both boxes on the deck, but he doubted if they would come after them.

He looked at the clock and rolled over in bed. 2 A.M.

CHAPTER 7

Ian slept until 8 A.M. and left for Houlton without breakfast. He needed to get the summons and cash bails to the Clerk of Courts. Then he went over to the Elm Tree Restaurant for breakfast. He met Roland Pelletier there and they had an enjoyable breakfast. After three cups of coffee, he was still yawning.

After leaving the restaurant, he decided to do something different. He'd drive to Linneus and back across the South Oakfield Road and work the area behind Skitacook Lake. He could never understand why this area was not hunted harder. There were more and bigger deer here than anywhere else in his district.

He'd go down to the lake side first and see if any of the camps were occupied. In the middle of all the camps at lake side was one owned by people from New York. He had never met them, but they always seemed to have all the toys and expensive ones. The camp was being used. He heard a gun shot out on the lake on the other side or maybe by the outlet. He went back for his binoculars. He heard another shot. But they didn't sound like a high powered rifle. Maybe a shotgun or a big caliber handgun.

Through the binoculars he could see three people in a boat near the outlet. The boat started moving towards the cove on Ian's left. *They're looking for ducks.* There was another shot and a small flock of ducks took to air.

The boat slowed and someone reached over and picked up a duck. Then there was rapid fire of three shots from a handgun. One was duck hunting and one just blasting away at anything.

The boat started to cross the cove and it looked as if they

145

were coming back to camp. He worked his way over so he would be close. He waited and they came in to the wharf. They were all drinking. When the boat was tied securely and the three were on the lawn walking towards the camp, Ian stepped out and said, "Nice day for duck hunting." One look at the operator of the boat and Ian knew he was going to be a problem.

"Would you unload your shotgun and the handgun?"

"Why should we?" the operator asked.

"Because I'd feel much better and safer while talking with you three. And the biggest reason is because I asked you to."

The two with the firearms already had unloaded them.

".44 Magnum, huh? How do you like it?" Ian asked, trying to put him at ease.

"The bullets are expensive and it has a lot of recoil. Other than that, just fine."

"How do you like your automatic Browning shotgun? I had one once, but the damn thing was too heavy to carry around in the woods."

"My sentiments exactly."

"I'd like to check your licenses."

The two with the firearms did, Richard Lajoie with the .44 and Randy Decato with the shotgun. "And yours, also," and he looked squarely at the operator.

He sat there for a few moments as if he wasn't going to, and then he handed it to Ian. Tony Derocco.

"How many ducks do you have?"

"Three," replied Randy Decato.

"Tony, I don't see any life preservers. Do you have any?"

"They're in the shed. But we're all good swimmers," Tony answered.

"Well that may be, or not. But you are still required to have them in the boat and reachable. And you three have another problem. While it is legal to discharge firearms from your boat, you can not while under power. And I have been here long enough to see each of you shoot while the boat was under power."

About then, Tony Derocco started for the camp and Ian stepped in front of him. "I'm not through with you yet, Mr. Derocco."

"I was driving the boat, not shooting ducks," and he tried to step around Ian.

"I said not yet."

"I'm going into the camp," Derocco exclaimed.

"Not until I am finished. If I have to, I'll sit you on your ass." Ian took two steps towards Derocco and said, "Your choice, but you'd better make it now," and he took another step.

"Okay, okay," Derocco said. He wasn't happy.

"I'm going to summons you, Richard, and you, Randy, for hunting ducks from a boat while under power. And you, Mr. Derocco, for failure to have any life preservers."

Ian was busy writing out the summons and when he finished he said, "If you can't or don't want to come back for court, you can sign a guilty waver now and your cash bail will be used for the fine."

"How much is it?" Richard asked.

"$100 each for you and Randy, and $150 for you, Tony."

"That's outrageous. Why is mine more?"

"Because the fine is $50 per missing life preserver."

"I ain't paying it!" he replied.

"Well, Mr. Derocco, if you don't, then I'll have to take you into jail and you can make bail there, plus pay the bail commissioner."

"So you need $350 right?"

"Yes," Ian said.

"I'll have to go inside to get it," Derocco said.

"No, you stay here. Richard or Randy can go in," and he looked squarely at him.

Without saying a word, Richard gave his .44 to Randy and he went inside. Derocco was still fuming.

Richard was back out shortly with the money and handed it to Ian.

Ian counted it and put it in his pocket and then he had each sign the guilty waver.

"Remember what I said, gentlemen, and have a nice day."

When he was back in his pickup, the police barracks called.

"Houlton, 2256."

"Go ahead, Houlton."

"Your sergeant would like you to come see him at the Ashland Headquarters as soon as possible."

"10-4 Houlton, I'm just leaving Skitacook Lake. It'll be travel time."

He beat-footed for home. It would be sunset soon anyhow.

"Yeah, Ian. Because of the information you had about Jason Campbell selling deer, and information Warden Carroll Bates had, we were able to send someone in undercover. He has made a buy and you are to meet Warden Sergeant Dave Sewall and the undercover officer at the truck stop in Medway. Can you be there at 6 P.M.?"

"That won't be a problem."

"Dave and the undercover officer will have all the information."

Ian ate a hurried sandwich and a glass of milk and he was on his way to Medway.

*   *   *   *

Dave Sewall and the undercover officer were waiting in the parking lot when Ian arrived.

"Ian, this is U.S. Fish and Game Warden Chris Howd, Warden Ian Randall. Let's go inside and have a bite to eat as we talk."

While they waited for their meals, they talked. "After your Uncle was approached about buying a deer, Carroll Bates had more information that corroborated the information you had, and the Colonel and Major gave us the go-ahead with an undercover agent. I understand you are proficient with writing affidavits for search warrants."

"I've written 25."

Chris Howd gave Ian a pad of paper and he already had a lot of information Ian would need, with his office telephone number, his headquarters and supervisor. "First you want to look for a sawed-off double barrel shotgun he keeps under the bar. I paid Jason Campbell $500 at 2 P.M. today for a buck. I believe this has been going on there for a while."

"Who's your uncle, Ian?" Chris asked.

"John Kenoyer; he's an FBI agent."

"I know him. Not well, but I'd know him if he walked in here. He's tall, over six feet and bald."

"That's him."

Their meals came and Ian put his papers to one side.

After they had finished eating, Agent Howd continued, "In the shed out back, there is an untagged buck deer hanging. In the freezer in the house, there will be an untagged beaver pelt and an untagged bear hide.

"It is my belief, although I didn't see it, but I think someone is doing the killing and Mr. Campbell sells."

"How long will it take you to write the affidavit, Ian?" Sewall asked.

"I'll have it written tonight and then in the morning I'll go to Houlton and have Judge Julian Werner sign it."

"Okay, as soon as it is signed, call me on the warden service repeater and I'll have a crew together and we'll meet you at the D.O.T. garage in Crystal."

"Thank you, Mr. Howd, for your help," Ian said.

"It was my pleasure, and don't forget the sawed-off shotgun."

On his way home, he drove by the café/restaurant lounge to measure the exact distance from a known location and to be able to describe the premises to be searched; the house, shed and lounge.

It was 10 P.M. when he drove into his own driveway. It was going to be a long night and he started the coffee pot.

First, he had to exactly describe the premises to be searched and exact location, so there could not be a mistake. He had to list items to search for and describe why they are illegal to possess. Then he had to qualify the information and this was easy. Federal Game Warden Chris Howd and the probable cause that the person named in the warrant is responsible for the contraband that is to be searched for and seized. When he had finished writing and rewriting, it was 1:15 A.M.

* * * *

Ian was up early the next morning. After going to bed, he laid on his back for a long time thinking about the affidavit and had he included all the necessary elements. He didn't type, therefore the affidavit and request for a search warrant was hand printed. He also hoped the judge would not have any difficulty reading it. He had to hand print most of his requests for a search warrant. Finally, around 4 A.M., he fell to sleep but was awakened by a passing log truck and its engine brake. He looked at his watch and decided it was time to be up anyhow.

Even before fixing a cup of coffee, he read and reread the request for a search warrant and in particular the affidavit. He was satisfied. There was nothing that could be added to strengthen the probable cause.

He could only sit still long enough for a cup of coffee and nibble on a slice of toast. It was always like this, the morning when he'd have to have his warrant signed. He was as excited as a young boy waking up on Christmas morning.

At 8 A.M. he put his paperwork in a folder, signed on with Houlton and headed for District Court in Houlton. The judge would probably be in Presque Isle on Friday, but he thought to look in Houlton first.

The Clerk of Courts said he was in Presque Isle that day hearing some cases. He drove to Presque Isle and there was already a case in progress. Ian asked the clerk, "Ma'am, can you get a message to the Judge for me?"

"What is it?"

"I have a search warrant to be signed."

"As soon as this case is over, I'll tell him."

"Thank you."

Ian waited not so patiently, as he walked up and down the hall. After 20 minutes, a disgruntled defendant came out of the courtroom and walked up to the clerk's window. This was his signal the case was over and he re-entered the clerk's office.

"You can go right in."

"Good morning, Your Honor."

"Good morning, Ian. I understand you have a warrant you want me to sign."

"Yes sir," and Ian gave him the folder.

Judge Julian Werner sat down in his chair as he read the request and affidavit. "This is very interesting. My only question, why didn't your superiors want to take the word of your Uncle, a special FBI agent?"

"My Lieutenant said he didn't want to involve the FBI."

"I guess I can understand. Everything looks in order. Raise your right hand." Ian did. "Do you swear the information on this request for a search warrant and the affidavit is true and accurate to the best of your knowledge?"

"Yes sir, I do."

Judge Werner signed the search warrant and handed it to Ian. "Good luck."

"Thank you, Your Honor."

This was the cake, dessert from all the work that had gone into this case, and the icing would come when they actually seized the contraband articles.

As he drove south of Presque Isle via Rt. 163 to Ashland, and then to Rt. 11, Ian radioed Sergeant Sewall on the Warden Service repeater frequency "2256, 2241."

"Go ahead, '56."

"I have that material and will be driving time from Presque Isle."

"10-4. We'll be here."

Ian's excitement was obvious at the speed he drove through Mapleton and down Castlehill towards Ashland. The road was rough but Ian was only hitting the high spots. Between Ashland and Masardis, he met a northbound state trooper who recognized Ian and flipped his blue light on momentarily, meaning for Ian to slow down. He did until he was south of the Oxbow turn, then he picked his pace up again. He normally would have his blue light and siren on, but he didn't want to alert too many curious onlookers. As if his speed wouldn't do the same. Thankfully, all the traffic he met was traveling north and not south. His biggest worry was a moose stepping out onto the road.

When he topped Bates Hill south of Hall's Corner, he forced himself to slow down. There were too many houses and curious onlookers. He didn't want to lose the case because someone had gotten spooked because a game warden was traveling towards Patten so fast.

He turned left off Main Street on to Rt. 159 and the D.O.T. garage was just a half mile east of town. There were three warden pickups in the yard. He stopped next to them. Sergeant Dave Sewall, Wardens Gary Ballahger and Pete McPheters got out. "Any problems?" Dave asked.

"No, but I had to go to Presque Isle to find Judge Julian Werner."

"What did he have to say?"

"He said everything looked good and good luck."

"Okay, this is your warrant, you're in charge. Tell us how you want to do this," Dave said.

"Gary, I'll go in first and then you right behind me. You go immediately behind the bar. There is a double barrel 12 gauge sawed-off shotgun. Take control of this and hold onto it. Then you maintain security of everyone there. I want everyone to be kept in the lounge area and not roaming around."

Gary looked at Ian and nodded his head, "Okay."

"Dave, you and Pete do the searching but take one room at

a time until it's finished and then move on. I have the inventory list and will record every piece of contraband we find and where it was found and who found it."

"What are we looking for besides the sawed-off shotgun?" Pete asked.

"There should be an untagged buck hanging up in back or the shed, an untagged beaver pelt and an untagged bear hide in a freezer in the house."

"Gary, we don't need all of our vehicles up there. Ride with Pete. Let's go."

Just as the three wardens drove into the restaurant lot, an individual was just leaving. When he looked at Ian and the rest of the wardens, he looked apprehensive. Ian only knew him to be one of the Atwood brothers. They all were out of their pickups and heading for the front door. They were on a mission and no conversation. Ian and Gary were the first ones to enter and Gary, without a word from anyone, went behind the bar. Jason just stood there totally surprised. He had no idea this was coming, and he made no attempt to stop Gary. Gary was much larger in stature than Jason.

Ian walked over to the bar and said, "Jason Campbell, we have a warrant to search your premises."

"While we search, Jason, you will remain here with Gary," Dave said.

There was a disinterested individual sitting to the far end of the bar. He didn't seem to be concerned, but maybe a little interested. He watched everything that was happening. Maybe the untagged deer out back, he had intended to buy. But not now.

Dave and Pete went to the back first and Ian followed behind them with the paperwork. The buck deer was hanging exactly where Chris Howd said it would be. They next went to the house and located the freezer and confiscated an untagged beaver pelt and a bear hide. These were brought back to the lounge. "Jason, yesterday at approximately 2 P.M., undercover Federal Game

Warden Chris Howd bought a buck deer from you, which is now in our possession."

Just then, Pete McPheters found a marijuana plant in the house and brought that to the lounge.

"Jason, I'm going to summons you for:

1. Selling a buck deer.
2. Possession of an unregistered deer.
3. Possession of a .12 gauge double barrel sawed-off shotgun.
4. Possession of an unregistered beaver pelt.
5. Possession of an unregistered bear hide.
6. Possession of one marijuana plant.

While Ian was copying the inventory list of all items seized and writing out the summons, Dave and Pete put the buck deer in his pickup along with the other contraband.

The gentleman at the far right at the bar finally spoke, "I met one of your comrades last year at Little Reed Pond in T8-R10. My friend and I were flown in Sunday afternoon and had just finished setting up camp and were boiling a pot of coffee when this game warden came walking in from the woods. I can't remember his last name, but his first name was Dan."

"Yes, Dan Glidden."

"Yes, Dan Glidden. That was it. He sat down and had coffee with us and we talked for a long time. He was a nice man. We didn't know but maybe he was planning to sleep there that night. I mean, it was well after sunset and totally dark. Well, he gets up and says, 'Have a good week hunting and thanks for the coffee.' Then the son of a gun disappears into the woods and no flashlight. My friend and I just sat there looking at each other. We had flown into an isolated pond to hunt and this guy walks off into the darkness like it was nothing at all. That really impressed us, me in particular. My friend and I are from New Jersey and we had never experienced anything like this. You guys are all right in my opinion."

They drove back to the D.O.T. garage, "That was a piece of good work," Dave said.

"I'll take care of the paperwork and summons and the prosecution reports, and I think there's just enough time today to return this warrant to the clerk in Houlton. After arraignment Dave, I'll keep one summons and send you the others. Thanks, guys, for your help."

*   *   *   *

From the clerk's office in the District Court House, Ian drove home; he showered, ate supper, hid his pickup behind his house and went to bed. For the first time during his career, he was really feeling tired. The first time in 29-plus years that working without any time off in the fall was beginning to wear on him. He knew now that on his 30th anniversary next August, that it was time for him to retire. He still had a few more good years, but if he couldn't keep the pace that this fall was dictating, he couldn't be any less, and if he couldn't be the kind of warden that he knew he was. . .well, then it was time.

The phone didn't ring that night and Ian slept until twelve noon. He had never done that before. He spent the rest of that afternoon writing reports. There were more reports to write than he thought when he first started. At 3 P.M. it started raining, easy at first and by 5 P.M. the rain came down in thundering sheets. That evening on the weather report, the temperatures were suppose to drop and in the colder regions into the 20's. And there was the possibility that the rain could turn to snow before morning. A little snow would certainly improve the hunting. He knew some people who would not hunt until there was snow on the ground. He doubted if he would go hunting this year, as his freezer was already full with moose and deer meat. And that reminded him; he was going to take some moose meat out to the Patches at Umcolcus Lake. "I'll do that tomorrow."

Just then, he heard someone drive into the driveway. He

hoped it wouldn't be a lost hunter. Maria came in without knocking as it was still raining. "My, I wasn't expecting to find you home, Ian."

He hugged her and her sweet essence was sweeter than heaven. "I missed you, Maria."

"You aren't working tonight?" she asked.

"Not in this weather, unless there's a lost hunter somewhere. If the phone rings tonight I'm tempted not to answer it."

"You didn't have to work this weekend?"

"No. The management has made some seasonal changes. I work now Monday through Friday."

"You couldn't live with yourself if you didn't work, Ian.

"Here, you go back to whatever you were doing and I'll fix us something to eat."

Later than evening, as they were talking in the living room, Ian told her about him suddenly feeling tired and that he would be giving it all up the following summer at his 30 year anniversary, which would be August 1st. "I have always felt a little tired come the middle of November, but this year it's more than feeling tired. I feel run-down."

"Well, my word, Ian. Look how busy you have been. You told me yourself that you are not normally as busy."

"Well. . .what I'm saying is when I am retired, I want to spend a lot more time with you and Eric."

She snuggled closer to Ian. She understood what he was saying and she had never been so happy.

Later, because of the divine love they were both feeling for each other, when they made love that night, it was something more special than ever before. It was as if the whole world had stopped and life was revolving around them.

* * * *

The next morning, while Maria was making coffee and breakfast of pancakes and bacon, he went down stairs to put more wood in the wood furnace. The thermometer that morning had dropped to 20°. It was beginning to snow and off to the northwest the storm clouds were getting darker and that would probably mean a lot of snow.

After breakfast, they put two boxes of moose meat in the pickup and drove out to see Roscoe and Renée.

There was four inches of wet, heavy snow on the ground. As they traveled along the woods road, everything was so green and white and really quite beautiful.

"Are you going to say anything to Roscoe and Renée about you deciding to retire next summer?"

"No, the only people who know are you and Uncle Jim and Nancy. I don't want everyone to know."

It was a good thing it wasn't a long walk into the Patch's camp as both boxes of moose meat were getting heavy.

Roscoe and Renée were surprised to see Ian and Maria. "I thought you'd be chasing Sunday hunters today, Ian, with this new snow."

"I probably should be, but I thought you and Renée might appreciate some moose meat."

"We sure would, Ian. Oh, bless you," Renée said as she took the box from Maria.

The lake had froze over during the night, except for a small opening near the outlet cove. There were several ducks still swimming around the pool. "Maybe they don't understand they are suppose to fly south in the winter," Roscoe said. "It was only 15° here this morning. This new snow will make it good hunting tomorrow. I think I'll cross the outlet tomorrow and chase me down a big buck. With this moose meat and a deer, that would grubstake us until next fall."

"Have you heard any more rumors, Roscoe, about the Trouts wanting to get even?" Ian asked.

"We've only been out once since I told you about that and we ain't heard nothing more."

"It was probably just talk."

"I don't think so, Ian. I think there was a lot of truth behind that story."

"If weather permitting and if you and Renée can get out, would you join us for Thanksgiving at Uncle Jim and Nancy's?" Ian asked.

"We'd love to, Ian," Renée said.

"Weather and all permitting," Roscoe said.

"I did hear, on the last trip out, that you sure have been busy this fall. You've chased down some folks who have been needing to join the Three Day Club. Have you seen the Murckle brothers around this fall?" Roscoe asked.

"No, I think they are having to pay attention to trucking to pay off their fines and time lost sitting in jail. I may be wrong, but I don't think we'll be hearing too much from either one of the brothers," and Ian smiled to himself. And Roscoe saw the smile and wondered what Ian had done to make him feel so sure.

They had a light lunch with Roscoe and Renée, and then Ian said, "Well, it's time to catch a Sunday hunter." Roscoe looked at Ian questioningly, but he didn't say anything. But he knew Ian was up to something. *What mouse was he playing with now?*

Maria said nothing, but she too thought it sounded as if Ian knew exactly where to go.

"I'm going to drop you off at home. I should be back for supper." He kissed her and said goodbye.

He beat-footed it to the St. Croix Siding, parked and locked his pickup and started walking up the B&A railroad tracks to Pride's Siding. It was a mile hike and he hoofed it right along. Before reaching the siding, he left the tracks and circled in behind the camp on the east side of the tracks. There were two vehicles parked where he had left his, so he knew they were into camp. He had, in the past, had complaints about the hunters from this camp, Sunday hunting in the afternoon, particularly if there was fresh snow. He thought today would be an excellent opportune chance to catch one or two of them.

He knew of an apple tree that set back away from the

clearing at the siding in a little clearing of its own. As he was circling to get behind the camp, he heard a muffled single shot that came from the east of the camp and not too far away. Before he reached the apple tree, he found two sets of men's tracks, in a trail he didn't know about. If whoever just fired and if they killed a deer, they would probably drag it back along this trail.

He continued on until he found the apple tree and there was fresh blood in the snow and a drag trail leading back towards the camp. Well, he had one for sure. He went back where he could watch the trail and still see the camp.

The air temperature was warming and he was sweating. He hoped he wouldn't have to wait too long. The snow was beginning to melt, also. Off in the distance he could hear two men talking, but they were too far away to understand what they were saying.

He could still hear them talking. Apparently they didn't expect to find a warden out here today. He was getting excited and he had to pee.

The two hunters were close enough now, so Ian could understand what was being said. "I think my buck is a lot heavier than yours, Rodney," Bart said.

"They're both ten points and about the same frame. I wonder if they're brothers," Rodney said. "At least we didn't have as far to drag mine,"

"We'd better keep our voices down. We're getting close to camp," Bart said.

"Who in hell do you think is going to hear us out here?"

"There could be a warden around," Bart said.

"Not hardly. How many times have you ever seen a warden out here? They ain't got enough gumption to walk up the tracks."

"I don't want that old hermit at Howl Brook after us, either. Ole Parnell doesn't take kindly to people poaching in what he figures is his territory."

"I wouldn't worry too much," Rodney said. "Although I guess I'd just as soon get caught by the warden than I would by Parnell Purchase."

"We'd better string this one up with the other deer before it gets any darker."

Just then, Ian stepped onto the trail just behind the two. He walked up behind them and said, "Now that's a nice buck."

They both dropped the deer and turned around and Bart yelled, "Jesus Christ, man! Where in hell did you come from?"

Rodney exclaimed, "Who in hell are you? What do you mean scaring the hell out of us?"

The light was fading. "I'm Ian Randall, game warden. And before we do any more talking, I want you to give me your handguns."

Bart handed Ian a .410 Center Contenter. It was loaded with a slug and he removed it. Rodney handed him a Blackhawk .44 Magnum and it, too, was loaded. "Okay, let's drag this down to your camp. You can put it on the porch. Then we'll go back and get yours, Rodney."

They weren't happy, nor were they doing much talking. When they were on the porch, Ian said, "Okay, lets go get the other one."

They still weren't talking. Ian followed along behind them to a game pole set up in a thicket of spruce and fir trees. Without snow, he would never have found it. The two cut it down and dragged it back to the porch.

"Let's go inside fellas. There's not enough light out here for me to write out your summons."

It was warm inside and Bart started a Coleman gas lantern. "I'm summonsing each of you for Sunday hunting." He wrote out the summons and gave one to each.

"Tomorrow, I'll be back to pick up both deer. If you do anything, anything to either deer, I'll put you both in jail for a long time. And just in case, I'm going to cut off an ear from each deer. That way, I'll know if you try to tag it. Remember what I said."

"Can we continue hunting?" Bart asked.

"Yes, but not for deer."

"Then we might as well high-tail it out of here in the morning," Rodney said.

After Ian had left and was down the tracks out of sight, Bart said, "That was pretty ballsy of that son-of-a-bitch."

"We underestimated him, Bart. I never in the world would have thought that a warden would walk in here like that," Rodney said.

"And he expects us to just leave those deer on the porch? Like hell," Bart was fuming.

"We're going to do just that, Bart. I don't want no more trouble from him."

"What gets me though, Rodney, we have been doing this for years and we have never seen a warden in here."

"Well, now we have and it'll cost us."

*   *   *   *

Ian was only a half hour late for supper. "Did you find what you were looking for?" Maria asked.

"Yes. Two Sunday hunters and two deer. I'll have to go back tomorrow for the deer."

"How are you going to bring both deer back? You said it was a mile up the tracks?"

"In the morning, I'll go down to the B&A crew house in Oakfield and see if they'll take me up in a track truck. If they do, I'll give one deer to the crew. What time do you have to leave tomorrow?"

"By 2 P.M. if I want to be home by 6 o'clock."

"Do you want to ride up with us? We should be back in plenty of time."

"Sure. How did you now they would be up there today and would be Sunday hunting?"

"Through the years, I've received complaints about shots being heard near Pride Siding and it was always on Sunday and the beginning of the third week. I figured with four inches of new snow they wouldn't be able to stay in camp."

They were up early the next morning and after a hearty breakfast, they rode down to the crew house next to the tracks. Dale Drew was just walking from his vehicle. "Hello, Ian. What brings you out so early?"

"Good morning, Dale. We need a ride to Pride's. There are two ten point bucks that I have confiscated that I need to bring out. I'd be willing to give the driver one deer."

"Wait here. I'll be back out in a few minutes, after I get the crews out and see where the train is."

Ten minutes later, Dale came back out and said, "The crews will be working between here and Island Falls. The train is in the yard. And they're waiting for it to go through. We can get on the rails in Smyrna."

"Okay, I'll leave my pickup up there."

Ian parked his pickup and radioed Houlton. "2256, Houlton."

"Go ahead, '56."

"I'll be 10-7 with the B&A at Pride's."

"10-4, 2256."

Dale was already there getting the rail truck set on the rails. "Dale, I'd like you to meet Maria Bechard. Maria, Dale Drew."

This was a special treat for Maria. She had never ridden the rails like this or even aboard a train. The scenery through the woods was beautiful.

They saw many moose, one bear and a raccoon. "This is what used to be Howe Brook Village. The only one living here now is Parnell Purchase." She found it difficult to understand how there once was a village here and now everything was gone and growing back with trees and bushes, and Mr. Purchase still living here all alone.

As they were passing St. Croix Siding, Ian said, "This is St. Croix Siding and I left my pickup here and walked to Pride. Their pickup is gone. I told them what would happen if they didn't leave the two deer on the porch."

"How far is Pride?"

"One mile," Dale answered.

It didn't take them long to reach Pride's. Dale began to slow the rail truck. "There's the deer," Dale said.

He stopped the truck and they got out and walked up to the camp. "Those are nice deer," Dale observed.

"Those bastards!" Ian exclaimed.

"What's wrong, Ian?" Maria asked.

"Those bastards nailed both deer to the porch floor."

"Yeah, they used bridge spikes through the necks."

"And 16 pd. spikes through the stomach hide to the floor."

"We'll never pull those bridge spikes out, Ian," Dale said.

"I don't suppose you have an axe on the truck, do you, Dale?"

"Afraid not."

"Maybe they have one around here somewhere." They split up and were searching for an axe.

Maria was looking through the window and said, "I see an axe inside."

"Nothing in the wood shed," Dale said.

"Nothing around or under the camp, either."

"You must have a hammer, don't you, Dale?"

"I sure do," and he knew what Ian was going to do.

It took him three swings, and on the last try the padlock broke. Maria stood, a little surprised, with the authority that game wardens had.

Ian looked first at Maria and then Dale and smiled. They both smiled back. "This is fun," Maria said.

Dale grabbed the axe. "Do you want the head for anything, Dale?"

"Not really. But I would like one set of antlers."

"Okay, why don't you use the axe and cut the antlers off. I'll work on this one and cut the neck off at the breast, except for the bone, and you'll have to use the axe to get through that."

With four cuts, Dale had one set of antlers off and Ian had cut away at the neck with his knife, all except for the neck bone. While Dale was working on that, Ian worked on cutting through

163

the neck on the other deer. Then Dale cut the second set of antlers off and the last neck bone. Ian used his knife and cut away the stomach hide on both deer.

Dale and Ian loaded the two deer on the back of the rail truck. "What are you going to do with the heads and necks?" Maria asked.

"We have no choice. They spiked them to the porch floor and we have no way of pulling the spikes."

Inside the camp, Ian found more 16 pd. spikes and used several of those to nail the door closed, since the padlock was now broke. The three stood on the porch, looking at the deer on the rail truck, the nailed closed door and the heads and necks spiked to the floor. Dale said, "Boy, when these start to rot, it is going to smell around here."

"Yeah. I don't think Rodney and Bart thought about that. This will be a prank they played on themselves." Even Maria began to laugh. She was understanding why Ian enjoyed his work so much.

"Well, there's nothing more we can do here," Ian said.

They started back for St. Croix Siding backwards. "Are we going all the way to Smyrna backwards?" Maria asked.

"Oh no, just to St. Croix Siding, where we can turn around."

It was a surprisingly joyful trip back, in spite of the deer being nailed to the floor. The weather had changed and the air was unseasonably warm and most of the snow was gone. By sunset, it would all be gone.

Back at the crew stationhouse in Oakfield, Ian helped Dale put one of the deer in his pickup and the other in his own. They each took a set of antlers. "What are you going to do with this deer? Your freezer is almost full?" Maria asked.

"I have a friend at the senior apartment complex who will see that all the residents get some."

After a quick lunch, Maria said goodbye and left for home. "See you a week from Wednesday. I'll make two pies to bring to the dinner."

Ian wrote up a prosecution report and included the two deer being spiked to the porch floor and of having to break the padlock and then having to nail the door closed. He didn't leave anything out. "We'll see who gets the last laugh at court."

The snow was gone and the weather had changed and now was unusually warm. Not really good hunting weather. "The deer will be out tonight though, when the air is much cooler."

He was home early and had a leftover fish and broccoli casserole Maria had made. He had a stiff drink and sat down to watch the evening news. During the interludes he made a thermos of coffee and when the news was over, he left and drove to the picnic area by the mouth of the Camp Violette Road. He backed his pickup in behind the spruce trees and got out and walked around some. Across the road was an old apple orchard where there once was a farm. He had often seen deer here.

From here he could see if a vehicle entered the Camp Violette Road and looking south along Rt. 11 was an excellent habitat for moose, and there had been many vehicle-moose accidents and a few night time poached moose and deer. But he was hoping a vehicle would choose to ditch-hunt the Violette Road.

He poured a cup of coffee and sat on the hood. Coyotes were howling not far behind him. They probably had a kill. Although the temperature was still warm, the sky was cloudless. He took a sip of his coffee and leaned back against the windshield. The coffee tasted unusually good tonight. He took another sip and there was a noise across the road in the old orchard. He finished his coffee and put the cup inside the cab and staying in the shadows, he worked his way to the edge of the road.

A branch snapped and all went silent. Even the coyotes had stopped howling. There was something in the apple orchard; but was it man or animal?

He shifted the angle of sight and in that movement, he thought he had seen a reflection. But he knew from past experience, that when you moved your eyes quickly in the dark, you think you see a tiny light of reflection of something. Was this the case? He waited to make sure. Never moving his eyes from where he thought he had seen something.

There had not been a vehicle by since he had parked his pickup, in either direction. There was another sound like a crash from across the road. His adrenaline was beginning to surge and he suddenly had to pee.

He couldn't just stand there without knowing what was making the noise. Maybe some hunting party had made camp in the wide turn-around just inside away from the road. He wanted to be on the other side, closer, so he could see. Very slowly he crossed the road and waited momentarily in the ditch before climbing up the bank. There was no sound anywhere.

Still staying in the shadows, he worked his way across the bottom of the orchard, stopping every few steps to listen. When he had reached the alder bushes growing just beyond the orchard, he decided that whatever had made the noise had moved on. He returned to his pickup.

Before crossing the road he stopped to listen and then again about twenty feet away from his pickup. He could hear something coming from his pickup. He heard it again; a bear was clicking its teeth, and this wasn't a good sign. He turned his flashlight on and there were two bear in the back of his pickup. One larger than the other. Probably a mother and a yearling.

As he tried to get closer, the mother climbed up on the wooden box he had in the back and she was clicking her teeth and swiping her paws in the air, warming Ian to stay clear. They probably had smelled the two deer he had had in back.

"Hey!" he hollered. "Get out of my truck!" The she-bear didn't like that and she jumped down over the roof onto the hood and jumped to the ground. Ian ran for the outhouse about fifty feet away. He closed the door behind him and locked the door and then held onto it, also. *Well, that worked good.* With a .357 Magnum, he would have to place his shot, and at close range it might not stop her before she could maul him. His only choice was to wait. Then thinking about his predicament, he began to laugh.

166

He shined his light through an empty knothole and the bear was sitting on its haunches facing the outhouse about fifteen feet away. Ian began to laugh again. He hoped he would not have to spend all night in the outhouse.

What is that damn bear doing? The smell in that old outhouse was terrible. She must smell the human odor. But why was she so intent? The smell was beginning to bother Ian. He knew he would have to put his uniform in the wash to get the smell out. The human smell didn't seem to bother the bear. Then she was intent at getting to Ian. But why?

The bear stood up and walked up to the door and began sniffing. Ian could hear the bear sniffing. He was going to holler at it and try to scare it, but it didn't work so well last time he hollered at it. The bear backed up and sat on its haunches again.

An hour later, Ian shined his light through the hole again and the yearling cub had joined its mother; both staring at the outhouse. Ian began laughing again. He was really in quite a fix. He hoped the bear would leave before daylight. He'd hate to have someone find him held prisoner in an outhouse by two bears. When you think about it, it was rather comical. But the smell was making his eyes water.

He waited two more hours and the bear were now laying down. If only a log truck would go by, he was sure the bear would run off then. Finally at 2 A.M., when he shined his light out through the knothole, the bear were gone. He opened the door and shined his flashlight all around and at his pickup. There was no sign of either bear. He left the outhouse door open and ran for his pickup. No problem.

He started his pickup and laughed all the way home. He wasn't sure if he wanted to tell too many people about this night or not. He knew Maria, Roscoe and his Uncle Jim would enjoy hearing about it.

*　　*　　*　　*

Ian went to bed that morning still laughing about being held in the outhouse by a bear. He eventually fell asleep and slept until the phone woke him at 8 o'clock. "Hi Ian," it was Maria, "I just wanted to say hi and I love you."

"I do love you, Maria."

"What did you do last night?"

There was a long moment of silence. She knows. That's why she is asking. "I. . .oh, I went up by Camp Violette to watch for night hunters."

"Did you see anything?"

"No," and he began laughing.

"What's so funny, Ian?"

"I was held prisoner for five hours last night in an outhouse."

"My word! What happened?"

"A she-bear with a yearling cub. . . ." Then he had to tell her all about it.

When he had finished, she said, "You don't always catch the bad guys, do you?" and they both laughed.

When Maria said goodbye, Ian decided he had better go to work. He signed on with Houlton and drove towards Oakfield to fuel up. Then after filling his fuel tank, he decided to work the woods in Dyer Brook.

As he turned onto Rt. 2, the police barracks were calling. "Houlton, 2241."

"Go ahead, Houlton."

"I just received information of a serious hunting accident in Silver Ridge on the east side of Rt. 2. There's a field beside the last house on the left before reaching Fred Goodwin's residence and on the Pond Road. The person who called in the complaint was at the house on the left and has now gone back into the woods to be with his friend."

"I know where you are describing, Houlton. I'm a long way away, but I'll start that way immediately. Ah. . .Houlton, if you have contact with 2256, would you ask him if he could assist and start that way?"

"2256, Houlton, I copy."

"2256, you're to go direct with 2241."

"2241, Dave, I copied all the traffic and I'm on Rt. 2, Dyer Brook and will start that way."

"You'll probably get there first, but I won't be far behind you. I don't have anyone in my section any closer than you."

"10-4, Dave, I'm on my way. Clear, Houlton."

Ian turned his blue light and siren on to Silver Ridge through Island Falls. As he drove, he kept trying to imagine the circumstances of the shooting and how serious it was. People stopped to watch as he drove through Island Falls. Once he was south of town, there was less traffic and he increased his speed considerably. He didn't know how much more his old truck could handle. He thought it a little ironic; thinking about the bear last night holding him prisoner in the old outhouse and now he was responding to a life and death situation. There was no way of knowing from moment to moment with the life of a game warden. *No one had said who the victim was.*

As he was approaching the field road, he saw a group standing in the yard and pointing towards a field road. He turned lights and siren off and braked hard to make the turn. He had his window down and someone was hollering, "Follow the road to the bottom of the field. The ambulance just arrived."

Ian drove down the short field road to the parked ambulance that had backed up to the mouth of the skidder road. Ian jumped out and ran along the skidder road until he came to the paramedics working on a body.

"I'm glad you arrived when you did, officer. We need your help to carry him back to the ambulance," one paramedic said.

Ian helped to put the victim on the stretcher and the four of them each grabbed a corner and started out. The victim had lost a lot of blood and his face now was as white as snow. He had been shot in the leg and his boot was so bloody it looked like a big liver. He had lost so much blood, Ian didn't know how he could still be alive. He looked at his chest and he couldn't see any movement. But the paramedics had said he was still alive. Just barely. But would he survive the ride to the hospital?

Ian asked the other person there who was not a paramedic, "Did you call this in?"

"Yes, we were hunting together."

"When the ambulance leaves, I want you to stay here so we can talk. You're Joe Harley. What's his name?" meaning the victim.

"Danny Gillam," Joe said.

As they were getting to the ambulance, Warden Sergeant Dave Sewall was just walking by the ambulance. The victim was loaded and the doors closed and the driver started to leave, but he was stuck. Someone there had a small 4x4 Toyota and hooked a chain to the ambulance and he couldn't pull it and he was stuck. Ian hooked to the Toyota with his chain and hauled both vehicles out and to Rt. 2.

"Okay, Joe, let's go back to the scene and you walk us through it." At the scene, Ian found an empty 16 oz. Budweiser bottle and one full bottle. "Well, looks like he was sitting on this stump drinking Budweiser."

"Where were you, Joe?" Dave asked.

"Danny dropped me off at Spaulding Brook where it crosses Rt. 2. I hunted up along the east side of the brook and Danny was sitting on the stump where you found us."

"How many shots did you hear?"

"Only one, and I was maybe 50 to 75 yards away. Right after the shot, I heard Danny screaming for help. I came up here running."

"Did you know he was drinking Budweiser?"

"Yeah."

While Dave was talking with Joe Harley, Ian started looking closely at the scene. "Dave, it looks like he slipped on this rotten root. And it looks like he was sitting on this old stump."

"He probably heard you coming up the brook, Joe, and when he stood up, he slipped on this root and fell. Where did the bullet hit him?" Dave asked.

"In the calf muscle of his lower right leg. According to the paramedics, the bullet blew away most of the muscle, but never hit the bone," Ian replied.

Ian laid on the ground where he had seen Danny lying and he looked up hill and had an idea. On his hands and knees, he started searching the ground, working his way up hill. Every once in a while he would see a spot of blood. He broke off fir boughs and stuck them in the ground at each spot of blood. Then on a leaf of a low bush was blood and tissue. He had the bullet path now and it was pointing to another old stump.

On his hands and knees he started looking closely at the stump and then he found it. A bullet hole only a few inches above the ground. "Hey, Dave, I think I found the bullet." He showed him the path of blood and tissue and how there was a straight trajectory to the second stump.

He got out his folding knife and started cutting away the wood. He soon had the spent bullet. "What caliber is that rifle, Dave?" The rifle still lying where Danny had shot himself.

".444."

"I think that's what ballistics will find this bullet to be," and Ian gave it to Dave.

Ian wrote down Joe Harley's name, phone number and address and then said, "You're free to go, Joe. If we need any more information, we'll call. But this seems pretty clear right now."

Ian stuck a piece of orange flagging in the hole where he had extracted the bullet, and another orange flagging wrapped around the stump Danny had been sitting on.

"Can you think of anything else, Ian?" Dave asked.

"I think we have it all."

"I'll take the rifle and beer bottles with me," Dave said.

When Joe had left, Ian and Dave stayed back talking. "What caliber was Joe using?"

".30-30. I thought of that, also."

"I'll check with the hospital and see if he made it, and if he did, I'll have to question him," Dave said. "Write this up as soon as you can, Ian, and get it to me. And thanks for your help. Good work finding the bullet."

Ian closed the door to his pickup and looked at his watch. Almost 2 P.M. He hadn't realized he had been at the scene that long. This had been one of the simpler hunting accidents to investigate.

He still wanted to work hunters in Dyer Brook, but Dave had asked for his written report as soon as possible. So he drove home and hid his pickup behind his house and sat down at his desk. "I sure wish I had learned how to type. Then maybe my reports could be read."

He finished the report after supper and he decided not to go out tonight. He was tired. He went to bed early with the intentions of getting out before sunrise the next morning. But at 10:10 P.M. the phone rang. He awoke with such a start he almost had a heart attack. The phone rang six times before he could crawl out of bed. "Hello."

"Ian.....this is Scotty at the barracks. Are you awake yet?"

"Don't tell me there's a lost hunter."

"Not tonight. Two trucks hit the same moose at the sand shed on Rt. 11. The moose disabled both trucks and I've dispatched two wreckers from Houlton."

"Okay, Scotty, I'll get dressed and head up."

He got dressed without turning on a light. He grabbed his jacket and gun belt and strapped that on, and walked out to his truck. There was a beam of light shining down across the green field across the road at the far west end of the field.

He turned all his light switches off before starting the engine. He backed up and eased out to the road. A powerful light beam was being directed down across the field next to the woods on the west end. He looked through his binoculars and a vehicle had driven off the road into the field. The light was coming from the passenger window. He had seen all he needed to see and he started up the road slowly; not wanting the noise of his truck to spook them.

But first, "2256, Houlton," he said in almost a whisper.

And Scotty answered almost in a whisper, "What's up, Ian?"

"I'll be a bit late getting to the trucks. I have two night hunters in the field across from my house. As soon as I clear here, I'll head up."

"10-4, Ian," he whispered.

He drove off the road right behind the pickup. The high intensity light was still shining down across the field. He turned his headlights on and jumped out and hollered, "Game Warden! Don't you make a frigging move!"

He ran up to the driver's door and yanked it open. The passenger had the big seal beam light and the driver had the only rifle. Usually the passenger was the shooter.

"You both are under arrest for night hunting. You," and he shined his flashlight at the passenger, "turn your seal beam off and roll your window up."

When the passenger just sat there, Ian said again a bit stronger, "I told you to roll your window up and turn that light off! Now!" He did.

"You pass me your rifle. . .butt first."

The driver handed Ian a new Remington .30-06 with scope. It was loaded and the magazine was full. Ian removed the bullets and put them in his pocket. He put the rifle on top of the roof.

"Get out," the driver got out and Ian frisked him. He had four more shells in his pocket.

"You, slide over here and get out." He frisked him and confiscated a new Buck knife. He turned the vehicle off and removed the keys and put them in his pocket and locked both doors. He put the rifle behind his seat and told the two to get in. "Your names?"

"Francis Morin," the driver and shooter.

"Mark Hamel," the passenger.

Ian pulled out his handcuffs and told them to put it on each of their right hands. "Before I can take you to jail, I have a double truck-moose accident up the road. When I finish there, then we'll go to jail."

"2256, Houlton."

"Go ahead, Ian."

"I have the two night hunting subjects under custody with me and we are going to take care of the trucks now."

"Thanks, 2256."

Francis and Mark sat there, handcuffed together, in silence. "How old are you two?"

"Twenty-five," Francis said.

"Twenty-six," Mark said.

"Where are you two staying?"

"The Katahdin Lodge."

"Where are you two from?"

"Worcester, Massachusetts."

"Why did you pick that field tonight to hunt?"

"It just looked like an out of the way good spot to find a deer," Francis said.

"Did you ever drive by during the daylight and see that house across the road?"

"Yeah, we saw it, but when we drove by there was no one there. What. . .did someone call you from that house?" Mark asked.

"No. I live there. You guys aren't very good at this, are you?"

"I'd have to agree with you there," Francis said.

"2256, Houlton, I'm off at the sand shed."

"You two stay here and leave things alone."

Ian turned his blue light on to warn other vehicles of a hazard. Then he walked over to talk with the two drivers. "I was coming north and that damned moose ran out in front of me. I hit the brakes, but it was too late."

"When I hit it, the moose spun around and I hit it and it went underneath and tore off one fuel tank. The fuel isn't leaking, though."

Ian went back to his pickup and started filling out an accident report for each driver.

Both wreckers arrived before he was finished. When he did finish, he gave each driver a copy and hooked a chain to the moose and his pickup and hauled the moose down Rt. 11 to the Jim May Road about a half mile away.

Then he drove back to the scene with the blue light flashing to warn other vehicles. But none came through. It was after one in the morning before they were back at Terry Levesque's field and Francis' pickup. "I'll let you, Francis, follow me and Mark to Houlton, so when you get bailed out of jail, you'll have transportation."

"You'll do that for us, Mister?" Mark asked.

On the way to Houlton, Mark asked, "Now what?"

"You'll be booked and if you don't have enough money to make bail, the turn-key will explain how to have it wired to you. Once you make bail, you'll be free to leave. Your arraignment date is on your summons; the third week in December. At the arraignment you plead guilty or not guilty. If you plead guilty, the court will give you three days in jail. That's mandatory, plus a fine. If you plead not guilty, the judge will set a date for your trial, probably sometime during the winter."

"What about the rifle?"

"That belongs to the state now."

"We have enough money, but I don't know if Francis will want to plead guilty."

"Well, you'll have time to discuss it."

* * * *

It was after four in the morning before Ian got home. He went back to bed, after taking the phone off the hook.

Ian slept all that day and woke up in time for supper. Then he wrote up reports of the night before. Somehow, he doubted if Morin and Hamel would ever show up for arraignment. He had their bail money and rifle; he really didn't care if they showed or not. If not, a bench warrant would be issued that would be good for seven years. And he would be in retirement.

When he had finished his reports, he called Maria and told her about catching two night hunters in front of his house.

"Did you go back to see if that she-bear was still around?" She thought that was hilarious. A game warden held prisoner in an outhouse by a she-bear. "When I told Eric and my folks, they all laughed so much, tears ran down their faces."

"Are you going out tonight?" she asked.

"After catching those two last night, I think the word has gotten around to the other sporting lodges and camps that the warden is around. Besides, I'm tired. This is the end of the third week."

CHAPTER 8

It snowed a foot late Sunday night, and this usually meant the end to lost hunters and night hunters. Although Ian could remember continuing to work night hunters through the middle of December. That's when he lost his first wife. "Why do you still go out every night looking for night hunters when hunting season is all over?" his first wife asked.

The only answer he had, but could never tell her, was he had become obsessed with the game of cat and mouse.

With new snow, and only a few non-resident hunters about, this made it ideal for the local true hunters. The bucks would be in full rut and when they were after a doe that was in heat, his alertness and preservation was ignored. All that mattered was to find a willing doe to mate. Many hunters who successfully shoot big bucks each year know how vulnerable bucks are this late in the season.

The ground wasn't frozen yet and Ian knew it would be a mistake to plow his driveway. Years ago, he bought an old 1947 Chevy 2 ½ ton truck that had been cut down and a nine foot Fisher plow attached. Although it was only a two wheel drive, it would push as much snow as a 4x4. He started smiling to himself then, as he thought about how fun it will be to teach Eric how to plow snow with the old '47 Chevy.

He was finishing his cup of coffee when the phone rang. It was Maria. "You must have heard me thinking about you. Well, actually I was thinking about Eric."

"Oh. How's that?"

"I was thinking how much fun it will be to teach Eric to

drive my old '47 Chevy plow truck."

Maria didn't know what to say. She was so happy Ian thought so much of her son.

"Eric and I will be driving through Tuesday evening after work. I have already talked with his teachers and they said it would be alright to keep him out of school for three days, as long as he is back on the following Monday. This way, I'll bake my pies at your house while you're out wardening."

"I can't wait to see you."

"It'll be tomorrow, not next week," they both laughed.

*   *   *   *

As he patrolled around his district, he saw very few hunters. But there were many deer tracks in all the unplowed woods roads, and too many coyote tracks for his liking. "If this keeps up, some day there'll be more coyotes in northern Maine than deer. Why they were ever brought into the state is beyond me."

When Maria and Eric arrived late Tuesday evening, Ian was at home. "I thought you'd be out chasing night hunters."

"Not tonight. When there is snow on the ground, it is rather difficult to work night hunters."

They didn't stay up late. After Eric went upstairs to bed, they laid awake for a while in bed talking. Maria had never found it so easy talking to someone as she did Ian. He was never correcting her and he heard every word she said. She had never found this in another man. She wished he would retire tomorrow so they could start a life together.

*   *   *   *

The next morning they were all up early and Maria fixed a breakfast of scrambled eggs and bacon. "Where will you go today, Ian?" Maria asked.

"I thought I'd go into Howe Brook and see Parnell Purchase.

He may have a deer that needs to be tagged. Eric, would you like to go with me?"

"Would I! Hell. . .excuse me, heck yes!"

"Okay, you'd better wear your orange hat and I have a vest for you. We may see a partridge or two."

"Do you want me to put up a lunch for you two?" Maria asked.

"That would be good."

Ian took his rifle, just in case a foolish buck was standing in the road somewhere. He had a freezer full of deer and moose meat, so he didn't care if he shot one or not. With the freezer full, he would have to can it.

They drove out through the Jim May Road in T7-R5. He followed that to Bugbee's Road in T8-R5 and then to the Levesque Road. They saw more moose tracks in the snow than deer. Deer didn't really like the big clear-cuts in winter. In the summer, the clear-cuts offered an easy and fabulous chance to browse.

When they reached Howe Brook Siding, Parnell was walking down the tracks toward them. "You're just in time, Ian. I have a big buck down, up near Beaver Brook. I just came down to get my toboggan. It'll be easier dragging the deer over these ties.

"Who's this young fella, Ian?"

"This is Eric Bechard, Maria's son."

"This seems to be a favorite place for you to hunt," Parnell said.

Parnell was addressing young Eric now. "Not long ago, Ian and I both shot bucks up there and then had to drag them down here. There was a warden camp in here then. Across the tracks and near the lake. Through the years I've shot a good many things near Beaver Brook." Parnell was remembering the moose he had snared and set up the poachers with a hind quarter who had camped near the bridge on Levesque's Road and the many deer he had taken from there. But he, like Ian, was getting older and slowing down and now he knew better than to turn away help. Even if from a game warden. But, Ian was different? They had played pranks on each other, but there never was any hard feelings. Parnell had lived a lonely existence there at Howe Brook when the village had been dismantled and Ian had become a playmate.

"Before we hike back up to Beaver Brook, let's have a cup of tea first. How about you, Eric?"

"Yes sir, tea sounds fine."

They drank tea with fresh bread and when Parnell was rested he went out back to the shed and retrieved an old wooden toboggan. There was both old moose and deer hair on it. Ian pretended he hadn't noticed. It was a two and a half mile hike up the tracks and Eric thought this was exciting, but he was also amazed how Ian and Parnell in their advanced years showed no signs that this little excursion was anything but normalcy. Once they were there where the deer was laying beside the tracks, Eric had to sit down and rest his legs.

Parnell and Ian loaded the deer on the toboggan and began the trek back, without resting. This really surprised him.

Back at Howe Brook Siding, Ian said, "We might as well load your deer into my pickup and I'll take you out to Oxbow to tag it."

"Okay, and when we get back, I'll fry up some liver and onions with potatoes."

On their way to Miss Pearl's in Oxbow to tag Parnell's deer, Eric asked, "Is this what you do every day?"

"Well, this is just part of what I do, Eric. I'm not always chasing poachers."

While Miss Pearl was filling out the registration, Ian and Eric filled her wood box in the kitchen. She handed the tag to Ian to attach to Parnell's deer.

"Thank you, Miss Pearl," Parnell said.

The drive back was a quick one. Ian was hungry and said, "I can almost smell the liver and onions." Eric didn't understand what he was saying.

"You string this deer up in the shed, Ian, and I'll get lunch started."

"Eric, get that block and tackle." When Eric looked confused, Ian said, "Those pulleys with the rope."

Ian found an old whiffle tree that had blood and hair on it and decided Parnell had used it before as a leg spreader to hang a deer. He hoisted the deer up and told Eric, "You see that wooden notch? Wrap the rope once around the post and then a figure eight pattern on the notch.

"That's right. . .that should hold."

"I never heard of a block and tackle before, Ian, or a whiffle tree."

"Your grandfather must have them on his farm, doesn't he?"

"Yes sir, but he calls them by different names."

"Like what?" Ian asked.

"The whiffle tree he calls a 'tie-to bar' and the block and tackle, 'ropes and pulleys.'"

"That's close enough, I guess. Let's go inside."

Parnell was already frying the liver and onions and another fry pan of potatoes and cabbage.

"Make a pot of coffee. This all will be done soon."

Eric had never smelled food that smelled so good. Not even his mother's. Maybe it had something to do with the atmosphere. Cold temps, snow on the ground, an old log cabin and cooking on an old wood cookstove, and the smell of smoke.

While Ian was pouring the coffee, Parnell said, "Everything is done. Eric, bring over the plates and I'll fill them." Eric had never heard of frying cabbage.

"Do you want some coffee, Eric, or water?"

"Coffee," he was feeling like this was a special occasion, as long as he didn't tell his Mom.

They sat down at the picnic table and they all began eating. "This is a meal fit for a king, Parnell. But there is a taste I can't identify with."

"It's bear fat. I fried everything in a little bear fat. It makes a terrific baking lard, also."

Eric didn't care what Parnell had used. It all was so delicious.

Parnell was really hungry. "I've been up since 3:30 this morning." When Ian looked at him, he added, "Well, it's a long hike up to Beaver Brook."

There it was, another game. When Ian and Eric had seen Parnell walking back to the siding, his first thoughts had been if Parnell had been out hunting along the track right of way before sunrise. And now he was sure of it from Parnell's last comment. But to show concern now would only mean that Parnell had won this round in the game of cat and mouse. And the audacity of the guy to get him and Eric to help drag it back and then give him a ride to Miss Pearl's to tag it. Ian swallowed his pride and said, "Yeah, this is the bestest dear liver I have ever eaten."

"We would like to stay and help clean up, Parnell, but me and Eric, we have to leave."

Parnell walked with them out to his pickup. "Thank you, Ian and Eric, for your help." Parnell offered his hand to shake Ian's and then Eric's. "It's been fun as always."

Ian knew what he meant by that, but to say anything now would only belittle himself.

*   *   *   *

After Ian and Eric had left, Parnell sat out on the porch with a whiskey and water drink and laughing so hard it sounded like a party at the ole hermit's cabin on the hill.

Parnell had left his cabin at 4 o'clock and walked up towards the Beaver Brook Crossing, staying between the rails. He knew from his close to 30 years living at the village that deer head for the deer yard around Beaver Brook the day after a heavy snow storm. And just like he knew it would be, that buck was standing off the tracks on the bank looking up the tracks. To make the scene look real, he had to drag the deer back into the woods and gut it and then drag it back to the tracks. His deception had worked.

Ian drove out the 3A Road to Camp Violette and he showed Eric where the she-bear had chased him into the outhouse and told him how she had laid in front of the door for hours, not letting him out. Eric thought this was really funny.

As they started out the Camp Violette Road, Ian stopped and said, "Eric, look. There's the she-bear or sow and her cub."

"Apples under that tree. There used to be a farm here 70 years ago."

From the tire track traffic, it looked as if most hunters were riding around looking for a deer track to follow. So far all they had seen were moose and coyote tracks. When they turned the corner where Never's Lumber Camp had once been, the road was flooded. "Looks like the beaver are back again. This has always been a problem with beavers. Great Northern Paper Company owns this land and they'll be harvesting wood in here this winter. We'll come back here Friday and dynamite it."

"Can I come too, Ian?"

"Sure you can."

Ian had wanted earlier to drive across the Umcolcus Road back to the I.P. Road, but he decided to drive to T8-R6 and go across Cyr's Road to the I.P. Road.

Surprisingly, there was only one set of tire tracks on this road, and when Ian came to a washed out culvert, he stopped and got out to look closely at the tire tracks.

"What are you looking for, Ian?"

"Trying to decide which way this vehicle is traveling. Look here," and he pointed where the tire had spun crossing the wash out. "You tell me, Eric, which way is it traveling?"

Eric looked at both tracks and said, "The snow was spun back this way. So that means the vehicle is traveling in the same direction we are."

"That's good, Eric. Let's see if we can catch up to it. It was through here only a short time ago."

Once they left Cut Lake Inlet Brook and were on higher ground, they began to see many deer tracks. "I think the hunters in the vehicle ahead of us are what we call ditch hunters. They ride around until they find something to shoot."

When Ian saw they had turned off onto a deadend road, he had an idea. He backed his pickup up so it wouldn't be seen when the hunters came back out. "You'll have to stay here, Eric. This probably won't take long. I'm going in on this road and find a good place to give them a surprise check."

"Okay."

Ian circled through the woods so not to leave his tracks in the road. He found just what he was looking for. Two short spruce trees growing close together at the edge of the road. He stood behind them and the hunters when approaching him would not be able to see him and he could make a quick check to see if their rifles were loaded.

He didn't have long to wait, when he could hear a pickup coming back. He waited motionless. The approaching vehicle making more noise. It sounded like an old beater. One needing a tune up. Looking through the spruce branches, he could see the pickup coming. He had to pee but that would have to wait. The pickup was moving slowly, which was good for him. When the front of the pickup reached Ian, he stepped out right to the passenger's open window. The passenger hollered in surprise and Ian said calmly, "Game Warden, stop." When they did, "How's it going, fellas? Seeing anything?"

"Only tracks," the passenger said.

"Well, it'll all be over in three more days." Ian engaged them in some more small talk to set them at ease. They both were acting pretty nervous. Like two kids caught with their hands in the cookie jar.

"It's supposed to get cold tonight and that'll make the snow real crunchy and noisy tomorrow. Where are you boys from?"

"Ashland," the passenger said.

"I'd like to see your licenses, but first, pass out your rifles so I can check the actions." The passenger started to hand his out muzzle first and Ian said, "butt first."

He opened the action on a Savage .308 and there was a live round in the chamber and three more in the magazine. Ian put those shells in his right pocket and put the rifle on the roof. "Now pass yours out, butt first." The driver also had a Savage .308 and there was a live round in the chamber and two more in the magazine. Ian put those shells in his left pocket.

"Your hunting licenses please." They did.

The driver, Cliff Doughty's licenses was already punched which meant he had already tagged out. The passenger handed Ian his license and when Ian looked at it, he said, "I need your license. This is Mary's, your wife." That license wasn't punched.

The passenger handed Ian another license, Freeman Doughty. "Are you two brothers?"

"Yeah."

"Your license is punched, also, as is Cliff's. Looks to me like you two are trying to get a deer for your wife, Mary. Can you think of any reason why I shouldn't summons you both for hunting deer after already having shot and tagged one?"

Cliff spoke up quickly, "We ain't stepped foot out of this truck except to pee."

"Then why are both rifles loaded?"

"In case we see a coyote," Cliff snapped.

"How many coyotes have you two shot?"

"Some, not many," Freeman said.

"Have you any more bullets, other than what was in your rifles?"

"That's all we have, Mister," Cliff said.

"Well, I'll tell you what I'm going to do. I'm going to summons each of you for a loaded rifle in a motor vehicle and I'm going to confiscate both rifles to keep you honest. You show up in court in December and I'll give you your rifles back."

They weren't happy about that, but then again, there was nothing they could say or do about it.

"You're free to go now." Ian walked back to his pickup and put both rifles inside.

"Did you get them for anything, Ian?"

"Yes, loaded rifles in a motor vehicle. When they come to court, I'll give them the rifles back."

"Let's go home." It was almost dark.

Ian and Eric both were carrying a rifle when they walked through the kitchen door. "My, what have you two been up to?" Maria asked, a little astonished to see her son walking in with a rifle.

"Whoa, Mom! Did we ever have an exciting day." Eric told his mother all about it. Ian sat back smiling, letting Eric tell the whole story.

*   *   *   *

Maria had been busy all day. Before she could do any baking, she had to go to Patten to do some shopping. "As I drove through Main Street, people were looking at me with the strangest expressions on their faces."

After breakfast, Ian put the two rifles in his gun case and sat down at his desk to write out his reports for court. And then it was time to go to Uncle Jim and Nancy's house and much to his surprise, Roscoe and his wife, Renée, were there already.

While they waited for the turkey to finish cooking, Uncle Jim said, "Ian, why don't you regale us with how that she-bear held you prisoner in an old outhouse." Uncle Jim and Roscoe were laughing so hard they were several minutes before they could catch their breath.

"Hum, I thought I could keep that story from you two."

They all laughed all the way through the story; even Ian. "I still don't know why she did that. Probably never will understand it."

The dinner was extraordinaire and everyone was having an exceptionally good time. Even Maria and Eric were taking part in the story telling, laughter and a good feeling of cheer. When the main course was finished, the table was cleared and everyone agreed to wait for dessert and coffee until their stomachs had settled. Roscoe and Renée were really enjoying themselves. These people were closer to being family, than their own families were.

Roscoe was deep in thought and found it odd how his two best friends were game wardens. And he knew from this day on, he would have to change his life and stop his poaching and prank playing on Ian.

It wasn't until mid-afternoon before anyone wanted dessert. The coffee was hot and they all had a slice of pie, some had two or more. "These pies are sure good, Maria," Ian said.

Jim got up and looked at the thermometer and said, "The temperature is dropping. . .20°." He went downstairs and put more wood in the furnace.

That was a signal for folks to call it a day and head home. "Renée and I really have to be leaving so we'll have a little daylight left to see by."

"We should be going also, Uncle Jim and Nancy. It was a super dinner."

*   *   *   *

The temperature kept falling all night. The next morning, it was 15°. At breakfast that morning, Eric asked, "Ian, are we still going to dynamite that beaver problem we found two days ago?"

Before Ian could answer, Maria asked, "What do you mean dynamite?"

"We found a nuisance beaver flowage that is flooding the Camp Violette Road and Great Northern will be cutting wood in there this winter and will need the problem taken care of.

"Do you want to come with us?"

"No, you two boys go ahead. Nancy asked me if I wanted to go to Millinocket with her and Jim today. No, you two go and play. But be careful."

"Where do you keep the dynamite, Ian?" Eric asked.

"In my green box in the pickup." Maria looked at him in

surprise, but she knew better than to say anything. She was beginning to understand what it would be like being married to a game warden.

Before they could go and blow up the beaver dam, Ian had to take the summons and reports from two days ago to the clerk's office in Houlton. When that was done, "Well, there's no sense in driving the hot top all the way to the Camp Violette Road. We might as well go through the woods, from Harvey Siding in Monticello."

"Why haven't they plowed this road?" Eric asked.

"The ground isn't frozen solid yet, and the plow would dig up the road bed. The big trucks will pack this snow down and it'll freeze and form ice and that is what the contractors want. A frozen ice road."

"I like what you do, Ian. Do you suppose I could be a game warden?"

"When you're old enough, sure. It's a great life."

They made their way out through the 3A Road to the Camp Violette Road to the beaver problem on Beaver Brook.

Ian taped two sticks of dynamite to an alder pole and inserted a blasting cap in one stick. He handed Eric a coil of T.V. antenna wire. "Can you carry this?"

He had to make a wide circle to the dam to stay on dry ground. He walked out on the dam and found where the deepest water was and using another pole, he made a hole in the dam down to the bottom and put the dynamite pole in the hole. Then he wrapped the antenna wire around some bushes and wired it to the blasting cap two wires. Then as they made their way back to the pickup, Ian uncoiled the wire. The pickup was sitting too close. "Eric, do you ever drive your grandfather's tractor?"

"Yes."

"Can you back up my pickup, while I uncoil this wire?"

"Yes sir, I sure can," Eric was excited now.

"Keep going until I say that's good."

Ian uncoiled all of the wire and Eric had to back up about a hundred feet. "That's good. You can shut it off and pop the hood."

When the hood was up and Eric was behind the truck, Ian touched each wire to the battery terminals. The dynamite exploded and water, mud, rocks and beaver wood went flying up in the air and then came raining down. The air was thick with blue smoke. In less than a minute the water over the road was gone. Ian coiled the antenna wire and put that back in his green box.

While they waited for the water to drain, he pulled on his hip waders and got out his axe and two 330 Conibear traps. "What are you going to do now?" Eric asked.

"If we don't trap these beaver, then in two days this road will be flooded again and we'll have to dynamite it again. When the water has stopped draining, we'll set these traps in two runs. Then we'll come back tomorrow and tend the traps."

Ian set one Conibear to show Eric how it worked and then used a stick and hit the trigger. When the trap sprung closed it happened so quick, Eric jumped. "When setting one of these, you have to be real careful and not get your hand or fingers stuck in the jaws."

"Have you ever?"

He showed Eric his middle finger on his right hand. "See that large knuckle? I got snapped and it broke my knuckle while setting one of these once. I also caught my left hand in a 220 Conibear this fall trapping fisher and martin. If set right, these traps close around the beaver's neck killing it instantly. The water is down. Let's set these two traps."

Ian set one in the run to the house and another in a major run the beaver were using to go ashore. "There, these two sets spell beaver."

"Are you sure they'll come back after you dynamited their dam and drained the pond?" Eric asked.

"Oh yeah, they'll be back as soon as we leave."

Every road that had vehicle tracks in the snow, Ian followed the tracks to either where the tracks stopped and the vehicle turned around, or to the end of the woods road. Ian wasn't finding much for hunter pressure. Most of the people were road hunting. He drove out to Flying Hill, the north branch of Wadleigh Brook and Lost Pond. Then he swung south in T7-R6 and stopped at High Dam to see if Jack McPhee, the warden pilot, was in at camp. There wasn't a soul there. They drove out through Hay Brook Deadwater and Lane Brook. Still only vehicle tracks.

"We might as well head for home, we haven't seen a single hunter today. Only where they had been this morning."

Ian found it real nice to come home and Maria waiting for him. And refreshing not to have to prepare something to eat, particularly after a long and tiring day. But most of all, he enjoyed seeing Maria's beautiful smile whenever he walked into the house or a room. But in his gut he knew it wouldn't work out until he retired the first of August. He began counting the months. Nine.

On the evening weather report, the bureau was predicting 14-16 inches of snow to start after 8 P.M. and the temperatures would again drop to 15° after midnight. "Well, at least it'll be a dry, fluffy snow. For the next three days, I'll have to rescue stranded hunters and campers."

"What about the beaver traps?" Eric asked.

"I'll have to tend those first."

Maria was so glad Ian was enjoying taking her son, Eric, with him on patrol. When she was alone with Eric, all he could talk about was what he and Ian had seen or done that day. She also knew that tomorrow morning Ian would have to go alone to check the traps. And probably by snowsled.

Eric fell asleep on the couch before 8 o'clock that evening. "All this fresh air and trying to keep up with you, Ian, has tired him out. You are good for him."

When they awoke the next morning, there was 15 inches of dry snow and the temperature had not dropped as low as predicted. It was only 8°.

"Did you ever plow snow for your grandfather, Eric?"

"Some."

"After breakfast, I'll teach you how to plow with my old '47 Chevy."

"Oh boy!" he gulped down the rest of his breakfast.

"Now watch how I start this; put the gear in neutral because you'll have to use your left foot to push the starter plunger, see?" Ian showed him by tapping the starter with his toe. "You turn the key on, kick the starter and pump the gas about three times only."

The engine purred like a new one. "Now watch everything I do."

Ian plowed out the mouth of the driveway first so Eric would not have to be in the road and then he made a pass close to the house, deck and basement doors and pushed the snow way back. "Okay, your turn, Eric. I'll swap seats with you." Ian shut the engine off so Eric could start it.

He remembered everything he had seen Ian do. He lifted the plow and backed up almost to the road and dropped the plow and made another pass like Ian had done.

"I guess you don't need me anymore. If you get in a fix, holler to your mother."

"Okay."

Ian loaded his snowsled on his pickup and went back inside. "You left Eric plowing by himself?"

"Sure. He's alright and he's doing a good job."

Ian waved to Eric as he drove out of the driveway. Eric was too busy paying attention to what he was doing to wave back.

Even though the snow was dry and fluffy, he decided to unload his snowsled in the parking area near the old orchard. There was a bank there he could back up to and drive off and then back on when he had finished. He only took his axe.

His machine was sinking in the dry snow to the road bed and the fluffy snow came up over the cowling and windshields and in his face. He had to kneel on the seat to stay above the spray of snow.

191

The only tracks he saw were moose and red squirrels. At the flowage, two large deer had walked around the flowage browsing on cedar and raspberry bushes. He kicked the snow off the first set and chopped through two inches of ice and pulled the trap and beaver out. He compressed the springs and removed the beaver and took the beaver and trap back to the snowsled and put them in back. Then he did the same with the second set and removed another two year old. He figured that's all that would be there.

He returned to his pickup and loaded the snowsled and as he was leaving the radio started squawkin', "Houlton, 2256."

"Go ahead, Houlton."

"I just received a call from Bear Mountain Lodge in Moro that they have two overdue hunters. They left the lodge at noon yesterday to ride the roads in and around Rockabema."

"10-4, Houlton. I'm at Camp Violette now and I'll head in that direction."

There was more snow at Knowles Corner than further north. But then again, Knowles Corner was at a higher elevation and it was in the snow belt. He stopped on the plowed highway and put his tire chains on the rear. Better now than waiting until he needed them. He had asked for four new snow tires earlier, but he was told in another couple of weeks.

With tire chains on and in four-wheel drive, he wasn't having any problems, although at times when the bumper would hit the snow and send it up and over the hood. This was hilly country, but he wasn't having any problems. There were two 4x4 pickups at Hubert Farrow's camp, but they shouldn't have any problems now that he had broken out a trail.

The road by Gilman Pond was full of ruts, throwing him all over the road. Then he drove by the parking spot that's used by the owners of the two log cabins on Mud Lake. One closest to the dam had belonged to Gerald Mitchell in his younger days when he used to run beaver traps in this country. Only then, he had to snowshoe in and then out again.

He expected to find them down by the river. There were hills in both directions. Others had gotten stuck here before. Halfway down the hill on the west side of the river, he could see where someone had tried over and over to make the hill in the new snow.

Underneath the dry snow the road had turned to ice where they had been spinning their tires. They weren't at the bridge, so he crossed and started out the other way. A slight uphill all the way to MacDonald's Road. The road was level and halfway to the MacDonald Road he found a blue two-wheel drive pickup sitting in the right hand ditch. There were two people inside. The pickup was running for heat. They couldn't have much gas left. "You boys need a tow?"

"Sure do, mister."

As Ian walked by their pickup, he noticed all the empty beer cans on the floor. "Looks like you guys were out here doing more drinking than hunting."

"We had a few, mister, when we realized we were going to spend the night here."

"Before I do anything, I want to check your firearms," he reached in through the open door and removed one and opened the action. It was empty and so, too, was the second rifle. But he had also seen a box of .9 mm ammunition on the seat, closer to the driver. He looked at the driver and said, "I'd like to check your handgun, also. The .9 mm."

The driver hesitated at first and then handed it to Ian. It was loaded and with a full clip. He unloaded it and put the shells in his pocket. "Before I tow you out of here, I'm going to write out a summons for you for a loaded firearm in a motor vehicle."

"Your name?"

"Vince Gaceetta."

"Okay, Vince, I'll need your hunting license."

Vince had a Portland address. Ian wrote only a summons and not a cash bail.

Ian pulled around their pickup and then backed up to it and

hooked his tow chain. His front tires were pretty run down, so he put on his second set of chains. "Okay, when I get you out of the ditch, I'm not going to stop until we get to Rt. 11."

He tightened the chain and then allowed a bit of slack and then bumped it. All four tires and chains spinning and churning snow, ice and bits of rock.He towed them a hundred yards before they could bring their pickup up and out of the ditch. All the time Ian was churning up the road something terrible.

It was a steep, sharp turn onto the MacDonald Road but once he had made the turn, from there to Rt. 11 was all downhill. But he was still glad he had put all four chains on. There were times, especially around a turn, that the boy's pickup would slide to one side and almost in the ditch, if not for being connected to Ian's pickup.

At the mouth of the road there was quite a snow bank the plow truck had pushed back. Ian gunned his engine so he wouldn't get stuck. The boy's pickup was pulled through the snow bank in a cloud of snow.

As Ian was taking his tow chains off, Vince walked over, "Hey mister, sorry about that loaded handgun and all, and thank you for towing us out. That was one hell of a ride."

Ian threw the chains in back and drove down to Gerald Mitchell's to give him the two beaver. Gerald and Geraldine were sitting at the kitchen table drinking tea.

"Good morning young fella. How about a cup of tea?"

While Geraldine was fixing a cup, "I brought two beaver I trapped last night in T8-R5."

"Must have been where Beaver Brook crosses the Camp Violette Road. That's always a problem there."

"The fur looks prime, you should be able to get top dollar for the two."

Then on another note, "Would you like some moose meat?"

"Yes, but our freezer is full. Maybe later on if this is a cold winter," Gerald said.

"There can't be many hunters left today after that storm last night."

"No. Those that are in the woods are digging themselves out and not hunting. I just had to tow two boys out from the river crossing below the MacDonald Road. There'll probably be more stuck hunters before the day is over. Thank you for the tea but I should be back on the air just in case."

"Houlton, 2256."

"Go ahead, Houlton."

"Received another call. . .behind Levesque's old city about a half mile is another stranded hunter."

"10-4, Houlton. I'm cleared of that other complaint, and I'll head that way now."

This time he put all four chains on while he was parked on Rt. 11 at the mouth of the Levesque Road. With the chains he didn't need the front end locked in, and a couple vehicles had already made their way out. At the turn to Levesque City, someone had waded the snow, probably for help and had been taken out to a telephone.

Just like Gaceetta's pickup, this one, a 4x4 even, had slid off the road and both right hand tires were actually in mud from a beaver flowage that bordered the old road. There was a young man and woman sitting in the pickup. Ian turned around and backed up to them.

Before doing anything, he checked all three firearms. This time everything was empty. "Who hiked out of here?"

"My brother, Phillip."

"Did Phillip tag out?"

"Yeah, he shot a crotch horn the first week," Jim said.

"What did you tag?" Ian asked.

"A spike horn."

"So you were in here yesterday trying to fill Rebecca's tag?"

"What do you want me to say? We thought we might get lucky."

There was no sense in badgering him anymore. "If I get you to the Blackwater Road, can you take it from there?"

"I hope so."

Ian hooked the chain and locked his front end in again and like before he allowed a little slack in the chain so to bump the stuck pickup. He moved it with the initial bump and all four of his tires and chains were spinning and digging down to dirt and mud and covering Jim's pickup. Finally he was able to pull them up on the road and out of the mud. And he didn't stop until he was on the Blackwater Road. He threw the tow chain in back.

"2256 , Houlton."

"Go ahead, '56."

"I'm clear of this one behind Levesque's City. Is there anything else on this side of Rt. 11?"

"There isn't anything in your district right now."

*   *   *   *

Ian drove home and was surprised at the clean job Eric had done plowing. He even had pushed the snow across the lawn like he did.

"Did you have any beaver?" Eric wanted to know first.

"Yes, two two-year olds. And I think that's all there was. I gave the beaver to an old friend who will skin and stretch them and sell them next spring to a fur buyer."

"Are you done for the day, Ian?" Maria asked.

"Yes, unless I get called out again. This is one heck of a way to end the deer season. Although I did get a loaded gun case this morning.

"Thank you, Eric, for doing such a good job of plowing."

"It was fun. I like driving that old truck."

After eating supper, they all sat in the living room and Ian told them all about the day. "What will you do now that hunting is over?" Maria asked.

"I have to collect all the tagging information from the agents and get that to Ashland and then in ten days, after the trapping season is closed, I have to take all that information to Ashland

and all my cases for this month are in court scheduled for the third week of December."

"And how about your regular days off?"

"I start back on my schedule this week.

"The next time you come over, I'll go back with you and spend time with you and your family."

That night, as Ian laid on his back and Maria snuggled in close, tears were running down her cheeks onto Ian. He was asleep. She had never imagined in her entire life that she would find such happiness as this. She would like to marry now but she really understood Ian's reason for waiting until he retired. That was fine with her.

CHAPTER 9

Ian's last deer season was over and he wasn't at all regretful. Instead, because of his love for Maria, he wished that his 30 years was also at an end. But he wasn't going to dwell on it.

His deer tags and fur tags and information were up to Ashland. His sergeant had left him four new winter tires and those were on now. The temperature continued to be colder than normal and the beaver trappers were glad for that. Another snow storm had dumped 12 more inches of snow and since it was so cold, this snow was also dry and fluffy.

He took some time off and spent three days with Maria and her family in Kedgwick. He enjoyed helping her father on the farm. Something he hadn't done since he was a boy. Maria's folks were really pious and even at Ian and Maria's age, they were not allowed to sleep together. Anita, Maria's mom, had fixed up the guest room for Ian. This was alright, too. He was just happy to be here.

At the end of his visit, he had Maria drive back with him, so she would be able to use his Toyota to come and go. The following week, he had a lot of court cases that were due for arraignment.

That evening, as they lay naked in each other's arms, Ian said, "I never realized how much I needed you beside me as we slept and how much sexual desire for you was pent up, until we couldn't sleep together."

Maria began laughing and said, "I thought I was the only one thinking about that." They both laughed and kissed and Maria rolled over on top of Ian so she was sitting on him and she said, "Hey mister, I'm horny. What are you going to do about it?"

Maria had to return to Kedgwick the next morning and Ian, after filling up with gas, drove south on I-95 and made a U turn in the cross-over below Battle Brook. Beaver had moved in during the summer and now there was a large flowage between the south and north bound lanes and further downstream. He parked his pickup and went downstream first to look for beaver traps.

The water under the ice being warmer than the snow pack covering, the ice had melted and refroze. He found two large houses downstream and no one had it set up yet. There was also a beaver dam between the two lanes in the median. He crossed under the road staying on the ice. About halfway through there was another smaller dam. More like a check dam. He stepped over this and took two maybe three steps and the ice broke and he went down in the freezing water. He was off balance and went completely under. He didn't have gloves on and, oh God, were his hands cold. Every time he tried to climb back up on the ice, it broke and he went down again. He tried laying in the water and then rolled up on the ice. It held until he moved and he went completely under again. God, he was cold and he knew he had to get out before his hands were too numb to be of any use— and hypothermia. His only choice was to try and roll up on the ice again. If he went under again, he knew he would be too cold to try it again. He rolled up and rolled again and again, until he was against the dam.

As quick as he could he hurried to the other end and rolled in the fluffy snow, allowing the snow to soak up the water in his clothes. He was still cold and knew if his pickup was any further away, he would not make it back. He had to crawl up the bank through the snow on his hands and knees.

He finally reached his pickup and, thank God, he had not locked the doors, and the engine was already warm. The heat and blower fan was on high on the drive home. He was all day warming up. He decided not to say anything about his to Maria. She would only worry about him.

Two days later, he was in district court in the clerk's office signing complaints. The courtroom was already full and there was another 15 minutes before arraignments.

The state police court officer was there, as the sheriff's court officer. Most of Ian's cases were cash bails with waivers, but the two Pride Siding hunters, Rodney Roussel and Bart Madore, were there and sitting in back. When Ian walked into the room, Roussel and Madore grinned at him. Ian knew what that grin was all about.

Ian walked down front and sat down. The assistant D.A. came in and sat at the table on the left. The bailiff came in and stood by the side door near the bench.

Twenty minutes passed and people were becoming restless and nervous. Five minutes more and Judge Julian Werner sat down at the bench. "I apologize for the delays, but there are many cases here today and one sparked my interest more than the others. I'll take care of the Warden Service complaints first."

"Rodney Roussel. Come forward and stand between the two tables."

Ian stood and said, "Your Honor, there is a companion defendant with Mr. Roussel, Bart Madore."

"Oh yes, here it is. Bart Madore, you come down with Mr. Roussel." The judge waited for Madore to stand next to his co-defendant.

"Mr. Roussel and Mr. Madore, you both have been charged with Sunday Hunting. How do you plead?"

"Guilty, Your Honor," they both answered.

"Warden Randall, did you see them hunting or just track them on snow?"

"Your Honor, they both shot ten point bucks that day at Pride Siding."

"Why were you there, Warden? I mean, had someone complained?"

"It was a hunch, Your Honor. When I saw their vehicle parked at St. Croix Siding and being fresh snow, a mile up the tracks from St. Croix and apple trees at the old siding, to me spelled a Sunday hunter."

"Did they give you any difficulty?"

"Not at the time, no."

"I believe there's an explanation with that?"

"Yes, Your Honor. I was unable to take both deer with me a mile down the tracks to my pickup, so I told them both I would be back the next morning and expected to find both deer on the cabin porch."

"Were they both there in the morning?"

"Yes, Your Honor, they were. The two boys had driven a ten-inch bridge spike through the neck of each deer to the porch timbers. And then they spiked the hide to the porch, also. I had no tools with me and looking through the window there was an axe next to the wood stove. I had to break the padlock and I used the axe to cut through the neck and then cut away the hide that was spiked to the porch. I then put the axe back inside and had to nail the door shut. I also cut the antlers off both deer. I didn't want either of the boys to have them. The head and neck of both deer are still there spiked to the porch."

"This could be funny in different circumstances, but I think you two did this out of spite, a couple of smart asses. I think because of this little prank, you two should become members of the Three Day Club to be served immediately and I fine you each $200.

"While you're lying in jail each night, I want you two to think about that stinking mess when it rots next spring. Bailiff, escort these two to the clerk's office."

The rest of the Warden Service cases were routine and when the last one was taken care of, Ian left. He drove home and banked his house with snow. The temperature was still dropping and it was supposed to snow another foot tomorrow.

It was already snowing when Ian got up the next morning.

There was no sense trying to do any work in the storm, so Ian stayed home on call. About noon, wanting something to do, he strapped on his snowshoes and decided to break out his trail behind his house before the snow got any deeper.

All while he was snowshoeing, he kept thinking about what Werner had said about come next spring there'd be a smelly mess of rotting flesh spiked to their porch. Now he began to laugh thinking about it.

He never in this world thought Judge Werner would give them three days in jail. He doubted if those two would raise any more trouble in the future. It would be difficult to forget doing three days in jail for a prank that backfired.

The snow being as dry and fluffy as it was, it didn't take him long to break out the two mile trail.

By dark, the snow stopped and it was getting even colder. Ian decided to plow out and not wait for morning.

As it turned out, it was a good thing he did plow. The old truck didn't start so well below 10°, and the next morning it had dropped to -20°. If the rest of the winter was going to be anything like this, the deer wouldn't stand a chance.

The next two days he was on regular days off and he drove to Houlton (with the state truck) to do some Christmas shopping. He bought Eric a .20 gage single shot shotgun and a pair of snowshoes with harness, and a pair of leather gloves.

He bought Maria gloves also, a sweater, a jacket and something very special, an engagement ring, with an emerald center stone with a smaller diamond on either side.

He bought insulated work clothes for her father and cooking utensils for her mom. Christmas was in four days. Maria would be here to pick him up on the 22rd and they would drive back on the 23rd.

* * * *

The weather changed on Christmas Day. It was warm

202

and sunny and the snow was melting. When Maria opened her special gift, she screamed and cried with happiness. "Oh, Ian, it is so beautiful!" She kissed him.

"Well, are you going to marry me or not?" he asked.

"Of course, but one condition. Not until you retire on August 1st next summer."

Eric hugged Ian and he probably was as happy as anyone. There were tears in her mother's eyes and her father sat in his chair smiling.

"This ring is so beautiful, Ian."

"I thought by having your birthstone, an emerald, as the center stone would be more appropriate than a diamond. So, the week after I retire then."

*   *   *   *

The weather was unusually warm for the next four days and there was very little snow left. But on New Years Eve, the temperature dropped to -20° and by morning, it had dropped another 10°. And by noon the wind started to howl. The wind and cold continued for two days and then the temperature warmed enough to snow. And it snowed for three days. A true Nor'easter.

Ian couldn't do much patrolling. Every few hours he would have to plow. When the snow finally stopped, there was 30 inches of fluffy snow. He banked his house again.

Miss Pearl in Oxbow lived alone in a big farm house and she was about 82 years old. Ian, Dan Glidden and Terry Hunter would stop in often that winter and refill her woodbox in the kitchen, take out the ashes, shovel snow around the house and clean her walk ways. She would always fix a pot of tea and a hot meal.

A few days after the snow, the temperature had dropped to -20°. Ian was on his way to Oxbow and check in on Miss Pearl. As he drove by Matthew Brook, outlet of the pond just out of sight of Rt. 11, Ian saw someone had parked a vehicle and walked through the snow into the woods, and leaving quite a trail as there were no snowshoe tracks.

Curiosity getting the better part of him, he decided to follow. He knew there were new beaver in the pond and someone might have set up traps. Following the already opened trail through the snow, he didn't strap on his snowshoes either. In five minutes he could see the pond.

He continued following the trail onto the ice and to the right was a beaver trap set, only the poles showing above the ice and snow. He wanted to check the name that would be on the scarf of the pole, so he continued following their trail, putting his feet in the boot tracks in the snow.

The cold wind was blowing down the length of the pond and at -20°, the chill factor had to be about -35°. He took three more steps, following their trail, and suddenly he broke through the snow. There was no ice under the trail of foot tracks. He went down and the only thing saving him from going completely under, he had spread out his arms and caught solid ice. He pulled himself out and his legs were covered with black muck. He had no choice, so he sat on the edge of the ice and put his legs back in the water to wash off the black muck. Then he rolled in the snow, so the snow would soak up as much water as possible from his clothing. Now he was really cold. He looked at the hole he had fallen into and he decided since it was a square hole, the trappers must have cut it and maybe there wasn't enough water to set 330 Conibear traps. But why had they filled it in and planted a boot track in the snow, as if someone had walked over testing each step. Ernie and Ed Lilly, Masardis, was scarfed on one pole. He had his answer, but not whether they had intended catching him, knowing that if Ian saw a trail in the snow through the woods that he would follow and step into the square hole. Or had there not been enough water to set their traps. *But why the boot track on the snow in the hole?*

He hurried back to his pickup and turned the heat and blower fan on high. Miss Pearl's would be the closest place to get dry and warm.

He picked up an arm load of stove wood and carried that into the kitchen. Miss Pearl was glad to see him and concerned about him falling through the ice. He didn't tell her that he fell into a hole that the two brothers had cut. He didn't want that part of the story known. While Miss Pearl fixed lunch and tea, Ian stood beside the woodstove warming up and drying out.

*   *   *   *

The month of January was the coldest that Ian had ever experienced. The day time temperatures never rose above 0°, and each night they dropped to -20° to -35°. One morning the temperature dropped to -62°. There wasn't any reason to leave the house that morning. The wind blew night and day.

The water mains in Patten were freezing, buried at six feet. D.O.T. had a device that would measure the depth of frost in the ground. At the Oakfield garage they found the presence of frost at eleven feet, and thirteen feet in Ashland.

Up until February the deer, in spite of the cold, had had a good winter. But during February, heavy snow storms came back along with the frigid cold.

One day, while checking camps around Timoney Lake in Oakfield, Ian saw a tip up fish trap with a flag up near the head of the lake, set out in front of the only occupied camp that year at the lake.

Ian hiked back to his pickup and got his pack, binoculars and strapped on his snowshoes and broke out a trail on the opposite side of the lake, so he could watch who tended the fish tip up. After two hours, he cleared the snow making a cup shape depression and because he was so cold, he started a smokeless fire of snapping dry pine limbs.

He cut fur boughs to sit on, off the cold ground. He ate snow when he was thirsty and all the time no one tended the tip up. He thought Delbert Roy was living there that winter but he wasn't positive. Del owned a skidder and worked in the woods.

Four hours later and there still was no movement on the ice or at the camp. Looking through his binoculars, the snow around the tip up looked as if it had recently been kicked up. Because of his small fire, he wasn't as cold now, but he was powerfully hungry. What he wouldn't pay for a cheeseburger right now.

Three o'clock and then four o'clock and still no one came to even look at it. He knew Del would be home soon from the woods. Five o'clock and lights came on at the camp and a puff of smoke from the chimney. He knew now that at any minute someone would come out and tend the tip up.

Six o'clock, then seven and at eight o'clock, after ten hours of watching the tip up, Ian had had enough. He strapped on his snowshoes and snowshoed across to the tip up. When he saw what wasn't there he wanted to be mad, and then he wanted to laugh. The hole was never drilled all the way down to the water. The tip up set on top, like any tip up with a baited line and the flag tripped and waving in the wind. A practical joke. It was time to go home.

*   *   *   *

The following week, Ian stopped at Battle Brook again and there were three traps that had been set up on the flowage. All were set legal. He could hear skidders operating just a short distance from I-95, so Ian strapped on his snowshoes and hiked out through the old twitch trail and that opened up to a newer trail. He followed that and could see a skidder twitching a load of wood.

There were deer trails everywhere. He took off his snowshoes and walked in the deer trails, so not to leave any boot tracks. He slowly worked his way around the choppings and he recognized the skidder operator, Delbert Roy.

Ian found Del's warming fire beside the main twitch trail back to the yard. He waited in the thick fir trees until Del had passed by on his way to the yard. Then Ian stepped out and using his snowshoe for a shovel, buried Del's fire with snow.

Ian was careful not to leave any tracks and then he stepped back in the thicket and waited. He didn't have long to wait and when Del saw only steam hissing through the snow covered fire, he took his safety hat off scratching his head. He looked all around and there wasn't a boot track to be seen. Ian had all he could do not to laugh. When Del moved on, Ian left and went back to his pickup. There now, he felt better about spending ten hours watching a dummy decoy tip up.

Ian was used to a lot of snow but he had never seen a winter like this one. He made a sixteen foot measuring pole and behind his house where the wind had drifted some snow, he measured 105 inches, and in the woods out of the wind he measured 87 inches.

During March, he began to find dead deer standing up dead. There was so much snow, it supported the deer even though it was dead. This winter was going to put an awful hurt on the deer herd and he knew it would be many years before they recovered. And with increasing coyote predation, then the deer may never recover.

On April 7th, a Nor'easter hit with a fury of heavy wet wind-driven snow. Ian tried to keep his driveway open with the old '47 Chevy but the wind would blow snow on the engine, fouling the plugs. He'd just get it running again and the plugs would foul. He gave up and parked his state pickup out near the mouth of the driveway and backed the plow truck up between the house and garage before the plugs fowled again.

The snow was coming down so fast, D.O.T. had their big grader out just trying to keep the hill open and finally they gave up and closed the road.

The storm ended on the 9th and there was three feet of wet wind-driven snow from the deck on his house to the road. The old truck started but it couldn't even begin to move that much wet snow. He was glad he had parked his state vehicle out by the road. It took D.O.T. all day to open the hill and the road to Knowles Corner, Rt. 11.

Never in his life had he seen a storm like that and so far into spring.

In the middle of April, Maria drove over for a few days. "How would you like a trip to Augusta tomorrow?"

"Of course. What's the occasion?"

"I have an appointment at 2 P.M. to sign my retirement papers. This has to be done three months prior to retirement date."

Ian unloaded his snowsled and even washed his pickup. Something he seldom did. Washed and clean, it didn't have the game warden patina.

They stopped for lunch in Bangor at The Governor's Restaurant, off the Hogan Exit near the big mall. "Oh Ian, look how big that mall is. Wow, would I like to come shopping here."

"Well, when we're married, you can. And maybe Nancy would like to go with you."

She couldn't wait to come to Bangor shopping. A whole new world was opening for her.

She never imagined that she would see anything as impressive as the mall or the Capital complex in Augusta. Ian's appointment was across the street from the huge State House, with the Department of Personnel.

As he was signing his retirement papers, Maria thought there might be a little bit of regret. But he surprised her when he said, "There, that's done. I've actually been dreading this day. . .but you know, it is a relief."

They toured the State House and as they walked past Governor Brennan's office, they looked in and the Governor waved to them. Legislature was seating, so they didn't stay long.

Ian then drove down to 284 State Street, the Warden Service Headquarters. A few people recognized Ian and said hello and they all wanted to know who Maria was. Chief Warden Mickey Noble was in his office and he invited them in for a cup of coffee. "I heard you would be signing your retirement papers today."

Ian introduced Maria. "Maria, Chief Warden Mickey Noble.

Chief Noble, my fiancé, Maria Bechard from Kedgwick, New Brunswick."

"I don't blame you for retiring. When is the wedding?"

"A week after he is retired," Maria replied.

"I understand you have had an extraordinarily busy fall. And a lot of good work."

There was some small talk as they sipped their coffee and when the coffee was finished, Ian excused them. "We must be leaving, Chief; it's a long drive home."

"I'm glad you stopped by, Ian, and it was a pleasure to meet you, Maria."

They talked about future plans and making plans for Maria and Eric to start moving some of their personal things to Ian's. Not once did Ian mention his retirement in a negative manner. It was just the opposite. He seemed to be elated.

*　　*　　*　　*

Because of the deep snow pack, everyone was worried about spring rains causing floods. But the weather warmed so slowly, the spring runoff was gentle and there was no flooding. Except that is along the B&A Railroad between Dyer Brook and Masardis. The track foreman, Dale Drew, contacted Ian. "Ian, would you spend a day with me and the crew, dynamiting beaver problems along the track?"

"Sure, when do you want to start?"

"Tomorrow morning would work for us."

"Okay, I'll have to go to Steel Stone in Houlton and borrow some dynamite and caps. Then sometime when I'm in Augusta, I'll pick up enough dynamite to replace what we use. What time?"

"We start work at 7 A.M. And there won't be any trains running tomorrow, either."

It seemed about every half mile there was a nuisance beaver flowage, softening the rail bed. The B&A were still using old cast iron culverts and Ian had to be careful and not use too much dynamite which would shatter the old culverts and then the rail bed would crumble. In those culverts, he only used a half stick at a time.

By noon they were at Pride's Siding and there was a terrible stink in the air. Dale looked at Ian and then they both smiled and didn't say a word. Just north of Hawkins' Siding there was an out cropping of ledge. "Ian, can you blow this ledge point off? Every time we plow, the tip of the plow hits this ledge."

"Sure thing." He wedged a half stick in and covered it with mud and he blew off about a foot of ledge.

It had been a long, hot day and their last problem was about two miles north of Smyrna at the outlet of White Lake. The culvert was five or six feet below the rail bed and the water was almost up to the crushed rocks. Ian was tired and not thinking and he used a full stick of dynamite and when it detonated, the culvert was cleared and the debris was being flushed out. But the rail bed started to sag and wash away. The cast iron culvert had crumbled. Ian was apologetic and worried, but Dale and the crew only laughed.

*   *   *   *

The day after the rail bed fiasco, he received a letter from the state police advising they would be needing volunteers to work with the Secret Service at the National Governor's Conference in July. Ian thought about that for only a minute and decided that would be a great way to end his career, working for the Secret Service.

The trout fishing that spring was the best that Ian had ever seen. With a slow snow melt, the water in brooks and streams stayed high and cold. One weekend, when Maria and Eric came to visit, Ian took them fishing at the beaver flowage on Battle Brook. He parked off the shoulder on the south bound side. The bag limit was twelve fish and within an hour they all had their limits. That night they had a fish fry and invited Uncle Jim and Nancy.

"What have you heard from the Murckle Brothers, Ian?" Jim asked.

"They have been back some since they did their time in jail, but they keep a low profile when they are home. I don't think they even party like they did. They'll behave themselves for a couple of years, but I suspect some day they'll be back to their same old stunts. Only by then, they'll be someone else's problem."

Ian was counting down the days. He was fortunate and he knew it. A good life that he had had for 30 years would soon be over, and then he would start building another life with Maria. Because of Maria's love and goodness, he had gone beyond the point of feeling regrets about giving it all up, or questioning if he was doing the right thing.

*   *   *   *

Ian was going to work over Memorial Day weekend and then he was going to take most of the month of June off. Upon retiring, the state will compensate for a maximum number of vacation and C.T.O. (Compensation Time Off) earned in lieu of cash overtime pay, but even with taking most of June off, he still would lose time that the State would not pay him for.

There were a lot of people around Memorial Day weekend. The weather was dry and warm. The only bad thing about it was the swarms of black flies. Ian had never seen them so bad.

Ian's Sergeant, Charles Vernon, called Ian Sunday evening and advised him that he would not be able to help him the next day with the road check at Knowles Corner, and he had asked Sergeant Dave Sewall to help out. Ian was all set up by 8 A.M. and Dave showed up shortly after.

There wasn't too much traffic heading home after the long weekend yet. But by 11 o'clock, it was a steady flow of vehicles.

They had written summons for a few fish over the limit and a loaded handgun in a glove box. But at a little past 1 o'clock, three people, two men and a woman, in a pickup with New York plates stopped.

They had been visiting relatives in Fort Kent, and yes, they had been fishing, and yes, they had fish with them. "Will you pull your vehicle off to the side so we can check what you have?" Ian asked.

"Certainly."

All three people got out and opened the cap on the back and pulled out two large ice coolers, and from those they removed three, one-gallon plastic jugs of brook trout frozen in water. Just by looking at them, both Dave and Ian figured there were far too many fish.

"How are you going to count these boys?" the woman asked with a sarcastic tone in her voice.

Dave said, "Well lady, if we have to, this game warden just lives a short distance from here and we can take 'em to his house and thaw them. Or we can let the jugs sit for a while in that warm mud puddle over there. . .course, that will take some time."

A state trooper had showed up by now to help out with the road check, and while Dave and Ian were busy with the New York party, Trooper Al checked all the vehicles.

"Dave," Ian said, "I have an idea. I think Pete and Irene Gerow are home and I think they'll probably let us thaw these fish out in the kitchen sink with warm water."

Ian knocked on the door and Irene answered. Ian told her what they were doing. "We would like to use your sink and warm water to thaw these."

"No problem, Ian, help yourself."

Even this took time and the three New Yorkers were sitting on the bank beside their truck. Dave was helping Al with the road check.

After a half hour, Ian came back out and said, "There are 124 brook trout."

"We'll need to see your licenses please," Dave said.

The woman didn't have a license and vowed she had not fished. But a fisherman can still give anyone a legal limit of fish. The bag limit for Aroostook County was twelve brook trout. Dave and Ian decided to give the woman twelve also, and that left 88 over the limit for the two men, brothers.

"We didn't catch all those fish," Norman Drake said, "most of them our family gave to us."

"You aren't being summonsed for catching them," Dave said, "for possession. We agreed to give your wife a limit and we didn't have to do that."

Ian wrote out summons for Norman and David Drake. "Because you both are now non-residents, to assure your presence in court, I am arresting you for over the limit possession of brook trout. If you don't want or can't appear at arraignment, which will be on June 14th in Houlton, Maine, you can sign a guilty waver and your bail money will be transferred to be used as your fine, and you won't be required to appear."

"How much is the bail?" Mr. Drake asked.

"You and your brother are both charged with possessing 44 trout over the limit. That's $50 for the violation, plus $5 for each fish. That totals $270 each."

"We don't have that much money between the three of us and have enough to get home!" Mr. Drake exclaimed.

All while Ian was inside thawing the fish, Mrs. Drake, Linda, had been giving Dave a hard time. Now she said, "I would think you bozos would be out chasing poachers instead of harassing innocent people," and she kept going on.

Finally Dave had had enough and he said, "Ma'am, I have taken about all that I am going to take from you. If you continue, I'll arrest you for interfering. Is that clear?"

"Linda," her husband said, "leave it alone and be quiet or we'll all end up in jail."

"We don't have the money. So what happens now, Warden?"

Dave said, "Then I'll have to take you to jail in Houlton,

and you'll have to post bail there."

"Then that's what we'll have to do. I can call home and someone will bring it down."

Dave took Norman with him in his pickup and let David and Linda follow him in their pickup. Ian and Al continued the road check for another half hour and then stopped.

* * * *

Ian went back to work on June 14th for the arraignment of the Drakes. He doubted if they would be there. "Didn't expect to find you here today, Ian. I thought you were using up some of your vacation time," Dave said.

"I wouldn't miss this for the world. Are they here yet?"

"Norman and Linda are, but not David."

The courtroom was full and this morning the judge, Julian Werner, took care of the police complaints first and left the fish and game cases for last.

Finally, near noon, he got to the fish and game cases. "State versus Norman and David Drake."

Norman rose and walked down front where he had seen other defendants stand. "This complaint is against both you, Mr. Drake and Daved Drake. Where is David?"

"He went into the Army two days after returning home."

"Did he say anything to the warden that he would be entering the military and wouldn't be able to appear?"

"No sir, he did not."

"How do you plead?"

"Guilty. You have David's bail so I guess you'll just have to catch up with him," Norman said.

The judge was grinning and this usually wasn't a good sign for the defendant. "I tell you what, Mr. Drake," Judge Werner cleared his throat and continued, "I am going to issue a bench warrant for his arrest for failure to appear. He made absolutely no effort to inform the court or the game wardens that he would be unable to appear. And I am changing your summons, Mr. Drake, making you responsible for all 88 fish and David's bail money is now forfeited to the court. If you have all the money, you can leave and pay the clerk. Next case."

When Mr. Drake had left the courtroom, the judge looked at Dave and Ian and slightly nodded his head and smiled. As Ian was walking out, he said, "Thank you, Your Honor."

"I never expected that," Dave said.

"Judge Werner is the best judge I have ever seen. I have lost a few, but he told me once, 'You can't expect to win every case.' I have always been able to go into his chambers and talk with him about cases. He likes game wardens and he likes to fish and hunt," Ian said.

Ian was back on time-off the next day. He was remodeling the bedroom upstairs for Eric and building another kitchen cabinet. The old braided rug in the living room was rolled up and later taken to the dump. Maria's mother had been making her a new one during the winter. When Eric came to visit with his mother, he helped Ian build an addition onto the garage.

Ian was beginning to like having all this time to spend on home projects. He just hoped it wouldn't get old and he'd begin to regret not chasing after poachers any longer.

Maria had planted flowers around the house and yard and the evening before he had to leave on special duty with the Secret Service, he was walking around looking at how things had changed around his home. The trees had all grown. Some he had had to cut down. The flowers Maria had planted were beautiful and this year he had taken the time to weed the garden. When Eric was there, he too enjoyed weeding the garden. He was looking forward to the wedding as much as his mother Maria and Ian. Because it would mean Ian would be his new dad and he would live here with him.

The next morning, Ian ate a good breakfast and finished packing his clothes and gear. The uniform would be staying home. His revolver would be worn concealed under his sport coat. He had to be in South Portland at the University at the main conference building, at 1500 hours.

He left home at 0900 because he had to stop at the Warden Service Supply building on Forest Ave., right behind the State House, to pick up a case of dynamite and blasting caps, to replace those he had borrowed from Steel Stone Industries in Houlton.

It was a beautiful day for a drive and there was no particular hurry. He was glad he had washed his pickup yesterday. Inside and out. It surely didn't look new, but it was clean.

He stopped at Howard Johnson's Restaurant and service station, south of Auburn, and he pulled into a self-service lane. Before he could reach for the pump, a loud and obnoxious attendant hollered, "Hey you! That lane is closed!"

Instinctively, Ian wanted to jump down his throat for being so rude, but he let it pass. No sooner had he started pumping his own gas in another lane and another vehicle, with a young woman in it, pulled into the unmarked closed lane and again the attendant hollered, "Hey you! That lane is closed, get over here."

This infuriated Ian and others there were as infuriated. The attendant made a mistake and came close to Ian. Ian said in a firm, controlled voice, "You have a big mouth."

And much to Ian's surprise, the attendant said, "Yes I do." And Ian thought he would probably change. Others there were saying, "Yes, you are rude."

The woman thanked Ian and then he left. He arrived at the Conference Building fifteen minutes early. Almost everyone else was already there. State Police Lieutenant Demers was in charge of the special security people. "If you all would find a seat, we'll brief you on your duties. I'm passing out a list of all teams and what each of your duties will be, and maps of each area where events will be held."

"While I'm briefing you on this, an explosives sniffing dog is going around the campus and vehicles."

Ian was sitting beside Dan Glidden. "Oh shit! Dan, take good notes. I need to get my pickup out of here."

"Why?"

"I stopped at supply on the way down and picked up a case of dynamite and blasting caps."

Dan just chuckled, shaking his head. Ian found a place to park off the University campus. After Ian was back at the briefing, it lasted only another half hour. "You men are free until 0600 tomorrow. Breakfast will be at the dining hall. Be here at 0700 hours."

As luck would have it, Ian had one of the best security details. He was to be special security at each event, while some would be security guarding a residence or personnel.

The next morning at 0700, the group gathered in individual teams. A state trooper was in charge of the team Ian was with and their first detail was at the Civic Center in downtown Portland. The building itself was first swept clean and then the exterior. Ian was detailed at the back entry along with two others. Each of the others were stationed at each end and patrolled on foot back and forth along that end. Ian patrolled back and forth along the length of the building and the rear entrance.

Ian was not used to walking on concrete and after two hours, his feet were hurting. They felt as if each side of both feet was trying to turn inward, causing severe pain. There was a wide strip of green grass between the building and the sidewalk and Ian took his shoes off and started patrolling in stockings on the grass. He was holding his shoes in his hands when Governor Brennan and his entourage walked by and into the back entrance. Governor Brennan looked at Ian and he didn't seem to be too pleased. Well, it was not his feet that were hurting.

Shortly after that, when all the nation's governors were inside the center, the state trooper team leader came out back and told Ian his new detail was out in front at the main entrance. "No one is allowed to enter now."

He was teamed up now with Warden Carroll Bates. It was a hot day and Ian was sweltering in his sport coat. There was a huge canopy overhead which was shielding them from the sun, but in the afternoon, the sun was shining on them. Carroll was beginning to sweat, also. At first, there were a lot of passers-by that were curious why there was so much security around the center. Then people just seemed to accept it without question.

The governors ended their conference at 4 P.M. and the team was free now until 2 P.M. the next afternoon. In the evening, Dan and Ian toured a small part of Portland. It was just so different than the big woods they were used to back home.

The next day, they took a drive to Old Orchard Beach and walked out on the boardwalk and looked around at all the sun bathers. Other than those on the beach, everyone seemed to be so busy, moving from booth to shop, never taking a minute to enjoy anything for long before moving on to something else. Their lives were passing all around them and they were too busy to enjoy it.

The detail that afternoon was at Vice President George Bush's estate in Kennebunkport. "Those who are detailed at the check points on Ocean Avenue, that runs by the Bush Estate, you are not to allow any demonstrators through. This will be a high security area this afternoon and evening and we can not allow demonstrators in, causing traffic congestions. If you find a demonstrator on foot, do not allow them to carry in any signs or demonstration material. If they want to walk through without carrying anything, let them. If you make an arrest, a Kennebunkport police officer will be stationed at each end of Ocean Avenue and will transport the trespassers to jail. Thank you."

Ian was detailed at the north end of Ocean Avenue along with Warden Glen Feeney, Warden Carroll Bates, and a police officer. From the get-go, traffic was bumper to bumper and everyone was pleasant.

Between 7 and 7:30 P.M., an individual came walking along carrying a placard that said, 'Stop sending our dollars overseas and feed our hungry.'

Ian walked up to this man and said, "You can't carry that placard through."

"It is my constitutional right to demonstrate."

"That may well be, but not tonight. This is a high security area and no one is allowed to demonstrate. If you want to walk along the Avenue, you can. You just can't demonstrate or carry any placards."

"The only way you can stop me. . .arrest me," and he started to walk away.

Ian grabbed his arm and said, "You are under arrest for disorderly conduct."

"Officer Bernie, would you handcuff this guy and transport him to jail?"

The detail lasted until 10 P.M. and Ian rode in the back seat of a state police cruiser. It was hot and muggy and the back windows would not roll down. Before they arrived back at the campus, Ian discovered that he was a bit claustrophobic.

The air at 10:30 P.M. was still hot and humid and Ian found sleep difficult. He laid on his back for most of the night first reliving the last year since meeting Maria, and then his mind took him for a trip into the past when he first became a game warden. He had been very naïve for a while thinking nobody would lie to a game warden, and when he heard stories about good people breaking the fish and game laws, he found it difficult to believe such people could be so devious. But little by little he began to understand that many people faced with temptation, if they thought they could get away with keeping a few extra fish, partridge or shooting a second deer for their spouse or children, would take the chance and hope they wouldn't get caught. But this he knew didn't necessarily make that person a bad person or a reprobate.

Then he thought about his relationship with Parnell Purchase and Roscoe Patch. He began laughing then and to his surprise, he had been sound asleep. He laughed some more and rolled over and went back to sleep.

When he awoke in the morning, he started laughing again. There wasn't much to do after breakfast until later in the afternoon. That evening there was a lobster and clam bake with thick steaks. He and Dan went to L.L. Bean's in Freeport and were amazed at the size of the store.

At 3 o'clock everyone gathered in the conference room for briefing. "The lobster and clam bake will be at Fort Williams Park. Those of you who will be positioned behind the food tables, I want to stress that the Green Peace Ship is off the coast and they may try to disrupt the cook out. So be vigilant and watch for small boats trying to come ashore. Dogs and their handlers are at the park now going over the area. When each of you get into position, search your immediate area. If you find anything, radio your team leader.

"This is the last event, so after breakfast tomorrow morning, we'll have a short debriefing and then you'll be free to leave."

Ian had probably received the best position of all the security personnel that evening. He was stationed on a knoll between the food tables and the coast. He couldn't see the Green Peace Ship but that didn't mean anything. He watched as the dignitaries all passed by filling their platters with lobster, clams, corn on the cob and biscuits.The smell of all that seafood and steaks was delicious and it was making him hungry.

It took quite a while to feed all fifty governors and their entourage. The sun had set and the tide was going out. Not ideal water conditions for a small boat to come ashore. He walked back and forth behind the tables and keeping watch on the coast for intruders.

Even though the sun had set, the air was still warm. Too warm for Ian's comfort. He had to keep wiping the sweat off his face. Ian turned around to look at the crowd and he saw a pretty blonde woman that looked a lot like Loni Anderson. He tried to pick her out of the crowd again, but there were too many people standing around her. He turned his attention back to the coastline. So far everything was going smoothly. There had been no radio traffic at all about any intruders. Perhaps Green Peace had had second thoughts.

There was so much food there that there was no way it was going to be all eaten. *I wonder what the caterers will do with the rest of it. Those steaks on the grill are looking better than the lobster. It would be interesting to know how much this cookout is costing the taxpayers*, Ian was thinking.

The line by the tables had been empty now for quite a while. Everyone was congregated down at the other end, near a fire and there was music but Ian was too far away to see if it was a band or not.

One of the caterers came walking up to Ian with a platter of lobster, corn on the cob and a hot biscuit. "Here sir, take this and send someone else down to get a plate."

"Thank you. I wasn't expecting this."

"Well, it looks like there's going to be plenty left over."

"Thanks again," and Ian headed out to the perimeter road to relieve someone so they could go down and get a plate.

Wardens Dave Sewall and Eric Wight were at the lower end of the perimeter road when they saw Ian coming towards them with a plate of lobster. Eric said, "Is that for us?"

"No, this is mine. I'm suppose to relieve you so you can go down and get a platter."

They left and Ian sat on the ground enjoying his meal. He had always been allergic to seafood, especially crustaceans. But this was special and he was hungry. The corn was good, but the lobster was fresh and it had been cooked in seaweed, which had given the meat an added flavor. He had never eaten such delicious lobster. It was soft shell and he could easily break apart the shell with his hands, except for the knuckles. Although the meat in the tails were sweeter by far.

Just as he was finishing his last bite, he heard a shuffling noise coming towards him. He stepped back in the shadows to be ready. Just in case—in case it was some of Green Peace people intent on disrupting the clambake. Then he heard familiar voices. It was Dave Sewall and Eric Wight coming back. When Ian stepped out of the shadows, he noticed Eric was carrying a bag of something over his shoulders.

"We brought up a few lobsters," Eric said.

"They're just giving them away down there," Dave said.

The three sat on the ground and started cracking lobster shells. Dave and Eric also said that was the sweetest lobster they had ever eaten. They had brought with them enough lobsters so they were not bothering to crack the claws. The tails were easier and the meat sweeter. "We sound like a bunch of raccoons," Eric said.

"You know guys, I'm allergic to lobster."

"What happens?" Dave asked.

"It starts with a tickle in my throat and then my throat swells and my eyes get red, itchy and puffy. But these aren't affecting me at all."

"You going to die on us?" Eric asked jokingly.

They ate tail after tail and finally, when none of them could eat any more, there were still a few lobsters left.

There was a radio announcement. "This is Lieutenant Demers, to all security people, this event has ended and you are free to leave. I'll see you tomorrow after breakfast for a debriefing."

It was late by the time they were back at the dormitory and Ian was tired. Some of the officers were staying up and eating lobster, but Ian figured he had had his share. Never again would he be in a position to eat as many lobsters as he wanted. Or that he could afford. He went to bed.

* * * *

In the conference room after breakfast the next morning, Lieutenant Demers said, "This was a very successful event. There was one incident involving a demonstrator at the Bush Estate. He was arrested and taken to the Kennebunkport Police Department. It is very unusual to have an event as large and spread out as the locations were during this Governor's Conference not to have more problems and demonstrations."

"I want to thank each of you for your professionalism.

"Warden Ian Randall."

"Yes sir," Ian said and stood up.

"I will be needing a written report about Mr. Merrill and how you handled the situation as soon as you can. You don't have to write it here. You can wait until you're home."

"Again, I want to thank you all. We did good. You're dismissed and free to leave."

Ian had his gear already in his pickup. He had enjoyed his time here and this will be a grand way to bring a fulfilled career to an end. But he was missing home, Maria and the 'big woods'. Only there did he ever feel totally at ease.

He wormed his way through Portland's streets and he found his way to I-95. He was also glad to safely get the case of dynamite and blasting caps out of the city and away from explosive-sniffing dogs.

Not far north of the Gray exit he came upon a vehicle stopped on the break-down lane with a flat tire. There were two old women and an older man.

As Ian was walking up to the vehicle, the man said, "Can you help us, mister? None of us have ever changed a flat tire."

"Sure, but for your safety, you all should stand on the grassy shoulder." Ian got his handyman jack from his pickup and his four way tire wrench.

The old guy was surprised as he watched Ian. He had no idea how to jack the car up, let alone how to get the old tire off and the car back on all four wheels in twenty minutes.

"How much do I owe you?" the man asked.

"Nothing. Maybe some day someone will stop and help me," Ian said with a smile.

"Thank you very much."

He left the old people behind and he sat back in his pickup thinking about Maria. He had to stop momentarily at the Augusta toll plaza and the next stop would be Orono for gas and coffee.

*   *   *   *

He wasn't expecting Maria, but she was sitting on the porch when he arrived home. "How was your week working with the Secret Service?"

"It was certainly different. I had fun, but I wouldn't want to do it every day."

Maria fixed a light lunch for supper and they ate on the porch and then sipped coffee while he told her all about what he had been doing.

"You have three weeks left. Will you have that time off?"

"We have about everything that needs doing, done. Anything else can wait until after we're married. I want to work my remaining days."

She understood. She really did. *He has been married to that life for 30 years. I'll let him end it his way,* she was thinking. She smiled and snuggled close to him.

There were northern lights to the north. A ballerina's dance in the sky. "Those lights are really bright tonight," Ian said.

They sat in silence and Ian had his arm around her. They were just enjoying each other's company. There was a low noise way off in the distance. "What is that noise, Ian?"

"That's Ansel Snow, backing off the engines of the B&A Train as he tops the grade at Dudley Siding. From Dudley, all the way to Smyrna, is downhill. From Howe Brook to Dudley is uphill."

"After you've retired, Ian, do you think people will stop playing pranks on you?"

"I suppose. It wouldn't be any fun for them, me being retired and all."

"Do you think you'll miss it?"

"There'll be some things I'll miss, I'm sure. But I know it's time for me to retire. Besides, things are beginning to change and I'm from the old school, and I don't think I would adjust too well.

"I hope you won't be too upset if I sleep outdoors some," he said jokingly.

She poked him in the ribs and said jokingly, "You try it and I'll lock the door."

He knew he had chosen well with Maria, and he hugged her and kissed her.

CHAPTER 10

The next morning, Maria fixed a very special breakfast. She had been making sausage, a recipe that her mother had given her. This morning, she made waffles with raspberries and her special sausage. "This is all so good, Maria. I have never had waffles with raspberries. And the sausage is really delicious."

"The sausage, I made from my mother's recipe using moose meat with pork. The raspberries in the waffles lighten the waffle."

"It is all so good, Maria. When I retire, I'm going to get fat from your cooking."

"You get fat and I'll trade you in for a younger model." Ian was drinking coffee and he almost spit it up through his nose.

"You have 18 days, Ian, before your retirement is final. I am going to give you a gift now. Warden Service has been a mistress to you for 30 years. For the next 18 days, I am leaving you alone to come to terms with your career and retirement, and you'll have a lot to think about as you relive those years," Maria said.

*   *   *   *

Maria left right after breakfast the next morning and he went to work as usual. As he watched Maria drive off, he understood what she had said last night. But he was missing her already.

The good brook and stream fishing was over for the summer. The water, having warmed up and water levels dropping, brook trout would be back in the lakes and ponds or in a spring. So he decided to take a ride into Pleasant Lake. This, over the years, seemed to have been a favorite haunt for out of work wood cutters to poach a deer or moose. The road was so rough it kept many people out.

There were yesterday's tire tracks coming out but nothing going in. Oh well, he might as well go see what they had been up to. He drove all the way into Spring Brook. He could see where a vehicle had been parked for a few days. He crossed the brook to the two old cabins on the shore of the lake. *By the looks of the grass, it looks like someone had pitched a tent here.*

He checked the cabins and the locks were still on the door and the windows hadn't been broken into. He walked around some more and found a box full of empty .357 Magnum shells. He hoped whoever it was, was only target shooting.

Along the shoreline, next to the water, he found a pile of fish heads. *Well, they had some luck fishing.* He counted 23 and wondered how many more had been thrown out into the lake. *I should have been here yesterday.*

Whoever had camped here had cleaned up after themselves pretty good. The only thing he found besides the fish heads were the empty .357 shells.

He left Pleasant Lake and rode around Rockabema and checked out Hale and Green Ponds. Nobody at either one. He spent all day riding the wood roads without seeing anyone.

That night, he was sitting in the warm air out on his porch, listening to the silence and waiting for the B&A train to back off the engines at Dudley Siding. The phone rang just as he heard the train at Dudley Siding. "Hello."

"Ian, this is Roland Carr," he sounded all in a panic. "I live on the River Road in Oakfield."

"Yes, Roland, I know where you live. What can I do for you?"

"Ian," pause, "Ian, you gotta help me. Oh my God, Ian! They are all over the place. She's hung them by skidder chains around the neck in the trees. You gotta help me, Ian. I don't know what to do," Roland pleaded.

"Roland, you probably just had a bad dream. Go back to sleep and I think everything will be okay."

Ian didn't hear from Roland again until morning and then it was almost a repeat of the night before. He worked around the house gathering up all of his state equipment that would have to be turned in to Augusta. He kept one uniform and all of the boots he had. But everything else was put in a pile in the garage. Except for his uniforms, which he would have to wear until he made his final trip to the storehouse on Forest Avenue.

Roland Carr called again while Ian was eating lunch. He didn't know what he could do to help Roland. Early that evening, Bob Atfield called Ian. "Ian, Roland Carr has been calling here today, something about dogs hanging from skidder chains in the trees."

"Yeah, he called me last night, then again this morning and at noon. About the same thing."

"I think I better look into this. Would you meet me at the old school house and go down with me?" Bob asked.

"Sure. I'll head right out."

As Ian drove towards Oakfield, he couldn't begin to imagine what the problem was. It didn't take him long to get to the schoolhouse. Bob was there. "Get in, Ian."

"What do you think about this, Bob?"

"I have no idea."

Roland Carr didn't live too far below Oakfield and as they turned into his driveway, Roland and his wife were in the kitchen and Roland had his hands around her neck and it looked like he was choking her. Bob and Ian rushed in without knocking. As soon as Roland saw them, he recognized them and let go of his wife's neck. "Boy, am I glad to see you. We have been fighting off these intruders for two days. They're gone right now but they will be back."

"I called the sheriff's office a few minutes ago and I was told they would have someone here soon," his wife Arlene said. "I think he has the D.T.'s."

The deputy sheriff arrived and everybody moved outside. Ian looked at Roland. He was bug-eyed and searching the tree tops and the bushes around the lawns. "I think it is only the D.T.'s," Bob said, "but we need to get him out of here and where he can get some help."

"Why don't we load him in my cruiser?" the deputy suggested.

"Okay, but no cuffs. I think he'll fight us if we try to cuff him," Bob said. "When you back out on the road, Ian will run across the lawn towards you and I will tackle him and then I'll radio you that we caught one. This might help him to go quietly."

It was no problem getting Roland to get in the deputy's cruiser and when he backed out onto the road, Ian started running across the lawn and Bob tackled him. Roland saw this. Bob made the radio call and the deputy said, "He saw you tackle him, Bob, and he has settled down. Thanks."

"I hope he gets some help," Ian said.

"The deputy will have to take him to lockup first and then he'll be moved to the psychiatric ward. He'll be home soon."

*   *   *   *

A Quandry at Knowles Corner

A week after Maria had left, Ian decided it was time to go see Roscoe and Renée, so after breakfast, he decided to take a drive in on the Old Umcolcus Road. And instead of following it towards Umcolcus Lake, the woods operator for I.P., Maurice Bugbee, had put in a new road that went south through T7-R5 and connected up to an already existing road that came north from the I.P. Road, crossing a tributary of West Hastings Brook. Bugbee had some French cutters working off this new road and they just might be tempted at trying to take a moose home with them. Since this was the tail end of the work week.

There was some real nice wood in there for the crews. Tall,

straight spruce and heavy on the trunk. Beautiful thick maple, only there wasn't a paying market yet for high quality hardwood. Ian hoped the hardwood would be left standing for now. As he drove along, not in any hurry, *This is surely some grand deer and moose habitat.*

Beaver were already starting to dam up and plug one culvert, *Oh well, it will soon be another game warden's worry.* This trip seemed like a ride through nostalgia.

About a mile before this new road intersected with the I.P. Road, Ian found a rather unusual car parked alongside the road. It could have been only an early morning bear hunter, but whatever the reason for being there, Ian's curiosity was piqued. He backed up, so his pickup would be off the road also, and he eased the door shut quietly.

Ian knew what lay west of the road. This is where he had found the bear skeleton and the gold disc. He had no idea this morning that the person who had parked the car by the road would be a direct descendent of the person who had originally stolen the gold from the Spanish galleon in 1808. *Who had the Spanish stolen it from?*

Quietly, Ian went directly to where the squared off block of fir trees were growing, where the old cabin had once stood. He waited, concealed behind the tree thicket. This was a lot like waiting for a night hunter to come hunt the field he was in. From this vantage point, he could see the hole the bear had dug and he could look across the brook to the now grown-up area.

He waited patiently. He could hear something moving across the brook in what had once been cleared land and he didn't think it was an animal. Once in a while, he saw movement, but not enough to see what it was. He waited.

*   *   *   *

Horace crossed the brook to the grown-up clearing and began scanning the ground using a grid pattern across this piece also. He found old rusting horse shoes, and broken bits of chain. He was getting tired, but he was not discouraged. He crossed back onto the east side of the brook and stood and looked at the hole the bear had dug. As he stood there looking at the hole, he began to wonder if the treasure had been buried here and someone had, by chance, stumbled onto it. He began to scan the hole with his metal detector.

Ian knew now what this person was looking for. He quietly worked his way over to Holigard standing in the hole. Holigard's attention was so fixed on the hole and what he hoped to find, he didn't see Ian standing above him.

"Whatever it is you're looking for, mister, you won't find it in there," Ian said.

Holigard was shaken almost out of his shoes. He jumped back totally surprised and when he hit the bank, he sat down in the hole. When he could compose himself, he stood up and stepped up out of the hole.

"What do you know about what I'm looking for?" he said defiantly.

"Well, you see a couple of years ago, I had some bear problems, so I set a trap for that bear," he pointed to the bones. "That bear was a so big and strong, it broke the chain the trap was tethered to and run off. I followed his trail here. You see those two trees?" he pointed towards two white maple trees. "He got the trap caught in between those trees and started clawing at the ground and dug this hole." He was hoping to keep Roscoe's name out of this.

"That old bear couldn't have dug in a more convenient place."

"Why is that?" Holigard asked.

Ian pulled out the gold disc from his left pants pocket and held it out to show Holigard.

"Because he dug this up." Ian noticed the changed expression suddenly come over Holigard's face. "You don't have to worry. This is the only one. I know, because I dug and dug looking for more."

Randall Probert

Without thinking about what he was doing, Holigard withdrew his small handgun from his pocket and pointed it at Ian. Ian was wearing his service revolver, but it wasn't visible. Oftentimes, while hiking in the woods, he would put the loose end of the holster into his back pocket to keep it from bouncing around. He never carried hancuffs on his gunbelt, unless he was working night hunters, and he never carried extra bullets, nor radio or any other attachment. So naturally, Holigard thought him unarmed.

"Now, warden," Holigard said, "give me that disc. It belongs to me!"

"Why does it belong to you?" Ian asked defiantly.

"Because in 1808, Gus and Wilmot Hastings stole a chest of considerable wealth, that my fifth great grandfather, Captain Horace Holigard, had buried on Grand Manan Island. And now I have finally located it."

"And who did Captain Holigard steal it from?" Ian asked.

"That doesn't matter now. Those were different times. Now give me that disc," Holigard was almost shouting.

"And if I don't, are you going to shoot me over one piece of gold? I have already told you, there is no more in that hole. Maybe there hasn't been for more than 150 years. When the Hastings left here, maybe they took the chest with them and this one piece was left behind." Ian was stalling for time.

"No warden. I did my research. The treasure never left here. Now give me that gold!"

Ian tossed it at Holigard's feet. And when he bent down to retrieve it, Ian jumped him and grabbed his left arm with the gun. This move surprised Holigard and he dropped his handgun and Ian twisted his arm behind his back.

"That was a very stupid thing to do, Mr. Holigard. Now, I'm arresting you for armed robbery and terrorizing with a firearm. These charges should keep you secure behind bars for a good long time." Now Ian wished he had his handcuffs with him. But he'd make do without them.

"Now, Mr. Holigard, if I let go of your arm, are you going to act like a gentleman? Or do I deck you and carry you out of here over my shoulder?"

Holigard had no doubt that Ian meant every word he spoke. "I won't give you any trouble, warden."

"Good, you walk ahead of me, that way," and he pointed.

In a few minutes they were back on the gravel road, in sight of their vehicles. Ian radioed the state police dispatcher and requested a wrecker to tow Holigard's vehicle to the impound yard at the barracks.

"Do you have any idea how many years and how much effort. . .well, how long my family has been looking for this treasure?"

"I have no idea," Ian said.

"All this work, and now when I finally discover who stole it in 1808, and where it was buried, only to discover now, that it isn't here." Holigard was really beside himself with anguish.

"Maybe the two Hastings brothers discovered they couldn't farm these woods, they packed up and left," Ian said.

"No. That's not it. The brothers left their families here and went to fight in the War of 1812 and were killed. From all the research that I have done, I firmly believe that when the Hastings women and kids left, the treasure was also left, because they knew nothing about it. None of the gold or gemstones have ever turned up until recently." And Ian knew full well who had the treasure now and why Roscoe was so secretive about his sudden appearance of wealth.

"Well Mr. Holigard, you'll have a good long time to think about it and when you are eventually released from prison, you will never be allowed back in the United States."

* * * *

By the time he was able to leave Houlton, it was too late to do or go anywhere else, so he went home and had a light meal and sat out on the porch long after sunset. His mind was full of images and pictures of the last 30 years. They had certainly been good years. But as much as he really didn't want this lifestyle to end, he wanted more to start another lifestyle with Maria.

A coyote howled in the field across the road. Then another answered it and then all was silence. Then the B&A train backed off at Dudley's Siding.

The next morning he drove into see Roscoe and Renée.

"Breakfast, Ian?"

"Yes. That's one reason why I came in early this morning."

"Maria and I are getting married soon. I'll be retired here shortly and Maria said a week after that."

"I like Maria," Renée said, "she'll be good for you."

Roscoe sat back and watched Ian. He knew Ian had something else on his mind. But he could wait.

"Your breakfasts are always so good, Renée. I envy you both; living out here like this."

When they had finished eating, they sat outside on the porch drinking coffee. "I had a very interesting, and at one point, an apprehensive day yesterday. Have either of you ever heard of anyone named Horace Holigard V? OK, his fifth great-grandfather, Captain Holigard?" Ian looked first at one and then the other. They weren't giving anything away.

"I met Horace yesterday, not far from here. In fact, I had to arrest him for armed robbery and terrorizing with a firearm and took him to jail in Houlton."

"What did he rob?" Renée asked.

"Me, at gun point." Roscoe was bewildered now, and Ian saw the expression on his face.

"What did he take from you, Ian?" Renée asked.

Ian took out the gold disc from his pocket and handed it to Roscoe, "Here, he was after this. And according to him, there should have been a chest full of these."

"Where did you find this, Ian?" Roscoe asked.

"Near the West Hastings Settlement. That's where I found

Holigard. I told him that I had trapped a bear that broke the chain and ended up there at West Hastings Brook. I told him the bear had dug a hole and when I found him, this was all that was left of the chest. When he saw it, he pulled a gun and took the disc. I was able to surprise him and now he sits in jail. When he is convicted of armed robbery and terrorizing with a firearm, he'll spend many years in prison and will never be allowed in the United States again."

"We actually did meet him once, at King's Landing, New Brunswick, at a museum. He told us about the Captain's treasure being stolen in 1808. He said that at today's value, the treasure would be worth about $4.7 million. He told us quite a story, how dedicated the Captain was and how he was going to use it for the war effort of 1812 and all that."

Roscoe excused himself and went into the bedroom and in a few moments he returned and said, "The other day, while Renée and I were walking along the shoreline, we found some pretty rocks. We didn't know but you and Maria would like to have them as a wedding gift." Roscoe gave him six uncut diamonds and four uncut sapphire stones.

"These sure are pretty rocks." He put them in his pockets.

"I like your stone fireplace. Did you do all the work? It sure is nice."

"It should be, the material was really expensive."

"Oh?"

"Yeah, about four million dollars worth." Ian choked on his coffee and spit up.

They all laughed. "Where to now, Ian?"

"I think I'll ride into Howe Brook Village and tell Parnell I'm retiring and that it's been a great game."

"Don't be a stranger now, Ian. You and Maria and Eric come in often to see us."

"We will, and thank you."

"No, Ian, it is us that should be thanking you."

*   *   *   *

Ian drove straight into Howe Brook and up to Parnell's cabin. "Hello, Ian. . .this an official visit or something?" Parnell asked.

"Or something," Ian replied. It was hot and he unbuckled his gunbelt and took his uniform shirt off. Parnell was glad to see that this was going to be a friendly visit, and he was glad Ian had made himself comfortable. "I just made a pot of tea."

"Sounds good."

"How about a little brandy in the tea to spice it up?"

"Sure." There was nothing like a little brandy to loosen the tongue.

They talked for a while before Ian told him he was retiring and the following week he and Maria would marry. "I'm happy for you, Ian. If you give Maria as much attention as you have me through the years, you two will have a marvelous marriage."

They talked of the early days at Howe Brook and Ole John Corriveau. "When you arrested me for that deer in my canoe, I really was afraid of you and I was mad as hell because John had set me up on purpose. But I soon learned you were a very woods-wise person. And I don't think you'd see that in wardens today."

The afternoon was waning. Ian had lost track of time. He had enjoyed the afternoon talking with Parnell, but it was time to go home.

"Maybe you could come out and share Thanksgiving dinner with us, Parnell?"

"I'll plan on it."

Parnell followed Ian to his pickup and before he drove off, Ian said, "It was fun, wasn't it, Parnell?"

"It sure was."

*   *   *   *

The next day, Ian was feeling woebegone all day as he washed his uniforms and then packed them in a box along with his jackets and other clothing articles. He kept his best red coat. Everything was in his garage now waiting to be loaded into his pickup.

Feeling a lot of nervous energy, he got in his pickup and drove, as close as he could, to Pickett Mountain Lake in Moro PLT. He had to walk the last quarter of a mile, but he didn't mind. Years ago he had cleared out all the blow-downs and limbs from the old road that went to the outlet where there had been a portable sawmill 30 years ago.

He stood on the old sawdust pile near the outlet, and looked up the lake. *This is one beautiful spot. When I die, I want my ashes spread on top of the sawdust pile.*

He sat down and leaned against a spruce tree. After a few minutes, a lone loon came swimming toward Ian. He swam back and forth, keeping a watchful eye on Ian. The loon very seldom ever saw humans here, as the lake was so shallow, nobody hardly ever fished it. Although near the peninsula, at the upper end, there was a huge spring in the middle of the lake and in the evenings, with a fly rod, Ian had caught three and four pound brook trout.

Getty Oil was doing some prospecting to the right of the lake and supposedly there were huge deposits of copper, gold and oil found. "Some day this area will be a mine."

He sat in silence while watching the loon. At one point, the loon swam towards Ian and sat there looking at him. Then he made a slight faint cry. Barely audible. The loon was talking to him and tears began to form in his eyes. The loon cried again and then swam off.

Ian stood up and stretched and he had one more ride he wanted to make. He first drove to Whitey's Market in Oakfield to fill his pickup with gas so he wouldn't have to do it in the morning. Then he drove up Rt. 212 and turned onto the Clark Settlement Road. An infamous road for night hunting. He just idled along. Every turnout, every field, old farm and orchard held memories for him as he relived each. He understood now why Maria had decided to let him have these few remaining days to himself; to relive his career. She had been so right.

He stopped at Warden's Rock and relived the first two night hunters he had caught alone there, and the McMann brothers. Then a little further down the road, the big rock he had run into while chasing the McMann brothers a year later.

He turned west on the Moro Town Line Road and headed for Rt. 11. And along that road too, at every turn, field and hidey hole, he relived more memories. He thought about stopping to see Uncle Jim and Nancy and have supper with them, but he decided against it. He was feeling melancholy after reliving his career as a game warden and right now he just wanted to be alone.

He loaded everything into his pickup now, so he wouldn't have to do it in the morning. After a light supper, he sat out on the porch. The air was still warm, but his house was situated on a high hill about 1100 feet and there was always a breeze. He watched the evening news, took a shower, poured himself a brandy and went back out on the porch. The sun had set and the thousands of fire flies that evening were putting on quite a show. It reminded him of kids with sparklers at a 4th of July celebration.

He poured another brandy and waited to hear the B&A train back off its huge engines at Dudley Siding.

*   *   *   *

Alvin Theriault in Stacyville had agreed to follow Ian to Augusta and give him a ride home.

It was about a three and a half hour drive to the storehouse on Forest Avenue. And once there, it didn't take long to turn everything in. The head of the storehouse, Linda, said, "One thing about you game wardens, when it comes time to turn in your uniforms and gear, you all turn in everything that had ever been issued to you."

On the drive back, Ian and Alvin had a good time talking. "I know you were a game warden for 30 years, Ian. But do you have any regrets about retiring?" Alvin asked.

"If not for Maria, I think there would be regrets. But we're getting married soon and I'm looking forward to that. And she has a great son. Eric just turned eleven."

Alvin took Ian home and before Ian got out, he said, "I need to sign off at home one more time. 2256, Houlton."

"Go ahead ,'56."

"2256, Houlton, I'm 10-7 and retired."

"Congratulations, 2256."

"Thanks, Scotty."

"Thank you, Alvin."

Ian telephoned Maria and asked her to come over. He was retired.

That night, as they laid together in bed, Ian looked at the clock on his bedstand, 12:01 A.M. "I'm no longer a Maine Game Warden." Tears actually filled his eyes. Being a game warden was so much a part of who he was and had been. He rolled over and put his arm around Maria and held her close, knowing another new and exciting life was starting.

CHAPTER 11

They were married in Ian's house four days later and after the wedding, Ian, Maria and Eric drove to Kedgwick, New Brunswick to visit her folks. Then they left Eric on the farm while they honeymooned. There was much Maria wanted to show Ian in the Province.

Ian had already forgotten about putting on the uniform and living the life of a warden. He was enjoying his new life.

Three days after returning to their home at Knowles Corner, Eric was having to go to school already. "You see, Eric, school here starts three weeks early and during the potato harvest in September, schools close for three weeks, giving the kids a chance to work and earn money. I've known some kids to earn $50 a day picking potatoes."

The school bus turned around in their driveway and Eric ran out to greet it.

As Ian and Maria were having another cup of coffee, a Fed Ex truck drove in the driveway and the driver came to the door. Maria opened it and the driver said, "I have a package here for Mr. Ian Randall."

Ian signed the delivery slip and the driver left. "What is it, Ian? Another surprise?"

"I have no idea."

"Well, open it," Maria said.

Ian opened it and removed a pretty urn and a letter. He gave the urn to Maria and opened the letter.

The Three Day Club
A Warden's Worry

Dear Ian,

If you are reading this, then you must know that I have died. The doctor at Togus discovered I had cancer throughout my body. Too advanced to do anything about it. I am happy that I came to see my family and say hello and goodbye to my mother. There is no reason to feel sorry for me or sad. I have lived a good life. I lived it according to my needs, not someone else's. My only regret in life is when the village left Howe Brook. A part of me died then, also. The urn you now hold contains my ashes. I have only this one last request. That you put my ashes in the water at the mouth of Tracy Brook. This is where I placed John Corriveau's ashes when he died.

I hope you are enjoying your retirement and your new life with Maria. If you give her as much attention as you did poachers, you two will have a long and happy life together.

As the end was coming near, I had a visit from John Corriveau. He was looking young and strong. He said that when I was ready, he knew where we could find a nice young moose (huh huh). This may have only been a dream, but at the time I thought he was here with me in this room.

As you read this, we are probably together again, and enjoying a feed of moose meat.

You and John were the best friends I ever had. John gave me the cabin on the knoll after I was released from jail. I think he felt really bad about the trick he played on me. Maybe now I can tell him about the banshee.

Getting back to the cabin, Ian. It is yours and everything in all the buildings. The key should accompany this letter. There is still plenty of food in the root cellar.

No fresh meat; the D.A. ate the last of that. There are several canning jars filled with different kinds of meat. I won't tell you what they are. You'll have to figure that out for yourself. But don't go telling anybody what they are. I wouldn't want people thinking that I left my cabin to a poacher.

When you arrested me 28 years ago for the deer in my canoe, I instantly liked you. The manner in which you conducted your authority. If I showed any anger, it was not directed towards you. From that encounter with you and throughout my existence at Howe Brook, I have nurtured a growing admiration and respect for you and call you my friend.

Words are coming hard for me now and my eyes are beginning to cloud with tears.

It has. . .been a Great Game.

Your friend,
Parnell Purchase

Ian gave the letter to Maria. He had to wipe the tears from his eyes and face. As Maria read the letter, Ian sat in silence thinking about all the capers Parnell had pulled. Yes, he would miss his friend.

"Wow, that's quite a letter and it says so much about the person you are. Look, Nancy wants me to go shopping with her in Bangor tomorrow, and I'd really like to go. Why don't you see if Uncle Jim would like to go in with you?"

"Eric's feelings will be hurt if he doesn't come along, also," Ian said.

"He has school tomorrow and besides, I think this is something you need to do for you, as well as for Parnell. If the cabin is yours, we'll have many chances to go to it."

*　*　*　*

The next morning Eric's feelings were hurt but he did understand. Ian was surprised when he didn't make a fuss about not being able to go along.

He ran for the bus and Maria and Ian drove down to Jim and Nancy's. Maria got in with Nancy and Jim with Ian. As Ian drove, he gave Jim the urn to hold and the letter for him to read.

"You know, Ian, this is quite an honor. To have someone who you have arrested and chased for all these years to call you friend and to give you his cabin and belongings.

"What did he mean by the 'banshee'?"

"It's a funny story, really. John Corriveau had set Parnell up to take the hit with a deer in his canoe; he suspected full well that I was probably around. After Parnell got out of jail, he went back to Howe Brook and got even with Corriveau." Ian told Jim the whole story, and then they both laughed so much their sides began to ache.

Ian turned onto the Jim May Road instead of taking the Levesque Road. As they crossed the bridge at St. Croix, Jim said, "That river looks awfully low. I know that it's the end of summer, but there's hardly a trickle."

"The beaver probably have it dammed up where the quick water starts downstream of the lake."

They drove across the shortcut road and met two log trucks loaded with long length spruce heading for Levesque's mill in Masardis. Ian had to wait for the dust cloud to clear before they could continue.

At Parnell's cabin, they drove up and Ian unlocked the garage. There was the canoe and life preservers hanging on the wall, and two paddles. They put everything and the urn in the canoe and started walking it to the lake.

The air was warm but not humid and there was a slight breeze which kept the bugs at bay, and created a slight chop on the water. But all in all it was a very pleasant day. Ian broke the silence after they were half way across the lake. "Parnell would have been happy knowing that the day when we spread his ashes—that the day was so eloquent."

"I've often wondered why a man like Parnell would choose a life like this. I mean, he was a captain in the U.S. Army for God's sake. He gave it all up and a promising career to live like a hermit in the middle of the woods."

"I think it has a lot to do with the Korean War. He must have seen some pretty ugly goings-on there. At least he said something close to that in court. I'll give him this much. He was resourceful."

At the mouth of Tracy Brook the water was calm and smooth as glass; they were out of the wind. Jim held the canoe in position while Ian brought the urn from his pack. "You know it's odd, no matter what we do with our life, at the end we only amount to a few handfuls of ashes." His voice cracked.

He took the top off and sprinkled the ashes in the water. The ashes floated on top and gathered in to a circle and then a slight breeze came out of nowhere and the circle began to spin, like a top. Both Ian and Jim sat in silence watching this. Then, without any warning, a lead began to leave the circle and was taken by the current out into the lake; a long narrow train of ashes. "Goodbye, Parnell."

"Is Tracy any good fishing?" Jim asked.

"When there aren't any beaver dams on this end of it, in the spring it can be excellent fishing. And when they spawn in the fall, I've seen this brook solid black with trout. But then again, only when there aren't any beaver dams.

"There once was a sporting camp upstream aways on top of a knoll on the left side. The only thing left there now is rotten bed logs. Are you hungry, Uncle Jim?" Ian asked.

"Yes, I could eat a horse."

"Parnell said in his letter that there was plenty of food in the root cellar. I want to go over his things at the cabin also, so I know what's there. He might have left some papers or something."

They carried the canoe up and stored it in the shed and Jim started looking at Parnell's old 1955 Studebaker-Packard pickup. "It's just like new, Ian. My God, he couldn't have put many miles on it." There were probably a hundred traps hanging on the walls.

"Let's go see what there is in the root cellar," Ian said.

He unlocked the door and pushed it open. It was cool inside and there was still some ice left buried in the sawdust.

"There's, well this has to be canned moose meat. There's beaver, partridge, trout and mushrooms all canned. There are a few potatoes there, four heads of cabbage and two squash. And it all looks fresh. How about potatoes, squash and canned moose meat?" Ian asked.

"That sounds good to me."

There was plenty of kindling next to the stove and in the shed, connected to the cabin, was dry split stove wood. While Jim started the fire, Ian began peeling the potatoes and squash. He put everything in pots and placed them on the stove. It was not hot yet.

While they waited for dinner to cook, they started looking through Parnell's effects. On the bottom shelf of an old night stand beside the bed, Jim found a photograph album. It was more scrapbook than photos, though. He took it out to the kitchen picnic table and sat down to look through it.

"Oh my God. It's all coming back to me now. Captain Parnell Peasley. It's been 32 years. I had completely forgotten."

"What's that, Uncle Jim?"

"Parnell. . .he was more, much more than what people knew of him as Parnell Purchase. He commanded the Red Fox Company in South Korea and he and his entire company were twice awarded the Bronze Star. I'm not reading this, Ian. I remember it!

"Do you remember Pierpole Silvanus? He became a Game Warden a year before you."

"Yes."

"Parnell was his commanding officer and Pierpole and his unit, the Grizzly Scouts, was the most decorated unit in the

Korean War. It's a small world sometimes, isn't it?" Jim said.

"Do you remember Pierpole's folks? Sterling and Wynola Silvanus?"

"They lived on the farm just up the road from where you grew up, didn't they?"

"Yes. Sterling and Wynola retired about the same time you were born. Wynola was with Sterling everywhere he traveled. They lived in the woods summer and winter."

"I was four, maybe five years old, when Sterling came home and then became a game warden. He gave me his chickens with the understanding that he and Wynola could have a dozen eggs each week and one chicken a month to roast. I could sell the eggs and keep the money. Sterling and Wynola were both living legends."

"They're both still living, aren't they?" Ian asked.

"Whenever I go back to Strong for a visit, I always stop and visit them. They're both in their 90's now, but you wouldn't know it to look at them. Pierpole retired after 20 years so he could take care of his folks in their old age.

"This album has some valuable history really. Here's a photo of the Grizzly Team. This album is full of newspaper articles, awards, copies of letters from command headquarters. This album says so much about Parnell's life. You should take this home and when you have the time, read through it. Parnell was surely more than what people thought. Who would have guessed that he was a commanding officer?"

Their dinner was ready and they sat down to a delicious meal of canned moose meat. Thanks to Parnell. Ian made a pot of coffee and after the dishes were cleaned, they sat back at the table sipping coffee. When they had finished their coffee, they continued looking through Parnell's effects. There were a few letters from home, but not many. The only firearm was Parnell's .35 Winchester and a half empty box of shells. "I'd better take this out with me, also."

Ian found another photo album and these were mostly of his

family. A few were of people Ian recognized who had lived at Howe Brook Village.

"What are you going to do with his pickup?" Jim asked.

"Leave it here for a while. Maybe we can use it for a woods vehicle when we come in for a few days. You know, Uncle Jim, you and Nancy can use this cabin any time you want."

"I'll take you up on that. I'd like to try fishing Tracy Brook next spring."

Jim was looking through a box of newspapers next to the stove and pulled one out that had some writing on it. "Hey Ian, look at this. Written on this newspaper is *Hit moose, down. 1 mile north of village.*"

"I know Ansel Snow from Ashland used to throw a newspaper for Parnell each morning. I wonder if he was telling Parnell where there was a dead moose, so he could salvage some meat."

"Here's another one. . .*Hit deer by Corriveau's camp.*"

"That has to be it. Maybe he didn't poach as much illegal game as I have always thought."

They locked the shed, root cellar and pulled the shades in the cabin before locking its doors. Ian had the .35 Winchester rifle and the album. He was already thinking he should send the album to the attorney who had forwarded Parnell's letter and request. He would see that his family would get it. But he'd think on it.

The Studebaker he had decided to give it to Eric. He would allow him to drive it in the woods while at the cabin and when he had his license, he'd let him bring it home.

After he had dropped his Uncle Jim off at his house, he drove home. But once on top of Matawamkeg Hill, he pulled over to the side and stopped. There were images floating across his inner vision. To help protect Roscoe and Renée's secret, he knew what he had to do.

When he got home, Maria and Eric were both already home. He hadn't realized he and Jim had been gone all day.

Maria and Eric came outside to greet him. "How'd it go?" she asked.

"Okay, sad. Here, this is about Parnell," and he gave her Parnell's album. "And for you, son, this was Parnell's rifle. A .35 Winchester." Eric's eyes bulged out like they would burst. He was speechless.

"Let's go inside. There is something I want to tell you about." Maria put the album on the kitchen bar top and Eric took his rifle up to his room. And Ian went into his office and opened the top drawer and removed a cloth pouch. Eric came downstairs.

"Sit, please. No, at the table," and Ian sat at the table, also.

"Two weeks ago, while I was visiting Roscoe and Renée, they gave us a wedding present." He paused there before continuing. He was so serious, Maria couldn't imagine what the concern was all about.

He looked at Maria and then at Eric and said, "Can you know something and never talk about it or say anything?"

Now Maria and Eric were so serious as they stared at Ian. "Can you?" and then he took the cloth pouch from inside his shirt and emptied the contents on the table.

"Can you know something and never talk about it?"

He told Maria and Eric, his family, the story of Holigard's treasure and the two Hastings brothers. As he told them the story, another part of himself was enjoying this new life with his family. The warden service mistress, now, long gone.

 *NOTES*

Note 1:

In 1983, I interviewed Mr. Braley (not his real name) at his camp on the Smyrna Center Road in Smyrna Mills, Maine. It became obvious real soon that Mr. Braley had indeed seen something. He was still showing symptoms of agitation and distress. Perhaps because he said the hands and head were not there. He said the body was clothed in a gray flannel shirt, dungarees, sneakers and a bra. Finding a headless corpse had really upset him.

Mr. Braley said he had started hunting that morning about 7 A.M. off the end of the Hermore Road in Hammond PLT. He said he had hunted through hardwoods and over a ridge and eventually came to Mill Brook. He said just before reaching the brook, he had seen the remains of an old woodstove and an old steel drum, and the woman's body was in the drum.

Mr. Braley said he panicked and was not really sure where he went from there. He thought he had walked north to the Smokey Hauler's Road in Smyrna, to Darrell Toner's camp. His camp on the Smyrna Center Road was 3 miles away. He said he walked out to his camp, and had someone drive him back to the Hermore Road for his own vehicle.

I took Mr. Braley in my pickup and we drove out to Toner's camp on Mill Brook and Mr. Braley and I followed the brook downstream. After we had hiked about a ¼ of a mile, Mr. Braley said nothing was looking familiar.

I then took Mr. Braley back to his camp and told him I would organize a search party and asked him to meet us the next morning at the end of the Hermore Road. A log yard.

I advised my sergeant, Greg Maher, about the information and told him I honestly thought Mr. Braley had indeed found something. Since the case was not a hunting incident or a missing person complaint, Sergeant Maher gave me 2 days to work it. It was, after all, the first week of deer season.

That night, I continued investigating and learned that Kermit Brannen had lumber camps in the Mill Brook area in the 1950's, and there was a woman from New Brunswick who lived at the camps also, and helped the camp cook and did cleaning. Two of the men started fighting over her and one Monday morning she did not show up for work. Kermit Brannen thought she had probably returned to New Brunswick because the 2 men were fighting over her. That would have been about 25 years before Kermit Braley found the body and the clothes would not still be intact and identifiable.

The next morning, Warden Roland Pelletier from Houlton, Mr. Braley and two state troopers (I'm not now sure of their names, but one I think was Cpl. Gary Craft, a K 9 handler) and I followed the old road into the woods and away from the yard. Mr. Braley's tracks were visible in the mud. When the tracks left the road the dog handler and Braley led the way. Roland took left flank and I took the right. Occasionally the dog would lose the scent and everybody would stop while Roland and I made circles until one of us picked up Braley's tracks again.

The dog led us to Mill Brook and the old stove, but no steel drum. And the dog was not able to follow or pick up Braley's scent trail from there to the Smokey Hauler's Road.

We backtracked to the log yard and from there we all went home. After the two days were up, no new information was obtained, nor the body, and there was not an unexplained missing woman.

In 2004, the Chief of Police in Portland, Chitwood, had obtained information of a missing 16 year old girl from the Portland area. This 16 year old girl was last seen picking potatoes in the Houlton area with an Indian from New Brunswick. In the same time frame when Mr. Braley found the body.

The sister of this suspect said her brother had killed someone. Chief Chitwood contacted Warden Sergeant Roger Guay, a professional K 9 handler in locating cadavers.

Roger contacted me and I gave him all the information that I could remember. After searching the log yard with his K 9, Roger advised me that the area had been lumbered over at least twice since 1984, and the original log yard had been bulldozed over, so any remains of the steel drum and body would not now be recoverable.

Apparently Chief Chitwood knew the name of the suspect and that he lived on a reservation in New Brunswick and when Chief Chitwood contacted the RCMP authorities in New Brunswick, the RCMP officer refused to go on the reservation to interview the suspect.

In my opinion, Mr. Braley had definitely found a corpse in a steel drum and this was corroborated by the suspect's sister that the body would be found in a drum over the bank at the log yard. At no time had the state trooper's K 9 indicated that it had hit on Braley's scent around or behind the log yard.

Was the steel drum containing the body ever there at the log yard? And where did Mr. Kermit Braley find the drum with the body?

Author, Randall Probert

Randall Probert lived and was raised in Strong,Maine; a small town in the western mountains of Maine. Six months after graduating from high school, he left the small town behind for Baltimore, Maryland and a Marine Engineering School, situated downtown near what was then called "The Block". Because of bad weather, the flight from Portland to New York was canceled and this made him late for the connecting flight to Baltimore. A young kid and alone from the backwoods of Maine finally found his way to Washington DC and boarded a bus from there to Baltimore. After leaving the Merchant Marines, he went to an aviation school in Lexington, Massachusetts.

During his interview for Maine Game Warden he was asked, "You have gone from the high seas to the air. . .are you sure you want to be a Game Warden?" Mr. Probert retired from Warden Service in 1997 and started writing historical novels about the history in the areas where he patrolled as a game warden, with his own experiences as a game warden as those of the wardens in his books. Mr. Probert has since expanded his purview and has written 2 science fiction books, *PARADIGM* and *PARADIGM2,* and has written a mystical adventure, *AN ESOTERIC JOURNEY.* Mr. Probert is also currently working on another historical novel, *EBEN McNINCH,* which should be available in the fall, 2014.

Acknowledgments

I would like to thank John and Regan Martin, Brian Colby and Laura Ashton for your help with this book.

Other Books by Randall Probert

A Forgotten Legacy

An Eloquent Caper

Courier de Bois

Katrina's Valley

Mysteries at Matagamon Lake

A Warden's Worry

A Quandry at Knowles Corner

Paradigm

Trial at Norway Dam

A Grafton Tale

Paradigm II

Train to Barnjum

A Trapper's Legacy

An Esoteric Journey

Made in the USA
Middletown, DE
02 February 2022

60331715R00144